PENGUIN BOOKS

NOTES ON A SCANDAL

'Outstanding, brilliantly understated and blackly funny' *Daily Telegraph*

'I read it twice. Has the epic quality of Greek tragedy and does what good fiction is supposed to do: remind us what fools we are as we lumber through our lives. It would be sad if it wasn't funny; funny if it wasn't sad' *Guardian*

'The best new novel I've read this year is Zoë Heller's *Notes on a Scandal*. It's sharp, funny, moving – and elegantly written' Miriam Gross

'Heller's novel is a story of obsessive friendships and sexual intoxication, told by a gloriously unreliable narrator. It's funny, touching, beautifully observed and radiated with a wholly undepressing gloom' Richard Eyre

'The best novel I've read in the past twelve months. With this one book Heller joins the front ranks of British novelists, right up there with Amis and McEwen' Edmund White

'Sinister and surprising, distinctly chilling with pin-sharp observations. A highlight in the year's fiction, a classic of emotional imprisonment' *Daily Express*

'Stunningly good' Anne Robinson

'[*Notes on a Scandal*] is witty, strong on atmosphere, cunningly narrated and formidably observant. A sad story, and a wickedly enjoyable one' John Gross

'Compelling, dark, sexy' *Observer*

'A quiet masterpiece, brilliantly observed and written' Sarah Sands, *Daily Telegraph*

'From the first sentence to the last, the story and the writing of it have a thrilling intensity that holds the reader's rapt attention' Paula Fox

'Highly addictive . . . a funny, unnerving, acutely intelligent novel of psychological suspense' *New York Observer*

'Wickedly funny, a sly satire. Heller writes in a brand of social satire reminiscent of British masters like Evelyn Waugh and Muriel Spark . . . not only very funny and original, but also demonstrates shrewdness, intelligence and nerve in tackling a difficult and tricky subject, and carrying it off' *Milwaukee Journal-Sentinel*

'The perfect "smart" book for beach reading' *San Francisco Chronicle*

'A nuanced portrait of the power plays in unbalanced relationships . . . shares many qualities with Kazuo Ishiguro's *The Remains of the Day*. A tartly readable portrait of terminal neediness, as sharp and merciless as any of Zoë Heller's columns' *Los Angeles Times Book Review*

'Insightful, piercing . . . utterly brilliant' *Booklist*

'[A] clever novel of social commentary and dangerous obsession . . . Heller offers a piercing look at a basic human failing: it's easier to criticize others than to look honestly at ourselves' *People*

'Equally adroit at satire and at psychological suspense, Heller charts the course of a predatory friendship and demonstrates the lengths to which some people go for human company' *New Yorker*

Notes on a Scandal

ZOË HELLER

PENGUIN BOOKS

PENGUIN BOOKS

Published by the Penguin Group
Penguin Books Ltd, 80 Strand, London WC2R 0RL, England
Penguin Group (USA), Inc., 375 Hudson Street, New York, New York 10014, USA
Penguin Books Australia Ltd, 250 Camberwell Road, Camberwell, Victoria 3124, Australia
Penguin Books Canada Ltd, 10 Alcorn Avenue, Toronto, Ontario, Canada M4V 3B2
Penguin Books India (P) Ltd, 11 Community Centre, Panchsheel Park, New Delhi – 110 017, India
Penguin Books (NZ) Ltd, Cnr Rosedale and Airborne Roads, Albany, Auckland, New Zealand
Penguin Books (South Africa) (Pty) Ltd, 24 Sturdee Avenue, Rosebank 2196, South Africa

Penguin Books Ltd, Registered Offices: 80 Strand, London WC2R 0RL, England

www.penguin.com

First published by Viking 2003
Published in Penguin Books 2004

1

Typeset by Rowland Phototypesetting Ltd, Bury St Edmunds, Suffolk
Printed in England by Clays Ltd, St Ives plc

ISBN-13: 978-0-14-104468-2

For Larry and Frankie

Foreword

1 March 1998

The other night at dinner, Sheba talked about the first time that she and the Connolly boy kissed. I had heard most of it before, of course, there being few aspects of the Connolly business that Sheba has not described to me several times over. But this time round, something new came up. I happened to ask her if anything about the first embrace had surprised her. She laughed. Yes, the *smell* of the whole thing had been surprising, she said. She hadn't anticipated his personal odour and if she had, she would probably have guessed at something teenagey: bubble gum, cola, feet.

When the moment arrived, what I actually inhaled was soap, tumble-dried laundry. He smelled of scrupulous self-maintenance. You know the washing-machine fug that envelops you sometimes, walking past the basement vents of mansion flats? Like that. So clean, Barbara. Never any of that cheese and onion breath that the other kids have . . .

Every night since we came to Eddie's house, Sheba has been talking to me like this. She sits at the kitchen table looking out on the green darkness of Eddie's garden. I sit across from her, watching her nervous fingers score ice-skating loops in the plastic tablecloth. It's often pretty strong stuff she tells me in that newsreader's voice of hers. But then, one of the many things I have always admired about Sheba is her capacity to talk about low things and make them seem perfectly decent. We don't have secrets, Sheba and I.

The first time I saw him undress, you know what I thought of,

Barbara? Fresh garden vegetables wrapped in a clean white hanky. Mushrooms fresh from the soil. No, really. He was edible. He washed his hair every night. Imagine! It was limp with cleanness. The vanity of adolescence, probably. Or no – perhaps the anxiety of it. His body was a new toy still: he hadn't learned to treat it with the indifferent neglect of adults.

Her account was wending back to familiar terrain. I must have heard the hair rhapsody at least fifteen times in recent months. (I've never cared for Connolly's hair, myself. It's always struck me as slightly sinister – like that spun-fibreglass snow that they used to sell as Christmas tree decoration.) Still, I kept giving her the cues.

'And were you nervous, when you were kissing him, Sheba?'

Oh no. Well, yes . . . Not exactly. [Laughter] Can you be nervous and calm at the same time? I remember being quite relieved that he wasn't using his tongue. You do need to know someone a bit, first, don't you? It's too much otherwise. All the slobber. And that slightly embarrassing sense of the other person trying to be creative in a limited space . . . Anyway, I relaxed too much or something, because the bike fell – there was this awful clatter – and then, of course, I ran away . . .

I don't say much on these occasions. The point is to get Sheba to talk. But even in the usual run of things I tend to be the listener in our relationship. It's not that Sheba is cleverer than me. Any objective comparison would have to rate me the more educated woman, I think. (Sheba knows a bit about art – I'll give her that; but for all her class advantages, she is woefully ill-read.) No, Sheba talks because she is just naturally more loquacious and candid than I am. I am circumspect by nature and she . . . well, she isn't.

For most people, honesty is such an unusual departure from their standard *modus operandi* – such an aberration in their workaday mendacity – that they feel obliged to alert you when a moment of sincerity is coming on. 'To be completely honest,' they say, or 'To tell you the truth,' or 'Can I be straight?' Often they want to extract vows of discretion from you before going any further. 'This is strictly between us, right? . . . You must *promise* not to tell anyone . . .' Sheba does none of that. She tosses out intimate and unflattering truths about herself, all the time, without a second thought. 'I was the most fearsomely obsessive little masturbator when I was a girl,' she told me once when we were first getting to know each other. 'My mother practically had to Sellotape my knickers to me, to stop me having at myself in public places.' 'Oh?' I said, trying to sound as if I were used to broaching such matters over coffee and a KitKat.

It's a class characteristic, I think – this insouciant frankness. If I had had more contact with posh people in my life I would probably be familiar with the style and think nothing of it. But Sheba is the only genuinely upper-class person I've ever known. Her throwaway candour is as exotic to me, in its way, as a plate in an Amazonian tribesman's lip. She's meant to be taking a nap at the moment. (She's not sleeping well at night.) But I can tell, from the creaking of the floorboards overhead, that she's pottering about in her niece's room. She often goes in there in the afternoons. It was her bedroom when she was growing up, apparently. She'll spend hours at a time handling the little girl's things – reorganizing the vials of glitter and glue in art-kits, making inventories of the dolls' plastic shoes. Sometimes she falls asleep up there and I have to go and wake her for dinner. She always looks rather sad and odd, sprawled out on the pink and white princess bed, with her big, rough feet dangling over the edge. Like a giantess who has blundered into the wrong house.

This place belongs to her brother, Eddie, now. After Sheba's father died, Sheba's mother decided it was too big for one person and Eddie bought it from her. Sheba is bitter about that, I think. It isn't fair, she says, that just because Eddie is rich, he should have been able to buy their shared past for himself.

Eddie and his family are away in New Delhi at the moment. The American bank he works for has posted him there for six months. Sheba rang him in India when her trouble started, and he agreed to let her stay in the house until she found something permanent. We've been here ever since. It's anyone's guess what we will do when Eddie returns in June. I gave up the lease on my little flat some weeks ago and Sheba's husband, Richard, is in no danger of taking us in, even temporarily. We probably don't have enough money to rent a new place and, besides, I'm not sure that any landlords in London would have us, right now. I try not to worry, though. Sufficient unto the day is the evil thereof, as my mother used to say.

This is not a story about me. But, since the task of telling it has fallen into my hands, and since I play a minor role in the events I am going to describe, it is only right that I should offer a brief account of myself and my relationship to the protagonist. My name is Barbara Covett. (From time to time one of my colleagues will call me 'Barb' or, even less desirably, 'Babs', but I discourage it.) Until I retired this January, I had been living in Archway, north London, and teaching History at St George's, a comprehensive school in the same neighbourhood, for the last twenty-one years. It was at St George's, a little less than eighteen months ago, that I met Bathsheba Hart. Her name will probably be familiar to most of you by now. She is the forty-two-year-old pottery teacher recently charged with indecent assault on a minor, after being discovered having a sexual affair with one of her students – a boy who was fifteen years old when the affair began.

Since it first came to light, Sheba's case has received nigh on unstinting media coverage. I try to keep up with all of it, although, frankly, it's a pretty depressing task. There was a time when I placed a certain amount of trust in the integrity of this country's news organizations, but, now that I have seen at close hand the way in which reporters go about their business, I recognize how sadly misplaced that trust was. Over the last fortnight, I must have spotted twenty errors of fact about Sheba's case, in the newspapers alone. On Monday of this week, some bright spark at the *Daily Mirror* described Sheba as a 'buxom bombshell'. (Anyone who has ever so much as glanced at her knows that she is as flat as the Fens.) And yesterday, the *Sun* ran an 'exposé' on Sheba's husband, in which it was claimed that Richard, who lectures in Communications Theory at City of London, is 'a trendy prof who gives sexy seminars on how to read dirty magazines'.

In the end, though, it's not the carelessness or even the cheerful mendacity of the reporting that astounds, so much as the sanctimony. Good Lord, the unrelenting sanctimony! I understood, when all this came out, that there was going to be a fuss. I did not expect Sheba to receive sympathy. But I could never have predicted the hysterical prurience of the response. The titillated fury. These reporters write about Sheba as if they were seven-year-olds confronting the fact of their parents' sexuality for the first time. 'Despicable' is one of their big words. 'Unhealthy' is another. Sheba's attraction to the boy was 'unhealthy'. Her marriage was 'unhealthy' too. The boy had had an 'unhealthy' interest in winning her approval. Any species of sexual attraction that you can't find documented on a seaside postcard fails the health test, as far as these people are concerned. Any sexual arrangement existing outside the narrow channels of family newspaper convention is relegated to a great, sinister parenthesis of kinky 'antics'.

Journalists are educated people, aren't they? College graduates, some of them. How did their minds get so small? Have *they* never desired anyone outside the age range that local law and custom deemed suitable? Never experienced an impulse that fell outside the magic circle of sexual orthodoxy?

It was the papers that finally did Sheba and Richard in, I believe. After she was given bail the two of them tried to soldier on for a while. But it was too much – too much for any couple – to bear. When you think of the reporters camped outside their house, the awful headlines every day – 'Sex Teacher Passes Her Orals With Flying Colours', 'Teacher Takes Keen Interest In The Student Body' and so on – it's a wonder that they lasted as long as they did. Just before Sheba made her first appearance in the magistrate's court, Richard told her that her presence in the house was making the children's lives a misery. I believe he thought this was a kinder rationale for throwing her out than his own feelings of revulsion.

That was when I stepped in. I put Sheba up for a week or so in my flat and then, when she got Eddie to let her stay in his house, I came with her. How could I not? Sheba was so pitifully alone. It would have taken a very unfeeling individual to desert her. There is at least one more pre-trial hearing – possibly two – to be got through before the case goes before the Crown Court and, frankly, I don't think Sheba would make it on her own. Her barrister says that she could avoid going to the Crown Court altogether, if she pleaded guilty to the charges. But Sheba won't hear of it. She regards a guilty plea – even one that includes a clear denial of 'coercion, duress or bribery' – as unthinkable. 'There was no assault and I've done nothing indecent,' she likes to say.

In becoming Sheba's caretaker these last few weeks, I have inevitably drawn some of the media glare to myself. It seems to be a source of some amusement and discomfort to the journalists that a respectable older woman with nearly forty years' experience as an educator should choose to be associated with Sheba. Every single reporter covering this case – *every single one* – has made a point of describing, with varying degrees of facetiousness, my handbag: a perfectly unexceptional, wooden-handled object, with a needlepoint portrait of two kittens on it. Clearly, it would suit them all much better if I were off somewhere with the other jowly old biddies, boasting about my grandchildren, or playing bingo. Not, at any rate, standing on the doorstep of a rich banker's house in Primrose Hill, defending the character of an alleged child-molester.

The only possible explanation that the journalists can find for my having voluntarily associated myself with Sheba's debauchery is that I am, in some as yet shadowy way, debauched myself. In the weeks since Sheba's arrest, I have been required, on several occasions, to speak to reporters on her behalf and, as a result, I am now known to readers of the *Sun* as 'the saucy schoolteacher's spin-doctor'. (Those who know me can attest to what an unlikely candidate I am for such a soubriquet.) My naive hope, in acting as Sheba's spokeswoman, has been to counter some of the sanctimonious hostility towards my friend, and to shed a little light on the true nature of her complex personality. But alas, my contributions have done no such thing. Either they have been cruelly and deliberately distorted, or gone unnoticed in a torrent of lies propagated by people who have never met Sheba and would, very likely, not have understood her even if they had.

This is chief among the reasons why I have now decided to risk further calumny by writing my own account of Sheba's downfall. I am presumptuous enough to believe that I am the person best qualified to write this small history. I would go so far as to hazard that I am the *only* person. Sheba and I have spent countless hours together over the last eighteen months, exchanging confidences of every kind. Certainly, there is no other friend or relative of Sheba's who has been so intimately involved in the day-to-day business of her affair with Connolly. In many cases, the events I describe here were witnessed by me personally. Elsewhere, I rely upon detailed accounts provided by Sheba herself. I am not so foolhardy as to claim for myself an infallible version of the story. But I do believe that my narrative will go some substantial way to helping the public understand who Sheba Hart really is.

I should acknowledge straightaway that, from a moral point of view, Sheba's testimony regarding her conduct is not always entirely reliable. Even now, she is inclined to romanticize the relationship and to underestimate the irresponsibility – the wrongness – of her actions. What remorse she expresses tends to be remorse for having been found out. But, confused and troubled as Sheba still is, her honesty remains utterly dependable. While I may dispute her *reading* of certain events, I have found no cause to doubt the factual particulars of her account. Indeed, I am confident that everything she has told me regarding the how, when and where of this affair is, to the best of her knowledge, true.

It's getting on for six o'clock now, so it won't be much longer. In half an hour – an hour at the most – Sheba will come down. I'll hear her shuffling on the stairs first and I'll put my writing away. (Sheba doesn't yet know about this project of mine. I fear it would only agitate her at the moment, so I've decided to keep it a secret until I'm a little further along.) A few seconds later, there she'll be in the living-room doorway, in her nightdress and socks.

She's always very quiet at first. She's usually been crying.

It's my job to cheer her up and bring her out of herself, so I try to be very upbeat. I'll tell her about something funny that happened at the supermarket today, or make a bitchy remark about the neighbour's yappy dog. After a bit, I'll get up to start preparations for supper. With Sheba, I've found, it's best not to push things. She's in a highly nervous state at the moment – extremely sensitive about being 'pressured'. So I don't ask her to come into the kitchen with me. I just go in and begin clattering. She'll wander about in the living room for a while, humming to herself and fiddling with things and then, after ten minutes or so, she will invariably relent and slope in after me.

I don't cook anything fancy. Sheba's appetite isn't up to much and I've never been one for sauces. We eat nursery food mainly. Beans on toast, Welsh rarebit, fish fingers. Sheba leans against the oven and watches me while I work. At a certain point, she usually asks for wine. I have tried to get her to wait until she's eaten something, but she gets very scratchy when I do that, so these days I tend to give in straightaway and pour her a small glass from the carton in the fridge. You choose your battles. Sheba is a bit of a snob about drink and she keeps whining at me to get a grander sort. *Something in a bottle, at least*, she says. But I continue to buy the cartons. We are on a tight budget these days. And for all her carping, Sheba doesn't seem to have too much trouble knocking back the cheap stuff.

Once she's got her drink, she relaxes a bit and starts to take a little more interest in what I'm saying. Sometimes, she even asks for a job and I'll give her a tin to open or some cheese to grate. Then, quite abruptly, as if we had never dropped the subject, she'll start talking about Connolly.

She doesn't seem to tire of the story. You wouldn't believe how many times she is willing to go back over the same small event, examining its details for clues and symbols. She reminds me of one of those Jewish fellows who devote years of their lives to analysing a single passage in the *Talmud*. She's always amazing to watch. So frail these days, and yet, when she's talking, so bright-eyed and erect! Sometimes she gets upset and there are tears. But I don't believe that the talking harms her. Actually, I think it does her good. There is no one else to whom Sheba can say these things. And it helps her, she says, to describe it all, exactly as it was.

One

The first time I ever saw Sheba was on a Monday morning, early in the winter term of 1996. I was standing in the St George's car park, getting books out of the back of my car when she came through the gates on a bicycle – an old-fashioned, butcher-boy model with a basket in the front. Her hair was arranged in one of those artfully dishevelled up-dos: a lot of stray tendrils framing the jaw, and something like a chopstick piercing a rough bun at the back. It was the sort of hairstyle that film actresses wear when they're playing sexy lady doctors. I can't recall exactly what she had on. Sheba's outfits tend to be very complicated – lots of floaty layers. I know she was wearing purple shoes. And there was definitely a long skirt involved, because I remember thinking that it was in imminent danger of becoming entangled in her spokes. When she dismounted – with a lithe, rather irritating, little skip – I saw that the skirt was made of some diaphanous material. Fey was the word that swam into my mind. *Fey person*, I thought. Then I locked my car and walked away.

My formal introduction to Sheba took place later the same day when Ted Mawson, the deputy head, brought her into the staffroom at afternoon break for a 'meet and greet'. Afternoon break is not a good time to meet schoolteachers. If you were to plot a graph of a teacher's spirits throughout the school day, afternoon break would be represented by the lowest valley. The air in the staffroom has a trapped, stagnant quality. The chirpy claptrap of the early morning has died away and those staff members who are not milling about, checking their timetables and so on, sprawl in lugubrious silence. (To be fair, the sprawling is as much a tribute to the shoddy construction of the staffroom's three elderly foam sofas as an expression of the teachers' low morale.) Some of the teachers stare, slack-shouldered, into space. Some of them read – the arts and media pages of the liberal newspapers mainly, or paperback editions of the lower sort of fiction – the draw being not so much the content as the shield against having to converse with their colleagues. A great many chocolate bars and instant noodles in plastic pots are consumed.

On the day of Sheba's arrival, the staffroom was slightly more crowded than usual, owing to the heating being on the blink in Old Hall. (In addition to its three modern struc- tures – the gym, the arts centre and the science block – the St George's site includes two rather decrepit red-brick buildings, Old Hall and Middle Hall, which date back to the school's original, Victorian incarnation as an orphanage.) That afternoon, several teachers who might otherwise have remained skulking in their Old Hall classrooms during break had been driven to seek refuge in the staffroom where the radiators were still operative. I was off in a far corner when Mawson ushered Sheba in, so I was able to watch their slow progress around the room for several minutes, before having to mould my face into the appropriate smile.

Sheba's hair had become more chaotic since the morning. The loose tendrils had graduated to hanks and where it was meant to be smooth and pulled back, tiny, fuzzy sprigs had reared up, creating a sort of corona around her scalp. She was a very thin woman, I saw now. As she bent to shake the hands of seated staff members, her body seemed to fold in half at the waist like a piece of paper.

'Our new pottery teacher!' Mr Mawson was bellowing with his customary, chilling good spirits, as he and Sheba loomed over Antonia Robinson, one of our Eng Lit women. Sheba smiled and patted at her hair.

Pottery. I repeated the word quietly to myself. It was too perfect: I pictured her, the dreamy maiden poised at her wheel, massaging tastefully mottled milk jugs into being.

She was gesturing at the windows. 'Why are all the curtains drawn?' I heard her ask.

Ted Mawson rubbed his hands, nervously.

'Oh,' Antonia said, 'so the kids can't look in at us and make faces.'

Bill Rumer, the head of Chemistry, who was sitting next to Antonia on one of the foam sofas, snorted loudly at this. 'Actually, Antonia,' he said, 'it's so *we* can't look out at *them.* So they can smash each other up – do their raping and pillaging – and we're not required to intervene.' Antonia laughed and made a scandalized face.

A lot of teachers at St George's go in for this sort of posturing cynicism about the pupils, but Bill is the chief offender. He is a rather ghastly character, I'm afraid – the sort of man who is always sitting with his legs aggressively akimbo, offering a clearer silhouette of his untidy crotch than is strictly decent. One of the more insufferable things about him is that he imagines himself tremendously naughty and shocking – a delusion in which women like Antonia are all too eager to conspire.

'Oh *Bill*,' Antonia said now, pressing her skirt against her thighs.

'Don't worry,' Bill said to Sheba, 'you'll get used to the gloom.' He smiled at her magnanimously – the grandee allowing her into the little enclosure of his bonhomie. Then, as his eyes swept over her, I saw his smile waver for a moment.

Women observing other women tend to be engrossed by the details – the bodily minutiae, the clothing particulars. We get so caught up in the lone dimple, the excessive ears, the missing button, that we often lag behind men in organizing the individual features into an overall impression. I mention this by way of explaining why it was only now, watching Bill, that the fact of Sheba's beauty occurred to me. *Of course*, I thought. *She's very good-looking.* Sheba, who had been smiling fixedly throughout Bill and Antonia's droll exchange, made another nervous adjustment to her hair. As she raised her long, thin arms to fuss with the chopstick hair ornament, her torso lengthened and her chest was thrust forward slightly. She had a dancer's bosom. Two firm little patties riding the raft of her ribs. Bill's eyes widened. Antonia's narrowed.

She and Mawson continued on their journey around the room. The change that took place in the teachers' faces as they set eyes on Sheba confirmed my appraisal of Bill's appraisal. The men beamed and ogled. The women shrank slightly and turned sullen. The one exception was Elaine Clifford, a St George's alumna who teaches lower school Biology. Assuming what is her characteristic stance of unearned intimacy, Elaine stood very close to Sheba and began to blast her with impudent chatter. They were only a few feet away from me now.

After a moment, Mawson turned and beckoned. 'Barbara!' he shouted, cutting off Elaine in mid-stream. 'Do come and meet Sheba Hart.'

I stepped over and joined the group.

'Sheba is going to be teaching pottery,' Mawson said. 'As you know, we've been waiting a long time to replace Mrs Sipwitch. We feel tremendously lucky and pleased to have got her.'

In response to these words, a small, precise circle of scarlet appeared on each of Sheba's cheeks.

'This is Barbara Covett,' Mawson went on. 'She's one of

our stalwarts. If Barbara ever left us, I'm afraid St George's would collapse.'

Sheba looked at me carefully. She was about thirty-five, I estimated. (She was actually forty, about to be forty-one.) The hand that she held out to be shaken was large and red and somewhat coarse to the touch. 'How nice to be so needed,' she said, smiling. It was difficult to distinguish her tone, but it seemed to me that it contained a note of genuine sympathy – as if she understood how maddening it might be to be patronized by Mawson.

'Sheba – is that as in Queen of?' I asked.

'No, as in Bathsheba.'

'Oh. Were your parents thinking of the Bible or of Hardy?' She smiled. 'I'm not sure. I think they just liked the name.'

'If there's anything you need to know about anything concerning this place, Sheba,' Mawson continued, 'you must ask Barbara. She's the St George's expert.'

'Oh, smashing. I'll remember that,' Sheba said.

People from the privileged orders are always described as having plums in their mouths, but that wasn't what came to mind when I heard Sheba speak. On the contrary, she sounded as if her mouth were very empty and clean – as if she'd never had a filling.

'Oh! Love your earrings!' Elaine said now. She reached out, like a monkey, to finger Sheba's ears and, as she raised her arms, I caught a glimpse of her armpits which were violently pink, as if inflamed, and speckled with black stubble. I do hate it when women don't keep their personal grooming up to scratch. Better the full bushy Frenchwoman's growth than that squalid sprinkling of iron filings. 'They're so pretty!' Elaine said of the earrings. 'Where d'you get 'em?'

Sandy Pabblem, the headmaster, is very keen on having former pupils like Elaine on the staff. He imagines it reflects well on the school that they should wish to return and 'give something back'. But the truth is, St George's alumni make exceptionally poor teachers. It's not so much that they don't know anything about anything. (Which they don't.) Or even that they are complacent about their ignorance. (I once heard Elaine blithely identifying Boris Yeltsin as 'the Russian one who doesn't have a thingy on his head'.) The real issue is one of personality. Invariably, pupils who come back to teach at St George's are emotionally suspect characters – people who have surmised that the world out there is a frightening place and who have responded by simply staying put. They'll never have to try going home again because they're never going to leave. I have a vision sometimes of the pupils of these ex-pupils deciding to become St George's teachers themselves – and these ex-pupils of ex-pupils producing more ex-pupils who return to St George's as teachers, and so on. It would take only a couple of generations for the school to become entirely populated by dolts.

I took the opportunity, while Sheba was explaining her jewellery, to examine her face more closely. The earrings *were* beautiful, as it happened: delicate little things made of gold and seed pearls. Her face was longish and thin, her nose ever so slightly crooked at the tip. And her eyes – no, not so much the eyes, as the eyelids – were prodigious: great, beige canopies fringed with dense lash. Like that spiky tiara that the Statue of Liberty wears.

'This is Sheba's first teaching post,' Ted said, when Elaine had stopped talking for a moment.

'Well, it'll certainly be a baptism by fire,' I remarked.

Ted laughed with excessive heartiness and then abruptly stopped. 'Okay,' he said, glancing at his watch, 'we ought to get on, Sheba. Let me introduce you to Malcolm Plummer . . .'

Elaine and I stood watching for a moment, as Sheba and Mawson moved off. 'She's sweet, isn't she?' Elaine said.

I smiled. 'No, I wouldn't have said sweet.'

Elaine made a clicking noise with her tongue, to indicate her affront. 'Well, I think she's nice,' she muttered.

During her first couple of weeks at school, Sheba kept very much to herself. At break-times, she often stayed in her pottery studio. When she did come into the staffroom, she usually stood alone at one of the windows, peeking round the curtains at the playground outside. She was perfectly pleasant to her colleagues – which is to say, she exchanged all the standard, weather-based pleasantries. But she did not automatically gravitate to another female teacher and start swapping autobiographies. Or put her name down to join the St George's contingent on the next NUT march. Or contribute to sarcastic group discussions about the headmaster. Her resistance to all the usual initiation rituals aroused a certain amount of suspicion among the other teachers. The women tended to the opinion that Sheba was 'stuck up', while the men favoured the theory that she was 'cold'. Bill Rumer, widely acknowledged as the staff expert on such matters, observed on more than one occasion that 'there was nothing wrong with her that a good boning wouldn't cure'.

I took Sheba's failure to forge an instantaneous friendship as an encouraging sign. In my experience, newcomers – particularly female ones – are far too eager to pin their colours to the mast of any staffroom coterie that will have them. Jennifer Dodd, who used to be my closest friend at the school, spent her first three weeks at St George's buried in the welcoming bosoms of Mary Horsely and Diane Nebbins. Mary and Diane are two hippies from the Maths department. They both carry packets of 'women's tea' in their handbags and use jagged lumps of rock crystal in lieu of anti-perspirant. They were entirely ill-suited – temperament-wise, humour-wise, world view-wise – to be Jennifer's friends. But they happened to get to her first and Jennifer was so grateful for someone being nice to her that she cheerfully undertook to ignore their soy milk mumbo-jumbo. I dare say she would have plighted her troth to a Moonie during her first week at St George's, if the Moonie had been quick enough off the mark.

Sheba displayed no such new-girl jitters and for this I admired her. She did not exempt me from her general aloofness. Owing to my seniority at St George's and the fact that I am more formal in manner than most of my colleagues, I am used to being treated with a certain deference. But Sheba seemed to be oblivious of my status. There was little indication, for a long time, that she really *saw* me at all. Yet, in spite of this, I found myself possessed by a strange certainty that we would one day be friends.

Early on, we made a few tentative approaches to one another. Somewhere in her second week, Sheba greeted me in the corridor. (She used 'Hello', I was pleased to note, as opposed to the awful, mid-Atlantic 'Hiya' that so many of the staff favour.) And another time, walking from the arts centre after an assembly, we shared some brief, rueful comments about the choral performance that had just taken place. My feelings of connection to Sheba did not depend upon these minute exchanges, however. The bond that I sensed, even at that stage, went far beyond anything that might have been expressed in quotidian chit-chat. It was an intuited kinship. An unspoken understanding. Does it sound too dramatic to call it spiritual recognition? Owing to our mutual reserve, I understood that it would take time for us to form a friendship. But when we did, I had no doubt that it would prove to be one of uncommon intimacy and trust – a relationship *de chaleur* as the French say.

In the meantime, I watched from afar and listened with interest to the gossip that circulated about her in the staffroom.

For most of the staff, Sheba's dignified self-containment acted as a sort of force-field, repelling the usual impertinent enquiries about home life and political allegiance. But elegance loses its power in the presence of the properly stupid, and there were a few who were not deterred. From time to time, I would spot certain staff members zooming in on Sheba in the car park or playground, stunning her into submission with their vulgar curiosity. They never achieved the immediate intimacy that they were seeking. But they usually managed to extract some piece of information as a consolation prize. It was from these eager little fishwives that the rest of the staffroom learned that Sheba was married with two children; that her husband was a lecturer; that her children were educated privately; that she lived in 'a ginormous house' in Highgate.

Inevitably, given the quality of the intermediaries, much of this information arrived in somewhat scrambled form. On one occasion I overheard Theresa Shreve, who teaches Educational Guidance, informing Marian Simmons, head of Lower Sixth, that Sheba's father was famous. 'Yeah,' she said. 'He's like, dead now. But he was a very important academic.'

Marian asked what discipline he had worked in.

'What?' Theresa said.

'What was his academic subject?' Marian clarified.

'Ooh, do you know, I don't know!' Theresa said. 'He was called Donald Taylor and he invented the word "inflation", I think.'

Thus did one gather that Sheba's father was Ronald Taylor, the Cambridge economist, who had died five years before, shortly after turning down an OBE. (His official reason had been that he didn't agree with the honours system, but the newspapers speculated that he was offended at not having been given a knighthood.)

'I think you'll find, Theresa,' I interrupted at this point, 'that Mrs Hart's father's name was Ronald. He didn't "invent inflation", as you say. He devised an important theory about the relationship between inflation and consumer expectation.'

Theresa looked at me with the sullen expression that so many people of her generation wear when one attempts to assail their ignorance. 'Uh-huh,' she said.

The other thing that became known in those early weeks was that Sheba was experiencing 'class control issues'. This was not entirely unexpected. Because Highgate is part of its catchment area, people often assume that St George's is one of those safe, soft comprehensives, full of posh children toting their cellos to orchestra practice. But posh parents don't surrender their offspring to St George's. The cello-players get sent to St Botolph's Girls or King Henry's Boys, or to private schools in other parts of London. St George's is the holding pen for Archway's pubescent proles – the children of the council estates who must fidget and scrap here for a minimum of five years until they can embrace their fates as plumbers and shop assistants. Last year, we had 240 pupils sit their GCSEs and exactly six of them achieved anything higher than a grade E pass. The school represents – how to put it? – a very *volatile* environment. Attacks on the staff are not uncommon. The year before Sheba arrived, three Year Eight boys, leaning out of one of the science lab windows, pelted the school secretary, Deirdre Rickman, with Bunsen burners. (Her resulting injuries included a fractured clavicle and a head wound requiring fourteen stitches.)

The boys naturally present the worst problems. But the girls are no picnic either. They're not quite as disposed to violence, but they are just as foul-mouthed and they possess a superior gift for insult. Not long ago, a girl in my Year Nine class – an angry little virago-in-training by the name of Denise Callaghan – called me, without any apparent forethought, 'a chewy-faced old bitch'. This sort of thing occurs very rarely in my classroom and when it does I am able, in almost every case, to stamp it out immediately. But for more junior members of the St George's staff, maintaining basic order is an ongoing and frequently bloody battle. For a novice like Sheba – a *wispy* novice with a tinkly accent and see-through skirts – the potential for disaster was great.

Later on, I learned the details of what happened in Sheba's first class. She had been put in what is grandly called the school 'studio' – a pre-fabricated hut adjoining the arts centre, which, for some years, since the departure of the last pottery teacher, had been used as a storage room. It was rather dark and musty, but Sheba had made an effort to cheer the place up with museum posters and some geranium cuttings taken from her garden that morning.

She had worked very conscientiously on her lesson plan. Her intention was to begin her first class of Year Nines with a short talk about what pottery *was* – the primal, creative impulse that it represented and the important role that it played in the earliest civilizations. After that, she was going to let the children handle some clay. She would ask them to construct a bowl – any sort of bowl they liked – and whatever they managed to produce she would fire in the kiln, in time for the next class. When the bell rang for first period, and her pupils began trickling in, her mood was bordering on elation. This, she had decided, was going to be great *fun*.

She waited until she judged that most of the class was present before standing up to say hello. But as she was introducing herself she was interrupted by Michael Beale – a wiry boy with a sinister, grey front tooth – who rushed towards her from the back of the class, shouting, 'I fancy you, Miss!' She chuckled gamely and asked him to take a seat. But he ignored her and remained standing. Shortly thereafter, another boy joined him. Having looked Sheba up and down, this lad – it was James Thornham, I think – announced to the class, in a sardonic monotone, that their teacher had 'little tits'. Even as the class was showing its appreciation for this witty observation, yet another boy stood up on one of the work tables and began chanting, 'Show us your tits.' Apparently this met with a derisive response from some of the female class members who called upon the boy in question to 'show his willy' and made offers of a magnifying glass for the purpose.

Sheba was having to hold back her tears by this stage. She sternly enjoined the class to settle down and for a moment, to her surprise, there was semi-quiet. She was starting to introduce herself again when a girl of South East Asian parentage, whom Sheba had identified as one of the more demure and well-behaved pupils, leaned back in her chair and shouted, 'Oi! Miss is wearing a see-through skirt. You can practically see her knickers!' The entire class broke out in cheers. 'Miss, how come you're not wearing a slip? . . . Come on, Miss, show us your tits . . . Miss, Miss, where d'you get that skirt? Oxfam?' Sheba did begin to cry now. 'Please,' she kept shouting above the din. 'Please. Would you please stop being so beastly for a *minute*?'

At the time, I was aware of none of these particulars. But I received a general idea of Sheba's troubles from the gleeful staffroom hearsay. The word on Sheba was that she was a short-fuse type. An exploder. One lunchtime, a fortnight into term, I overheard Elaine Clifford describing what one of her Year Eights had told her about Sheba.

'The kids go wild on her, apparently,' Elaine said. 'She like, begs them to be good. And then the next thing, she loses her rag. Curses at them. "Bloody" this and "F" that. All sorts.'

This worried me a good deal. The Head tends to be pretty soft on cursing. But strictly speaking, uttering expletives in the presence of the children is a sackable offence. It is not so uncommon for teachers – particularly inexperienced ones – to start out negotiating with unruly pupils and then, when that approach fails, to resort abruptly to anger. But, in most cases, these transitions have an element of calculated, or affected ferocity. The teacher is *performing* rage. If children see someone like Sheba truly losing control – shouting, swearing and so forth – they are delighted. They sense, not incorrectly, that a victory has been won. I wanted very much to take Sheba aside and tell her, tactfully, where she was going wrong. But I was shy. I didn't know how to broach the matter without seeming like a busybody. So I kept my own counsel and waited.

In Sheba's third week at the school, a Geography teacher called Jerry Samuels was patrolling the school property for truants when he passed the arts centre and heard what sounded like a riot inside Sheba's hut. When he went in to investigate, he found the studio in uproar. The entire Year Eight class was having a clay fight. Several of the boys were stripped to the waist. Two of them were endeavouring to topple the kiln. Samuels discovered Sheba cowering, tearfully, behind her desk. 'In ten years of teaching, I've never seen anything like it,' he later told the staffroom. 'It was *Lord of the Flies* in there.'

Two

You never appreciate what a compost your memory is until you start trying to smooth past events into a rational sequence. To make sure that I maintain maximum accuracy in this narrative, I have started putting together a timeline of Sheba's year at St George's. I store it – along with the manuscript – under my mattress at night. The timeline is just a little thing on graph paper but I believe it's going to be very useful. Yesterday, I bought a packet of stick-on gold stars at the newsagent's. I shall be using these to mark the truly seminal events. I've already used a star, for example, to indicate the first time that Sheba and I spoke in the staffroom. After that, there's a bit of a blank until Sheba's fourth week at St George's which is when, if my calculations are correct, she met Connolly for the first time.

The occasion for this meeting was a session of the school's Homework Club. Notwithstanding her difficulties in maintaining order, Sheba was expected to participate in the full range of staff duties – playground patrol, canteen shift and, perhaps most daunting of all, Homework Club supervision. 'Haitch Cee', as it is known to the pupils, is held in a Middle Hall classroom, every weekday between the hours of 3.30 and 6 p.m. It was set up a few years ago by the Head, with the official purpose of 'providing a quiet working environment for those who might have difficulty finding one in their own homes'. It is a deeply unpopular institution among the staff, mainly because it tends to double as a dumping ground for children who have received detentions. Club supervisors usually find themselves having to deal with the school's worst pupils at a point in the day when those pupils are at their most restive and difficult.

There were ten children in the Homework Club on the afternoon that Sheba was supervising. Almost immediately after she began taking attendance, a violent dispute broke out between two Year Nine girls, one of whom was accusing the other of putting chewing gum in her hair. For the next three-quarters of an hour or so, Sheba's attention was taken up with keeping the girls physically apart from one another. It was not until she sent one of the girls to the head of Year Nine that things settled down and she had leisure to notice the other children in the room. There were now three girls and six boys present, all of whom, according to the teachers' notes that they had brought with them, were attending HC as punishment. They returned Sheba's gaze with reflexive surliness. Only one boy, at the very back of the room, sat working quietly. Sheba remembers being touched by his child-like posture of concentration – the way his tongue was peeping out from his mouth and his left arm was curled protectively around his labours. This was Steven Connolly.

A little while later, when she had issued the usual reminder about assigned tasks having to be completed by five o'clock, she got up and wandered over to where the boy was sitting. He winced slightly when he saw her approaching, and drew himself upright. 'What?' he said. 'I'm not doing nothing wrong.' From across the room, Sheba had assumed he was a Year Eight or Year Nine pupil. But at close range, he seemed older. His upper body had a solid, triangular look. His hands and forearms were unexpectedly large. She could see the beginnings of bristle on his chin.

Sheba has always maintained that Connolly is a terrifically attractive boy and, to be fair to her, several female newspaper columnists have made observations to similar effect. ('Glowering and exotic' one woman in the *Mail* called him a few weeks back.) I don't see it, I must confess. I have never been physically drawn to any of my pupils of course, so I may not be the best person to assess the boy's charms. Yet, I rather think that if my tastes *had* run in that direction, I would have fixed upon someone a little prettier: a delicate-boned, downy-faced boy in the lower school, perhaps. Connolly is not pretty in the slightest. He is a coarse-looking fellow, with lank hair the colour of pee and a loose, plump-lipped mouth. His nose, owing to a childhood accident (an ardent game of kiss-chase, an unanticipated pot-hole) is quite severely squished. His eyes are heavy-hooded and so down-turned as to bring to mind a tragedy mask. Sheba insists that he has superb skin and it is true, I suppose, that he has been spared the sort of suppurating carbuncles to which boys of his age are prone. But what she refers to as his 'olive complexion' has always struck me as rather dingy. I can never lay eyes on the boy without wanting to give his face a good going-over with a hot flannel.

On Connolly's desk, Sheba saw a torn out magazine advertisement for a sale at Harrods. It was illustrated with one of those highly stylized, pen-and-ink sketches of a woman in a fur stole: all hourglass waist and scornful expression. Connolly was copying the image into the back page of his Maths workbook. Sheba assured him she had not come over to tell him off. She just wanted to see what he was up to. His sketch was good, she said. The embarrassment, or perhaps the pleasure, caused by this praise made him squirm. (Sheba remembers him twisting his head from side to side, 'like a blind person'.) 'But you know,' she went on, 'you don't have to copy things. Why don't you draw something from life? Or even your imagination?' Connolly's face, which had momentarily softened under flattery, closed up again. He shrugged irritably.

Sheba struggled to correct herself. 'No,' she said, 'because, I mean, I bet you could do really brilliant things. This is very, very good.' She began asking him a few questions about himself. What was his name? How old was he? She expressed some disappointment that he wasn't in her pottery class. What option was he taking instead? Connolly looked stricken when she asked this and muttered something that Sheba couldn't make out.

'What's that?' she asked.

'Special Needs, Miss,' he repeated in a croak.

Contrary to some of the reports that have since emerged, Connolly was not 'backward' or 'retarded'. Along with a good 25 per cent of St George's students, he had been identified as having 'literacy issues' – difficulties with reading and writing – and was therefore eligible for daily Special Needs sessions. On questioning the boy further, Sheba discovered that Special Needs also prevented him from participating in Art classes. She told him that she was surprised about this and suggested that something might be done to rectify the situation. Connolly was shrugging non-committally when Sheba was suddenly called away. One of her Year Eight charges was attempting to burn a Year Seven with a disposable lighter.

That night, she says, she remembered her brief interaction with Connolly and put a little note in her diary reminding herself to enquire about the possibility of rejigging his time-table. It was wrong, she felt, that the boy should be prevented from pursuing a subject – perhaps the only subject – for which he had some aptitude. She wanted to help.

Such do-gooding fantasies are not uncommon in comprehensive schools these days. Many of the younger teachers harbour secret hopes of 'making a difference'. They have all seen the American films in which lovely young women tame inner-city thugs with recitations of Dylan Thomas. They, too, want to conquer their little charges' hearts with poetry and compassion. When I was at teacher training college there was none of this sort of thing. My fellow students and I never thought of raising self-esteem or making dreams come true. Our expectations did not go beyond guiding our prospective pupils through the three Rs and providing them with some pointers on personal hygiene. Perhaps we were lacking in idealism. But then it strikes me as not coincidental that in the same period that pedagogical ambitions have become so inflated and grandiose, the standards of basic literacy and numeracy have radically declined. We might not have fretted much about our children's souls in the old days, but we did send them out knowing how to do long division.

Sheba never did succeed in having Connolly's schedule altered, of course. She went as far as going to see Ted Mawson, who is responsible for devising the school timetable. But Mawson brusquely dismissed her request, explaining that to design simultaneous timetables for 1,300 children was 'like playing three dimensional chess' and that if he started dithering over this one's lost Art class or that one's missed Woodwork, he would never get the job done. Anxious not to be difficult, Sheba apologized furiously. 'This *is* a comprehensive school,' Mawson told her in a jokily reproachful tone as she backed out of his office, 'not the bloody *Lycée*.' Sheba seems to have been rather outraged by this last comment, detecting in it a dig at her privileged naivety. At the time, she promised herself to pursue the matter further – with the Head, if necessary. But she never did. Other things came up, she says. She got too busy. Or perhaps, one conjectures, like so many would-be reformers before her, she simply lost interest.

A few days after meeting Connolly for the first time, Sheba found a picture in her pigeon-hole. It was a rudimentary pencil sketch of a woman, executed on lined foolscap, in the romantic style often favoured by pavement artists. The woman had vast, woozy eyes and long, long arms that resolved themselves in odd, fingerless trowels. She was gazing into the distance with an expression of slightly cross-eyed eroticism. Ballooning out from her low-cut blouse was a good amount of heavily cross-hatched cleavage. In the bottom right-hand corner of the page the anonymous author of the sketch had written in large, unwieldy italics the words, *Foxy Lady*.

Sheba understood, more or less straightaway, that she was the foxy lady in question, that the picture was intended as a portrait, and that it had been drawn by the blond-haired boy from the previous week's HC. She was not alarmed. On the contrary, she was pleased and rather flattered. In the brutal atmosphere of St George's, the gesture struck her as eccentrically innocent. She didn't seek Connolly out to thank him for the drawing. She assumed that, since he had sent it anonymously, any acknowledgement on her part would embarrass him. But she expected that he would, sooner or later, make some approach to her. And sure enough, one day shortly before the half-term break, she found him dawdling outside her studio as she was leaving for lunch.

Sheba remembers Connolly being poorly dressed for the weather. It was a blowy October day and he had on only a T-shirt and a flimsy cotton jacket. When he lifted the T-shirt to scratch absent-mindedly at his belly, Sheba saw how his pelvic bone jutted out, creating a wide, shallow cavity just above his groin. She had forgotten that about young men's bodies, she says.

'Did you get that picture, then?' Connolly asked.

'What,' she said, feigning surprise, 'you mean it was from you?'

Connolly allowed, coyly, that this might be the case.

Sheba told him it was a lovely picture and that if he really

29

had drawn it, he ought to have signed it. 'Wait a minute,' she said. She unlocked the door and went back into the studio where she took the drawing out from the bottom drawer of her desk. 'Why don't you sign it for me now?' she asked.

Connolly, who was still standing in the doorway, looked at her uncertainly.

'Why, Miss?' he asked.

Sheba laughed. 'No reason. I just thought it would be nice. You don't have to. But usually artists like to take credit for their work.'

Connolly came over to the desk and looked at the drawing. It was not as good as some of the other things he had done, he told her. He couldn't do hands. Sheba agreed that hands were very hard and went on to utter some encouraging words about the value of practice and of studying life models. At a certain point, she noticed him gazing at her own hands. She was shy, she recalls, because they were so rough and unkempt. She put the picture down and folded her arms. 'I had a word with Mr Mawson about changing your timetable,' she said. 'Apparently it's not as easy as I thought.' Connolly nodded, unsurprised. 'But I haven't given up,' she added quickly. 'I'm definitely going to keep trying and in the meantime the most important thing is for you to keep drawing.'

There was a short silence. Then Connolly confessed hesitantly that his picture had been intended as a portrait of her. Sheba nodded and told him that she had guessed as much. The boy became flustered and began to stammer. In a clumsy attempt to put him at his ease, Sheba made a joking comment about the generous bosom he had given her. 'Wishful thinking,' she said. But this only exacerbated the boy's embarrassment. He turned quite purple, apparently, and did not say anything for a long time.

Sheba was tickled by this episode. It was a novelty, she says, to be so candidly admired. When she first told me this, I remember expressing some incredulity. I could believe that Richard's affection might have grown complacent over the years, or perhaps just so reliable as not to count. But surely she wasn't suggesting that she had been in want of admirers before Connolly? Sheba? Who made the men in the St George's staffroom gaga with her flimsy blouses? No, she insisted. *That* was quite different. There had always been men who made furtive google eyes at her, men who made it clear that they found her attractive. But no one, before Connolly, had ever truly *pursued* her. She used to think it was out of respect for her having a husband. But it had to have been something else. If everybody was so reverent of the institution of marriage, how did all the adultery get committed? Perhaps, she said, the more plausible explanation lay with the kind of men she had consorted with. Most of Richard's friends were academic types, and they were all terrified at the thought of being 'cheesy' or insensitive. If they flirted, it was always an arch, joking sort of thing. Even when they told you that your dress was nice, they put it in quotation marks in case you took offence and slapped their faces.

There had been one fellow, several years before, a visiting professor of Linguistics from Finland who accompanied her home from the opera one night after Richard had been forced to retire early with food poisoning. He had made a fairly unambiguous pass at her, as she was getting out of the cab. But even that had come to nothing. Sheba said that she had sensed something resentful about him, as if he begrudged her for having the power to attract him. The moment she resisted – or hesitated, actually – he had become very nasty and rude. He had suspected all along that she was 'a tease', he told her. Only Connolly, who was either too young, or too obtuse, to appreciate the outrageousness of his ambition, had dared to reach out to her with any charm or persistence. *He* hadn't been scared of her, or angry with her. He didn't tie himself in rhetorical knots trying to be equal to her beauty. When he looked at her, it was as if he were gobbling her up, she said. 'Like a peach.'

∞

Throughout the first half of the winter term, I had been building up my confidence to tackle Sheba on the matter of class discipline. In the final week before the half-term holiday, I believe I might have done so. But on the Monday morning of that week, I became aware of a new development – one so unexpected and disappointing that it quite stopped me in my tracks.

I was standing in my classroom during the second period, which I happened to have free that day, when through the window I glimpsed Sheba walking across the playground from the science block towards Old Hall. She was with Sue Hodge, the head of Music. Until this moment, I had been unaware that the women knew each other. But something in Sheba's body language – a certain animation in her gestures – suggested to me now that they were on quite familiar terms. They were walking close to one another, so close that Sue's over-stuffed canvas handbag was bumping against Sheba's skinny hip. Sheba didn't seem to notice this. She was laughing at something that Sue was saying, throwing back her head so that I could see her long white neck and the two dark pinholes of her nostrils. Sue was laughing too. She's a big woman and mirth tends to have a rather unseemly effect on her. Together, they made a sound raucous enough to penetrate the windows of my classroom. *Ha ha ha.* After a few moments, I grew fearful that they would catch me spying and I drew the curtains.

I am not an alarmist by nature and I was careful not to draw any dramatic conclusions from the scene I had witnessed. But three days later, on Thursday, I overheard Bob Baker, a Science teacher, remark, in a rather catty way, to Antonia Robinson that Sheba appeared to have 'chummed up' with Hodge. One recent afternoon, Bob said, Sue had put Sheba's bike in the back of her car and given her a lift home.

This was confirmation of my grimmest suspicions. Sheba had picked Sue Hodge to be her intimate. *Sue Hodge!* Had it emerged earlier in the term, I might have assumed that this liaison was a mistake: another one of those short-lived pacts dictated by exigency rather than true fellow feeling. But given how long Sheba had maintained a stately separateness from the rest of the staff, the friendship had to be acknowledged as a considered and deliberate choice on her part. My initial shock swiftly gave way to indignation. For weeks, Sheba had saved herself, fended off all advances, only to succumb to *this* ridiculous creature?

I used to run into Sue Hodge quite a lot. Being smokers, we both tended to nip off at lunchtimes for a fag at La Traviata, the Italian café down the road from St George's. We never sat together. There was something of a *froideur* between us, dating from an occasion a few years earlier, when Sue had caught me sniggering over one of her class worksheets entitled, 'Dem Bones: the cultural roots of the negro spiritual'. Sue is a frightfully pretentious woman – always making the children do expressive dances to Pink Floyd and singing 'American Pie' with them, playing her horrid little banjo. Underneath all that free and easy hippy malarkey she is actually the most awful prig – the sort of woman who wears Lady-Lite panty liners every day of the month, as if there is nothing her body secretes that she doesn't think vile enough to be captured in cotton wool, wrapped in paper bags and thrust far, far down at the bottom of the waste-paper bin. (I've been in the staff toilet after her and I know.)

Also – and this was what made Sheba's interest in her particularly incomprehensible – Sue is terrifyingly dull. A living anthology of mediocre sentiments. A woman whose idea of an excellent *bon mot* is to sidle up to someone on a hot summer day and bark, excitedly, 'Hot enough for ya?' Many years ago, before the negro spirituals incident, I had the misfortune of spending half an hour waiting with Sue at the bus stop. At some point she actually turned to me and declared, in the halting, exultant manner of a person who was just then minting a delicious epigram, 'You wait – when the bus finally comes, there'll be five of them right behind it.'

On the Friday of that week, I was sitting at my usual lunchtime table at La Traviata when Sue arrived with Sheba. They were whooping and guffawing about something as they entered the restaurant. The imminence of the holiday had apparently put them in exuberant spirits. Or perhaps, I thought, a certain kind of self-conscious hilarity was the signature mood of their friendship. Even after they had sat down they continued to break out periodically in giggles. Sue kept glancing around the restaurant, as if to make sure that their riotous fun was receiving sufficient attention. To avoid providing any gratification on that score, I took out a book and began to read. Although I hardly looked in their direction for the duration of my meal, I continued to be aware of their laughter. By the time I left the restaurant, there were five cigarette stubs in the little tin ashtray on my table, and my mood was dark.

In order to fully convey the effect that this episode had upon my spirits, I should explain that some years ago, I was dealt a very severe blow when my friend Jennifer Dodd announced that she wanted no further contact with me. She and I had been extremely close for more than a year and there had been no warning of this volte-face. I was bewildered. She had recently taken up with a young man – a painter and decorator who had been doing some work on her sister's house in Richmond – but she insisted that he was not the cause of her sudden change of heart. Beyond some mysterious references to my being 'too intense', she refused to furnish *any* explanation for her decision. When I attempted to plead my cause, she clammed up and the more I cajoled and questioned, the colder and more unpleasant she became. In the last conversation we ever had, she actually threatened to take out a legal injunction against me if I did not leave her alone. And then one Saturday, about six weeks later, I was sitting on the train, going to do some Christmas shopping in the West End, when Jennifer and her new beau boarded at Mornington Crescent.

They sat on the other side of the car, just a few seats down from mine. As soon as she spotted me, Jennifer turned her head and looked in the other direction. But the young man – Jason was his name – proceeded to stare at me in an insolent and challenging fashion. He was a shiny-faced, empty-eyed sort of chap, with one of those 'developed' bodies that men acquire from heaving dumb-bells about in gyms. The one time we had met previously, I had taken great pains to be polite to him, and afterwards I had communicated my misgivings to Jennifer in the gentlest manner possible. So it was unclear why he should now be adopting this aggressive posture towards me. Not wanting to appear intimidated, I returned his stare with an icy glare of my own. And then, evidently in some sort of fury, he turned to Jennifer, grasped her by her shoulders and kissed her. The aim, it seems, was to assert his proprietorial rights over my friend. When he finally released her, he fixed me with a horrible smile and made an obscene gesture – right there in the crowded carriage, in front of everyone. I could hardly believe it. When the train drew into the next station, I fled. For half an hour after that, I sat on a bench on the Goodge Street platform and wept.

Watching Sue snuggle up to Sheba at La Traviata, I was reminded of all this unpleasantness and the recollection acted as a kind of alarm. My relationship with Jennifer had been a good deal more important and profound than any nascent feelings of affection I might have been harbouring for Sheba. But the hurt that she had inflicted had been the same *sort* of hurt that I was experiencing now. My mistake with Jennifer had been to attribute to her an intelligence that had never really existed. For the last six weeks, I realized, I had been making the same mistake with Sheba. Thank God she had revealed her true colours at this juncture, before I had invested any more of my feelings! Once again, I told myself, I had made an error of judgement. Sheba was not my soul-mate. Not my kindred spirit. She wasn't, in fact, my sort at all.

After the half-term holiday, I desisted from all the little genialities with which I had been attempting to semaphore my goodwill towards Sheba. I deliberately allowed my warm feelings to curdle into contempt. Occasionally, I confess, I went too far and stooped to some slightly childish insults. I would cough with suppressed laughter when Sheba was speaking to someone. Or I would do a dramatic double take when she walked into the staffroom, to indicate my disapproval of her attire. Once, when the hem of her skirt was hanging down at the back, I made a great show of presenting her with a safety pin in front of several colleagues.

None of these petty gestures brought me much solace. Sheba did not rise to my provocations. Mostly, in fact, she didn't seem to notice that she was being provoked. She blushed the time I gave her the safety pin. But then she smiled and thanked me profusely, as if she hadn't registered my animus at all.

Eventually, in desperation, I tried a more forthright attack. Sheba came into the staffroom early one morning before the start of classes and stood next to me at the kitchenette counter, rinsing out one of the tannin-stained cups that were designated for general use. Most of the St George's staff members brought in their own mugs from home, but for some reason Sheba never bothered. I was about to comment sardonically on the dubious hygiene of her drinking vessel, when Brian Bangs, a Maths teacher, pushed in between us.

'Hiya, ladies!' he boomed. 'Good weekend?'

Bangs is a rather pitiful man. He sports a more or less permanent shaving rash and he is always very, very nervous. Even his most minor conversational sallies have an agonized, over-meditated quality and he tends to pitch his voice one or two uncomfortable decibels above the standard register. Talking to him is rather like attempting to converse with a school play. I nodded at him curtly, but Sheba was more magnanimous.

'Hello, Brian,' she said. 'Not a bad weekend, thanks. And yours?'

'Oh great, yeah,' Bangs replied. 'I went to Arsenal on Saturday.'

'Yes?' Sheba said.

'Great match,' Bangs said. 'Yeah, terrific . . .'

Sheba nodded.

'We won Liverpool three nil,' Bangs shouted woodenly. He made a fist and punched the air triumphantly. 'Yesss.'

'Ahh.' Sheba was concentrating now, on squashing a tea-bag against the side of her cup. 'How satisfactory.' She spooned out the tea-bag, poured in some milk.

'That's . . . that's a lovely blouse you have on,' Bangs said. He was pointing, rather rudely, at Sheba's chest.

'What?' Sheba was momentarily nonplussed. She picked up

a corner of her blouse, as if to remind herself of what she had on, and gazed at it sceptically. 'Huh. Well, thank you.'

'Is it new, then?' Bangs said quickly.

'No, I've had it for years, actually.'

'Yeah? Is that right? Well, it doesn't look old at all. It's dead nice. You should wear it more often.'

'Oh . . . okay,' Sheba said, laughing.

I had finished making my tea. Elaine Clifford and a French teacher called Michael Self approached the counter now, to prepare their instant coffee. But I remained where I was, listening with a kind of irritated fascination to the exchange between Sheba and Bangs. It amazed me that Sheba would bestow kind attention on such a cretin, while ignoring me.

'So, em – what do you think of *my* shirt?' Bangs was saying. He stepped back from us and, with his hands on his hips, made two twirling rotations in imitation of a fashion model. It was the kind of larky behaviour that men like him – ungainly, fundamentally without comic gift – are best advised to avoid.

The garment for which he was seeking Sheba's approval was a sky blue office shirt with a stiff white collar and one large breast pocket on which a designer logo had been emblazoned. Judging from the symmetrical fold marks that scored his chest, it was a brand-new purchase.

Sheba put down her mug and examined Bangs gravely. 'Oh yes,' she said. 'Lovely.' She wasn't at all convincing. She spoke as if she were praising a child's potato print.

But Bangs responded to her approbation with undoubting, ingenuous delight. 'Yeah? You like it?'

'*Yes*,' Sheba said. 'It's great. Very smart.'

'I wasn't sure about . . . the collar and everything, you know. I thought it might be a bit flash for me.'

'Oh no,' Sheba said. 'It's a great shirt.'

I couldn't stand it any longer. The two of them were

twittering away at each other as though I didn't exist. I groped for something witty with which to reassert my presence. 'Your children are educated privately aren't they, Sheba?' I blurted.

Sheba leaned towards me with a smile, holding a cupped hand to her ear. 'Sorry, Barbara,' she said, 'what was that?'

'I said, you send your children to private schools, don't you?' There was a silence.

'Isn't that right?' I added.

Bangs and Elaine and Michael looked at me, startled. Then all three of them smirked. At this stage, everyone on the staff knew about Sheba's two children attending private schools – the French teacher Linda Preel had got it out of her early on in the term – but no one had yet bearded her on the issue. They were all too sissy. Personally, I have no quarrel with private education. My first job in teaching was at a fee-paying school in Dumfries and, had it not been for certain personal difficulties that I experienced with staff members at that institution, I might well be teaching there still. For my simple-minded colleagues, however, private education is a sin pure and simple. It's up there with fur coats and fox hunting, on their all-time top ten list of Things They Reelly Reelly Disapprove Of.

Sheba turned to me, with a slightly puzzled look on her face. 'Yes,' she said. 'My daughter is at boarding school, actually. She was at Maitland Park Comp for a bit, but she didn't like it there much.'

'I see,' I said. 'And your son? Has he also stated an objection to state school oiks?'

Sheba smiled evenly. 'Well, Ben goes to a special place –'

'Ahhh!' I interrupted. 'A *special* place.'

'Yes.' Sheba paused. 'He has Down's Syndrome.'

Elaine and Michael's expectant grins sagged. Bangs looked as if he might faint.

'Oh,' I said. 'I'm sorry, I . . .'

Sheba shook her head. 'Please, don't be.'

Elaine and Michael and Bangs had reorganized their expressions into maudlin frowns of sympathy. I wanted to slap them.

'No, sorry,' I said. 'I didn't mean that I was sorry –'

'I know,' Sheba stopped me. 'It's just one of those bits of information to which there is no good response.'

There it was again – the perverse refusal to acknowledge my hostility. She seemed to me like some magical lake in a fairy tale: nothing could disturb the mirror-calm of her surface. My snide comments and bitter jokes disappeared soundlessly into her depths, leaving not so much as a ripple.

I would like to say that I was ashamed of myself. I am certainly ashamed now. But what I felt at the time was rage: the boiling rage of defeat. After this incident, I stopped trying to goad Sheba and stayed away from her. Sometimes, if we ran into each other in the school corridor, I would acknowledge her with the slightest inclination of my head. But more often, I gazed stoically into the middle distance and hurried past.

Three

The irony of my having agonized over Sheba's friendship with Fatty Hodge, when all the time she was preparing to fornicate with a minor, does not escape me. It is sad and rather galling to reflect that I wasted all that time on the mystery of Sue's allure, while the much more lethal liaison was brewing away beneath my nose. I am not prepared, however, to say that my concerns were *altogether* misdirected. It seems to me that if Sheba had made a wiser choice of girl friend – if she had chosen me over Sue from the start – it is quite possible that she might have avoided the Connolly imbroglio. I do not mean to exaggerate the beneficial effects of my friendship, or, for that matter, the deleterious influence of Sue. I have always been careful to avoid simple, catch-all explanations for what Sheba did and it would certainly be foolish to offload the responsibility for her actions onto anyone else. But if, at this very challenging period in her life, Sheba had been receiving the emotional support of a sensible adult, I do believe she would have been a good deal less tempted by whatever specious comforts Connolly had to offer. In fact, when I look back on this period, I am struck not by the inappropriateness of my anxieties concerning Sheba but, on the contrary, by how accurately I had intuited her vulnerability. All the anguish I felt about her and Hodge – all the frustration I felt at being shut out of her life – is revealed, now, to have been very much *au point*. I alone, of all her friends and family and colleagues, it seems, had sensed her desperate need for guidance.

Right after half-term, Connolly turned up at Sheba's studio

again. She was alone in the hut at the end of the school day, collecting up some animal figurines that her Year Sevens had made, when he appeared. He had some pictures that he wanted to show her, he said. It had been raining on and off throughout the day. His hair was sticking close to his head and there was a sweet smell of damp clothes about him. When he came close, she caught a whiff of his breath and that smelled sweet too – candied almost, Sheba thought. They sat down and looked at his sketches – all of which, in deference to her advice, he had drawn from life models. Then they examined some of the Year Seven's pandas and lions, laughing together at the particularly clumsy ones. At a certain point, Sheba started trying to explain the principles of glazing. She was impressed by how attentively he listened. He seemed genuinely interested, she thought. Interested and eager to learn. *This*, she told herself, was what she had hoped teaching would be.

Shortly before Connolly left that afternoon, he looked up at a British Museum poster of an ancient Roman urn and remarked on how odd it was to think of an actual person – 'a real bloke, thousands of years ago' – creating the artefact. Sheba glanced at him warily. Until now, none of the children had shown the slightest interest in her posters. Connolly's comment was so much the sort of sentiment that she had wanted to inspire, that she half suspected him of mocking her.

'It does your brain in, doesn't it?' he added now, flicking at his fringe. His face yielded no trace of satirical intent.

'Yes,' she replied, eagerly. 'Yes. *Exactly*. You're right. It *does* do your brain in.'

He prepared to leave. Sheba told him to drop by with his sketches whenever he wanted. 'Perhaps the next time you come,' she added, 'we'll have a go at making something with clay.' Connolly nodded, but made no other response and Sheba feared that she had overstepped the mark. When

Connolly didn't show up on the following Tuesday or Wednesday or Thursday, she took it as confirmation that she had.

The next Friday, though, just as Sheba was loading the kiln, Connolly reappeared. He had been unable to come earlier in the week, he explained, because he had been tied up with detentions. Sheba, determined not to be overbearing this time, shrugged and said she was glad to see him. He had brought more of his sketches and, again, they sat for a long time examining his work, before going on to chat more generally about school and other matters. He stayed with her for almost two hours. Towards the end of his visit, Sheba was discussing the science of kiln temperatures when he interrupted her to comment on how nicely she spoke. She didn't need to be a teacher, he told her earnestly. She could get a job 'doing the weather on the telly, or something'. Sheba smiled, amused by his gaucheness. She would keep the career tip in mind, she told him.

When he returned the next week, he did not bring his sketch pad. He hadn't got round to any drawing that week, he said. He had just dropped in for a chat. Sheba, who was pleased that he no longer needed the pretext of seeking her artistic advice in order to visit her, welcomed him warmly. There was a book of Degas reproductions lying on her desk – she had brought it in, hoping to charm her Year Eight girls with ballerinas – and when Connolly picked it up, she encouraged him to look inside.

He began leafing through the book, stopping every now and then to let Sheba paraphrase the commentary on a particular painting or sculpture. She was very pleased with his response to a painting entitled *Sulking*. Reading from the book, she informed him that the relationship between the man and the woman in the picture was mysterious and that nobody knew for sure which one of them was meant to be the sulker.

After looking at the picture again, Connolly declared that there was no mystery – the man was clearly the sulking party. The woman was bending towards him, trying to get something from him and his hunched, irascible posture indicated his displeasure. Sheba was impressed by this analysis and she congratulated Connolly on being an acute observer of body language. After he had gone, she found herself chuckling aloud. Connolly's Special Needs teacher would have been very shocked, she thought, if he could have seen his learning-disabled pupil chattering so enthusiastically about Degas!

As time went on and Connolly's visits became routine, he was emboldened to volunteer more of his insights about art and his ideas about the world. Sometimes, when he and Sheba were talking or looking at pictures, he would get up suddenly and go to the studio window to comment on the shapes of the clouds, or the purplish colour of the early evening sky. Once, in what was surely a rather desperate moment, he even stroked the nubby mustard material of the studio curtains and pronounced it 'an interesting fabric'.

It is pretty clear to me that there was a strong element of calculation in these little bursts of wistfulness and wonderment. By which I do not mean to imply that the boy was cynical, exactly. Simply anxious to please. He had observed that Sheba liked him best when he was saying sensitive things about paintings and so on, and he was beefing up his moony ponderings accordingly. If this was cynical, then we must allow that all courtship is cynical. Connolly was doing as all people do in such situations – tricking out his stall with an eye to what would best please his customer.

For a long time, though, Sheba didn't see any of this. It did not occur to her that Connolly's schoolboy profundities or his 'passion' for the kiln, were anything other than heartfelt. And when, at last, it did occur to her, she seems to have been touched rather than disillusioned. To this day, she furiously defends Connolly's 'brilliance' and 'imagination'. If he did affect interests that weren't his, she says, the pretence demonstrated 'a very sophisticated social adaptiveness' on his part. The school is embarrassed by the idea that Connolly might be clever, she claims, 'because they've always written him off as dim'.

The school has never written Connolly off as dim, of course. The fact that he has been identified as a Special Needs pupil – that he receives help for his dyslexia – indicates quite the contrary. No one on the staff has ever been quite as excited about his intellectual capacities as Sheba, it is true. But then the plain fact is that Connolly is *not* a very exciting boy. He is a perfectly average boy in possession of a perfectly average intelligence.

Why, then, was Sheba moved to such an extravagant estimation of his virtues? Why did she insist on seeing him as her little Helen Keller in a sea of Yahoos? The papers will tell you that Sheba's judgement was clouded by desire: she was attracted to Connolly, and in order to explain that attraction, she convinced herself that he was some kind of a genius. This is reasonable enough. But it is not the whole story, I think. To completely understand Sheba's response to Connolly, you would also have to take into account her very limited knowledge – and low expectations – of people of his social class. Until she met Connolly, Sheba had never had any intimate contact with a bona fide member of the British proletariat. Her acquaintance with that stratum did not – and still doesn't – extend much beyond what she has gleaned from the grittier soap operas and the various women who have cleaned her house over the years.

Naturally, she would deny this. Like so many members of London's haute bourgeoisie, Sheba is deeply attached to a

45

mythology of herself as street-smart. She always howls when I refer to her as upper class. (She's middle, she insists; at the very most, upper-middle.) She loves to come shopping with me in the Queenstown street market or the Shop-A-Lot next to the Chalk Farm council estates. It flatters her image of herself as a denizen of the urban jungle to stand cheek by jowl in checkout queues with teenage mothers buying quick-cook macaroni in the shape of Teletubbies for their children. But you can be quite sure that if any of those prematurely craggy-faced girls were ever to address her directly, she would be frightened out of her wits. Though she cannot say it, or even acknowledge it to herself, she thinks of the working class as a mysterious and homogeneous entity: a tempery, florid-faced people addled by food additives and alcohol.

Little wonder that Connolly seemed so fascinatingly anomalous to her. Here, in the midst of all the hostile, north London yobs, she had found a young man who actually sought out her company, who listened, open-mouthed, when she lectured him on Great Artists. Who proffered whimsical *aperçus* about the curtains. Poor old Sheba regarded Connolly with much the same amazement and delight as you or I would a monkey who strolled out of the rain forest and asked for a gin and tonic.

Connolly understood all this, I think. I don't mean that he would have been able to articulate, or even to consciously formulate the role that class played in his relationship with Sheba. But that he sensed the anthropological dimension of Sheba's interest in him and played up to it, I have no doubt. When describing his family and home to Sheba, he seems to have been at pains to leave her naive notions of prole mores intact. He told her about his family's holiday caravan in Maldon, Essex, about his mother's part-time job as a dinner lady and his father's job as a taxi driver – but he omitted to mention that his mother held a college diploma or that his father was a history buff with a special interest in the American Civil War. These facts, now that they have emerged in the papers, are so astounding to Sheba – so at odds with the cartoon thugs she has been encouraged to envisage – that she chooses either to ignore them, or to dismiss them as lies. In a recent newspaper interview, Connolly's mother mentioned that when her children were young, she and her husband often played them recordings of *Swan Lake* and *Peter and the Wolf*. Sheba threw the paper down when she got to this bit. Mrs Connolly was lying, she said – trying to make her son's home life seem more wholesome and happy than it was. 'Steven's father hits him, you know,' she screeched. 'He beats him. She doesn't mention that, does she?'

This accusation is based on something that Connolly told Sheba once, at the beginning of their relationship. Sheba has spoken of this conversation often because Connolly's claim about his father's violence – true or not – prompted her first gesture of intimacy towards the boy. It was near the end of the winter term. Connolly had come to see her in the studio and the two of them were looking out of the window at the darkening playground, discussing the possibility that it might snow. Connolly mentioned that snow always put his father in a bad mood. When Mr Connolly 'had the hump', he added, he often hit him. Sheba was not particularly surprised by this admission. She had watched several made-for-television dramas about domestic violence, and considered herself well acquainted with council-house brutality. She murmured something consoling to Connolly. And then she reached out and rubbed his head. When her fingers came away, strands of his hair rose up with them in an electric spray. Sheba laughed and made a light-hearted comment about the static in the air that day. Connolly closed his eyes and smiled. 'Do that again, Miss,' he said.

Prior to this incident, Sheba had occasionally wondered about the extent of Connolly's sexual experience. Year Ten males at St George's vary pretty widely in their level of sexual sophistication. Some are still at the stage of giggling about 'the come tree' in the headmaster's garden (a cyclamen so-called because its scent has an alleged resemblance to the smell of semen). Some brag about receiving 'blow-jobs' and 'finger-fucking' girls. And then there are others who make convincing reference to their experience of sexual intercourse. Sheba had no way of knowing for sure where Connolly fitted on this spectrum, but she had been inclined to place him at the innocent end of the scale. Not technically a virgin, perhaps, but still fundamentally inexperienced. Now, something about his smile – the confident way he commanded her to touch him again – made her revise her original estimation.

Sheba declined to repeat the gesture. It was time for her to go home, she told him. She put on her coat and the funny Peruvian hat that she was wearing that winter. Then she locked up the studio and the two of them walked through the playground to the car park together. Even though she told him not to bother, Connolly hung around while she undid the lock on her bicycle. When they got out on the street, they paused awkwardly, unsure of how to effect their farewells. Sheba resolved the matter by prodding Connolly abruptly in the ribs and jumping onto her bike. 'Bye then!' she cried as she rode away. When she glanced behind her, she saw that he was lingering on the pavement where she had left him. She waved and, after a moment, he waved mournfully back.

It has always been a nice question as to when exactly Sheba became conscious of having amorous feelings for Connolly or, indeed, became conscious of his having amorous feelings for her. I have pressed her on many occasions for specificity on this issue, but her responses are maddeningly inconsistent.

At times, she will insist that she was guilty of nothing more than maternal fondness for Connolly and was utterly 'ambushed' when he first kissed her. At other times, she will coyly volunteer that she 'fancied' him from the start. I dare say we shall never know for certain the exact progress of her romantic attachment. But it seems clear that during these early days, Sheba was not very honest with herself about her feelings for the boy. The hair-stroking episode is a case in point. On her way home that evening, she felt troubled, she says. Unsettled. She kept going over what had just happened in her studio and telling herself that there was nothing to fuss about. She had ruffled the boy's hair for goodness' sake. Just as an auntie might. But why, then, she wondered, was she feeling so shifty? Why was it necessary to reassure herself? Things that are truly innocent don't need to be labelled as such. If everything between her and the boy was so simple and above board, why had she never mentioned his visits to Sue? She was feeling guilty about it. She was!

Had Sheba pursued this interrogation of herself with any rigour, things might have turned out very differently. But almost as soon as the promising line of enquiry had been opened, she abruptly shut it down. She had not mentioned Connolly to Sue, she told herself, because Sue would have been bound to respond with unnecessary anxiety. She would have said that the after-school meetings were 'inappropriate'. And Sheba absolutely knew that they weren't. What did it matter what other people might think, as long as *she* knew that the thing was harmless? People were hyper-vigilant these days, because of child abuse. In the rush to guard against the sickos, the world had gone slightly mad. There were people who wouldn't take pictures of their naked children any more, for fear of being shopped by the chemist. Surely she wasn't going to succumb to that sort of craziness and become her own tyrannous Neighbourhood Watch? She had ruffled his hair. His hair. She had only wanted to comfort the boy, she told herself. Perhaps she would have been less inclined to make the gesture with another, less appealing pupil. But what of that? She couldn't expect herself to be oblivious of what the kids looked like and smelled like. She spent all day confronting their corporeal reality: inhaling their farts, gazing, with pity, upon their acne. Some of them were vile-looking and some were attractive. What kind of saint wouldn't notice the difference? Any pleasure she took in Steven's physical self was no more or less suspect than the pleasure she had once taken in the plump, velvety bodies of her own babies. A sensuous pleasure certainly, but far from sensual.

One Friday afternoon, not long before the Christmas holidays, Connolly appeared at a Homework Club that Sheba was minding. The two had not encountered each other in a public setting since they had become friends and Sheba felt somewhat uneasy. Connolly arrived late, in the company of a skinny, grinning boy called Jackie Kilbane. According to the notes that they handed in, they had been caught earlier in the week sharing a cigarette together in the school's crumbling outdoor lavatories. They were now serving a fortnight's worth of hour-long detentions. Sheba detected something sly and furtive in Connolly's manner as he stood before her desk. When she smiled at him, he would not meet her eye.

As soon as he and the Kilbane boy had been registered, they retreated to the back of the room where they began rocking on their chairs and whispering. Sheba could not make out what they were saying, but she had an uncomfortable sense that it was obscene in nature and connected, in some way, to herself. The suspicion grew when Kilbane got up and approached her desk to ask for more paper. Kilbane is an unpleasant boy with an ugly, yellow face and an insolent, insinuating attitude about him. A thin line of fur skulks on his upper lip, like a baby caterpillar. He gave Sheba the creeps. As she burrowed in the desk drawer for paper, he seemed to be standing uncomfortably close to her chair, but only when she sat up did it dawn on her that he was attempting to look down her shirt. She handed him a sheet of paper and sharply ordered him back to his desk. 'All right, all right,' he said mockingly, as he strolled away. 'Don't get your knickers in a twist.' Sheba glanced at Connolly. He had been watching this exchange intently. As he met her eye, there was a hard, unfriendly look on his face. All the softness in his features had gone.

Sheba felt betrayed. She had thought him special and here he was exchanging spitballs, plotting with his horrid friend to get a peek at her bosoms. At the same time, she registered a definite twinge of – what was it? Excitement? Titillation? For a split second, she found herself imagining what it would be like to lie beneath him; to have his hands on her. She shook her head in fright. She ought not to have been so easy and sweet with him, she told herself. Now, she would have to draw back.

Towards the end of the first half hour, Kilbane and Connolly started play-fighting with one another – rolling around on the floor while the rest of the HC group screamed encouragement. Neither of them responded, she says, when she got up from her desk and stood over them, ordering them loudly to stop. Finally, she threatened to send for Mr Mawson if they did not immediately desist and accompany her outside. This worked. The boys got up from the floor, still laughing, and trooped out into the corridor. But once Sheba had closed the classroom door and was facing the two of them, she was at a loss. Her one thought had been to remove them from their encouraging audience. Now that she had done so, she struggled to find her next gambit.

I happened to be walking through Middle Hall, on my way to a meeting with the Head, when Sheba and the two boys emerged. I heard Sheba's voice, shrill with admonition, before I saw her. And then, when I turned the corner, I spotted the little confrontational knot at the far end of the corridor. Sheba's feet were planted firmly in the ten to two position, as if in preparation for a *plié*. Her hands were on her hips. She looked like the tarot-card symbol for wrath. The boys, who were well versed in the postures of this teacher–pupil tableau, were slouching against a wall, their hands thrust deep into their pockets.

Given that I was already in danger of being late for Pabblem, and given that my relations with Sheba had reached such a difficult pass, I was tempted to ignore whatever contretemps she was having with the two boys and simply walk on. But as I drew nearer I distinctly heard the taller boy call her a 'silly cow'.

'What was that?' I said sharply. Whatever my personal feelings towards Sheba, I was obliged to address the boy's incivility. It would have been a dereliction of duty to do otherwise.

The three of them looked round at me. Sheba had a slightly wild look in her eye and the tell-tale patch of scarlet on each cheek.

'Are these boys giving you trouble, Mrs Hart?' I asked.

'I'm afraid so, Miss Covett,' Sheba said. There was a quaver in her voice. 'They've been talking and generally creating a disturbance since the beginning of HC. And now they've started fighting.'

Together, we studied the two boys. The taller one, Kilbane, had been in one of my bottom stream History classes the year before. He was known to his classmates as 'Lurch'. The one with the blond hair, I did not know. He was not as confident as Kilbane and when I asked him his name, he spoke it quietly to the floor.

'Excuse me?' I said. 'Speak up, please.'

He raised his head. 'Steve Connolly, Miss,' he said. His voice still had a trace of boy in it – a scraping clarinet tootle.

I went through the usual process with the boys – cold outrage, warm threats, admonitions to 'shape up'. I suppose that I laid it on a bit thick for Sheba's benefit. As I spoke, Connolly kept his eyes on the floor, occasionally lifting his head to glance stealthily at Sheba. 'Look at me when I am speaking to you,' I told him.

Did I sense anything sexual in his attitude towards her then? Possibly. But dealings with male pupils of that age are rarely without some manner of sexual undertow. A secondary school is a kind of hormonal soup. All those bodies pressed in on one another – bubbling with puberty and low-level adolescent fantasy – are bound to produce a certain *atmosphere*. Even I, a woman in my early sixties and, by common consent, no oil painting, have been known to prick the testosteronal curiosity of my fifteen-year-old charges from time to time. It is something to which one becomes inured. Very occasionally, sexual tension will be released in a small explosion of some sort – a groping, a threat. There was one incident, back in 1982, when an absolutely evil little fellow in Year Nine named Mark Roth assaulted the young woman who was coming in at the time to give French conversation. (He was apparently on top of her when her screams alerted a staff member who happened to be walking by.) But that was a singular case. For the most part, the sexual angst of the school's student population is nothing more than an indistinct background hum: so much white noise.

After I was done lecturing the boys, I accompanied them back into the classroom and watched them settle down to their assigned tasks. My handling of this episode had not been altogether tactful. School etiquette demands that where one's moral authority with the children is demonstrably greater than that of a fellow staff member, one should endeavour to play down the fact. Instead, I had gone out of my way to flaunt my superior disciplinary skills. I went over to Sheba, who was standing at the front of the room. 'Don't hesitate to call me if these two give you any further problems,' I told her.

I assumed that she would be peevish. But as I walked away, she came after me, with a wide smile on her narrow face. At the door, she leaned in to me, and put her hand on my shoulder. 'Thank you *so* much for saving me, Barbara,' she whispered.

I was too taken aback to say anything. In fact, it was not until I had walked out into the corridor and closed the door behind me, that I remembered some sort of response might have been expected.

Four

I was late for Pabblem, of course. When I walked into his office he was kneeling on his special backless, ergonomic chair, emanating a prissy sort of dissatisfaction. 'At last!' he cried when he saw me. He proceeded to wish me good afternoon with the rather too careful politeness of someone who has plans to be nasty. 'Please . . .' He gestured to a chair (non-ergonomic, standard issue) on the other side of his desk. I sat down. The school's administration centre is housed in an ugly, L-shaped annexe to the science block and Pabblem's office, which is at the very end of the annexe, looks out onto a modest square of grass and flower-beds known as 'the headmaster's garden'. That afternoon, Phelps, the school caretaker, and Jenkins, his depressed assistant, were in the garden, installing a bird bath. I was able to track their comically incompetent manoeuvres over Pabblem's shoulder as he spoke.

'Good week?' Pabblem asked.

I nodded. I wasn't going to waste any energy being charming. 'Good, good,' he continued. 'I see you have a cup of coffee already, so now . . . let's get to it.'

Just a fortnight before, three other members of the History staff had taken eighty Year Tens on a field trip to the cathedral at St Albans as part of the term's project on churches. While they were there, a group of about fifteen children had escaped their supervision and gone on a shop-lifting rampage through the town centre. A few boys had been caught in the act and taken to the local police station where charges were pressed. The following day, Pabblem had been inundated with complaints and threats from St Albans shop-owners, and later in the week the school had been informed by the St Albans town council that it was banned from ever visiting St Albans again. I had not been present on the outing, but as the most senior staff member on the History faculty, I had been charged by Pabblem with writing a report on the incident. My official brief had been to account for the 'breach in discipline' and to offer suggestions for how such problems might be avoided in the future. My *real* task was to state for the record that no responsibility for this regrettable episode could possibly be attributed to Pabblem's leadership. The finished report, which I had dropped off with Deirdre Rickman that morning, had omitted, somewhat ostentatiously, to perform either function.

'First of all,' Pabblem said, 'I want to thank you for your hard work on this paper.' (Pabblem always calls the reports he commissions 'papers', as if life at St George's is a perpetual summit of international AIDS doctors.) 'Whatever objections I am about to raise,' he went on, 'I want you to know, they do not diminish my appreciation of your effort.' He paused here, to let me thank him for his Solomon-like fair-mindedness. When I remained silent, he gave a small, fake cough and continued. 'I must be frank with you, Barbara. When I read your paper I was a bit confused. Ultimately, I'm afraid, I was disappointed.'

There was a sudden, loud buzzing in the room. Pabblem sighed as he leaned forward to press a button on his intercom. 'Yes?'

'Colin Robinson's on the line,' Deirdre Rickman's voice announced.

'I can't talk to him now,' Pabblem said irritably. 'Tell him . . .' He ran his fingers through his thin, red hair. The harried chief executive. 'No, wait. Put him on.'

He picked up the telephone and shrugged at me apologetically. 'Colin? Hi!'

During the short conversation that ensued, Pabblem leaned his head to one side and clamped the phone between his shoulder and ear, freeing his hands to pat the tidy piles of documents on his desk into more perfect symmetry. I could feel goosebumps rising up on my arms as I watched his white hands make their prim, fussing gestures. I gazed out of the window. Phelps and Jenkins were still engaged in their mysterious charade with the bird bath. 'Great, yes. That'd be t'riffic . . .' Pabblem was saying. 'Colin, you're a star . . .'

When Pabblem first came to St George's seven years ago, the school board hailed him as 'the breath-of-fresh-air candidate'. The staff was cock-a-hoop. He was thirty-seven at the time – the youngest head the school had ever employed – and unlike his predecessor, the melancholy Ralph Simpson, he was said to be 'very big on communication'. In his former post as deputy head at a school in Stoke Newington, he had created a drama department and an award-winning 'neighbourhood ecology project'.

Since that time, Pabblem has certainly fulfilled his promise as an innovator. Thanks to him, St George's now boasts a daily salad alternative on the canteen menu and an annual magazine of creative writing called *The Shiner*. (The logo is a portrait of a little boy with a black eye.) There is also an annual 'Day of Subversion' – a day on which all roles are reversed and the pupils get the chance to teach their teachers. (Pabblem joins in the fun by adopting the persona of 'Lord of Misrule' and touring the classrooms wearing a jester's cap.)

Yet, even among staff members who like this sort of thing, Pabblem is not a popular headmaster. Beneath his easy-going exterior, he has turned out to be a thoroughly pedantic man – a petty-minded despot obsessed with staff punctuality charts and compulsory staff 'bull sessions' and time-wasting, bureau-cratic folderol in all its manifestations. At least once a term, Pabblem makes the entire staff attend a special lecture given by some sour-faced young person from the education authority. Because he is a progressive bully, the subjects are always things like Meeting the Challenge of Diversity, or Teaching the Differently Abled. Shortly before Sheba came to the school, he set up a system called Morale-Watch, which requires all staff members to fill out a weekly report card on their mental and spiritual health. (Any admissions of dissatisfaction are rewarded with agonizing follow-up interviews, so naturally everyone always fills in the cards with slavish avowals of personal joy.) The original Pabblem-boosters try to save face by saying that power has transformed Pabblem. My own sense is that power has merely given opportunity to an unpleasant, *Gauleiter* tendency that was always there. Either way, no one says he is fresh air any more.

When Pabblem had finished his phone conversation, he buzzed back through to Deirdre – 'No more calls unless they're urgent.' Then he turned to me. 'Okay!' He held up my report. 'So, Barbara, I think I am right in saying that you were asked to write an analysis of how discipline broke down on the St Albans trip, and, if possible, to offer some suggestions for how we might improve our security procedures on future excursions of this sort.'

'Actually –' I began.

Pabblem held up a palm, to silence me.

'But you didn't –' I said.

'Uh uh.' He shook his head. 'Hang on, Barbara, let me finish. Whatever exact phrases I used, I think I made it pretty clear that I was looking for a practically-oriented paper on school control issues. What you have handed in is, well . . . an attack on the St George's History syllabus.'

'I'm not sure what you mean by "practically-oriented" . . .'
I began.

Pabblem closed his eyes. 'Barbara,' he said. 'Please.'

Presently, he opened his eyes again. 'I think you'll agree,
Barbara, I run a pretty relaxed ship here. I am very open to
different approaches and ideas. But you know and I know, this
report is not what I asked for. Is it?' He moistened his index
finger on his tongue and began flicking through the pages of
the report. 'I mean, *really*, Barbara.'

I stared at him blankly. 'I thought what I wrote was very
much to the point,' I said.

He gazed, frowning, into the middle distance for a moment
and then he pushed the report across the desk to me. 'Look at
that,' he said. It was open to the last page which was headed
'Conclusion'.

'I don't need to,' I said. 'I wrote it.'

'No, no, I want you to read it again. From my point of
view. I want you to consider whether this is the sort of thing
that enhances my ability, as a headmaster, to respond to the
St Albans crisis.'

'I am prepared to believe that you didn't find it helpful. I
don't need to read it again.'

'Barbara,' Pabblem leaned forward in his chair and smiled,
tightly, 'please do as I ask.'

Odious little man! I crossed my legs and bent my head to read.

All the way down the margin of the page, Pabblem had
printed triplets and sometimes quadruplets of miniature exclamation points and question marks. The final paragraph had so
excited or enraged him that he had highlighted the entire thing
with yellow fluorescent ink.

Gavin Breech, whom I regard as the ringleader of the shop-lifting
expedition, is a very nasty little fellow: angry, violent and, I would

hazard, a bit mad. I doubt that he is susceptible to any of the rehabilitation procedures provided by St George's. Our best bet, in my opinion, would be to expel him. I stress, however, that this course of action does not guarantee an end to such incidents. The periodic eruption of unruly, and even criminal behaviour in our student body would seem to be a fact of school life for the foreseeable future. Given the socio-economic profile of our catchment area, only a fool would imagine otherwise.

'Well?' Pabblem said when I looked up. 'Is that a helpful contribution?'

'I think it could be,' I said. 'You asked me to offer suggestions and I did. I wrote what I truly believe.'

'Oh for goodness' sake!' Pabblem banged his white fist on the desk.

There was a silence, during which he smoothed back a strand of hair that had fallen into his eye. 'Look, Barbara,' he went on in a quieter voice, 'by commissioning you to write this paper, I was giving you an opportunity to make your mark on things.' He smiled. 'If attacked with the right kind of creative thinking, this is the kind of project that turns a teacher into deputy head material . . .'

'But I don't want to be a deputy head,' I said.

'That aside,' he said, the smile vanishing from his face, 'the sort of despair you preach here has no place at St George's. I'm afraid I'm going to have to ask you to have another go at this.'

'So you're censoring me.'

He laughed, mirthlessly. 'Come on, Barbara, let's not be childish. I'm giving you a chance to improve on your first effort.' He got up from his chair and walked to the door. 'The holidays are coming up. That should give you a good chunk of time to think about this. If you could have a new draft back to me at the start of next term, that'll be fine,' he said.

'If you don't like what I have to say, why don't you give it to someone else?' I asked.

Pabblem opened the door. 'No, Barbara,' he said firmly. 'I want you to do this. It'll be a good learning experience for you.'

∞

The following Monday, as I was being shown to a table at La Traviata, someone held out their arm like a toll-gate to bar my way. It was Sheba, sitting in a booth with Sue.

'Barbara!' she said. 'I've been looking for you! I wanted to thank you again for helping me out on Friday.'

I shrugged. 'You're quite welcome.' Then I gestured to the waiter who was showing me to my table. 'I should go.'

'Oh, but won't you sit with us?' Sheba smiled at me brightly. Sue, sitting opposite her, drummed her chubby fingers on the Formica table and frowned.

'Well . . .' I said.

'Oh please do,' Sheba said. 'We haven't ordered yet.'

Clearly, she had not been informed about the cold war between Sue and me. This came as both a relief and a vague disappointment. Was it possible that I had never even come up in their conversations?

'Are you sure?' I said. 'I don't want to barge in on you . . .'

'Don't be *silly*,' Sheba said.

'All right then.' I turned to the waiter. 'I'll sit here, thanks.'

'Smashing!' Sheba shifted over to make room for me on her side of the booth. Sue lit a cigarette. Her expression suggested the kind of deeply private, strictly incommunicable anguish of someone who has just slammed the car door on her thumb.

'Barbara was completely marvellous the other afternoon,' Sheba said, as we all examined the chalkboard menu on the wall above us. 'I was on the verge of going loony with two of my HC boys. And she came along and saved my bacon.' She turned to me. 'I hope I didn't make you late for the Head.'

I shook my head. 'I wish you had. Our meeting certainly didn't deserve promptness.'

'Oh dear,' she said. 'It didn't go well then?'

'He didn't like the report he made me write about the St Albans business.'

'What did you write?' Sue asked.

I provided a précis. By the time I finished, Sheba was laughing. 'Goodness, you *are* brave. Was he fearfully angry with you?'

'In his ineffectual, gingery way, yes.'

She laughed again. 'He *is* a bit of an idiot, isn't he? The other day, he cornered me in the headmaster's garden and asked me for my opinion of his spring planting plans. I thought it sounded awfully gaudy – endless tulips, you know – but I'm afraid I wasn't nearly as courageous as you. I said it all sounded *lovely*. He looked so pathetically pleased! It *is* maddening the way men do that – ask questions to which you are bound to reply with a lie.'

Sue giggled appreciatively.

'Actually,' Sheba went on, frowning now, 'I take that back. That's terribly mean-spirited of me. I'm sure I frequently fish for compliments myself –'

'Oh, no,' Sue broke in. 'It's true. Men are such babies. They need to be told how bloody marvellous they are all the time. They're insecure, that's the thing. They need their egos stroking, don't they?'

I waited for her to stop, so that Sheba could finish what she'd been about to say. But she kept talking. 'Women are too canny to be taken in by flattery. If Ted says something nice to me, I know he's after a bit of nooky. That's the other thing. Men are such *dogs*, aren't they? Brains between their legs!'

I have never enjoyed this kind of women's talk – the hopelessness of the other sex and all that. Sooner or later, it always seems to degenerate into tittering critiques of the male member. So silly. So *beneath* women. And funnily enough, the females who go in for this low-grade misandry are usually the ones who are most in thrall to men. I glanced at Sheba. She was listening to Sue's chatter with apparent interest. Was this the sort of conversation that had seduced her into becoming Sue's companion?

'Believe me,' Sue was saying, 'when Ted tells me, "Yes, you look lovely, dear," I *always* know when he's lying. Whereas if *I* tell Ted he looks like a Greek god, he falls for it, hook, line and sinker . . .'

Ted was Sue's live-in companion. In the days when we were still on amiable terms, she used to refer to him as her 'lover' or, worse still, her 'old man'. *Shut up, shut up*, I thought, as she chuntered on. *Shut up, you boring cow. Let Sheba speak.*

Presently she did.

'Well, you may be right, Sue,' Sheba said. 'But, sometimes, I think it's more my problem. It's not as if I'm *obliged* to give the answer that Pabblem or whoever is looking for. Maybe I'm just blaming him for my own lily-liveredness. Why do I always need to tell people what they want to hear? My husband says that I have a lot of empathy but I'm afraid that's just a nice way of saying that I want to please everybody.'

'Well, don't be trying to please the pupils,' I said, mindful of her discipline problems. 'That way disaster lies.'

The waiter came and took our orders. Sue wanted lasagne. (She's an awful glutton, Sue.) Sheba was considering a salad but when she heard me ask for minestrone, she decided to have the same. This maddened Sue, you could tell. And when the waiter walked away, she gave me a look of simpering reproof. 'What you were saying just now, Barbara – about not trying to please the pupils? I'm afraid I can't let that go. I have to disagree with you there. There's nothing wrong with making the kids happy, you know. When they're happy, they're receptive and when they're receptive, they learn. I believe, quite passionately, that creating the right sort of warm environment for learning is three-quarters of what teaching is all about.'

It had been a long time since I had actually heard any of Sue's claptrap. It was just as idiotic as I remembered.

'Hmm. That's very interesting, Sue,' I said. 'But then of course you have your marvellous instruments to help you soothe the savage beast . . . You do still have your banjo, don't you?'

Sue gave me a look. 'Yes I do, actually. But it's not a question of the instrument *per se* . . .'

'No, no, of course.'

'Oh, I wish I could play something,' Sheba said. 'My parents made me take piano when I was a girl, but –'

'Sheba, I didn't know that!' Sue's tone suggested mild outrage that any detail of Sheba's biography should, at this stage, remain unknown to her.

'Yes. Only until I was twelve, though. After that, they gave up. I was truly, truly untalented . . .'

'Oh no!' Sue protested. 'There's no such thing! You and I must try some duets together. It'd be such fun!'

Sheba laughed. 'You don't understand, Sue. It was the piano teacher who suggested I stop. I have no musicality at all. I live in dread of being asked to clap along to music in a public place.'

'Really?' I said. 'Same here.'

'Rubbish,' Sue said, ignoring me. 'I'm not going to let you get away with this, Sheba. You just had the wrong teacher.'

'No, take my word. I was a lost cause,' Sheba said. She turned to me. 'Were you made to play an instrument too, Barbara?'

'Afraid so,' I nodded. 'Recorder.'

'Well the recorder hardly counts,' Sue said with a quick, high laugh. 'That's like saying you studied the tambourine . . .'

'Oh no, surely not,' Sheba said. 'Aren't there world-class recorder players, just like there are world-class cellists and whatever?'

Sue frowned. 'Well yes . . .'

The waiter arrived now with my and Sheba's soup. 'How scrummy!' Sheba exclaimed, tasting hers. 'What a good idea this was, Barbara.'

Across the table, I could feel Sue giving me the evil eye. I smiled and shrugged and blew on my soup to cool it. I was beginning to enjoy myself.

∞

The Christmas holidays came. Sheba and her family spent Christmas Day at home, where they were joined by her husband's ex-wife and his two children by that marriage. I journeyed to Eastbourne, as I always do, to spend a few days with my younger sister, Marjorie. Marjorie and her husband, Dave, are devout members of the Seventh Day Adventist Church. They and their children – twenty-four-year-old Martin and twenty-six-year-old Lorraine – spend most of Christmas Day serving soup to homeless people as part of the church's 'outreach' programme. I stay in bed, watching television. I'm all for tolerating people who believe in fairy stories, but I do draw the line at joining in with the delusion. My sister and I have a tacit understanding about my non-participation in religious activities. She is prepared to put up with it, so long as I keep up the desultory pretence that I am feeling 'poorly'.

I have spent so many Christmases at her house lying on the front-room sofa, pretending to sip lemon and honey drinks, that by now my niece and nephew regard me as a more or less permanent invalid.

I returned to school for the new term, feeling somewhat low. Holidays always tend to put me in a brown study. I had not written the new report for Pabblem, so I was forced to go to him and lie about 'a family problem' that had prevented me from giving it my full attention. I had hopes that he would grow impatient at this stage and cancel the assignment. But no such luck. After making me grovel for a bit, he granted me a month's extension.

The one bright spot at this time was Sheba, who continued to show me great kindness. With increasing frequency I joined her and Sue for lunch at La Traviata. It was not the easiest of threesomes. Sue resented my intrusion and she never missed an opportunity to distinguish her relationship with Sheba as the one of greater warmth and importance. One of her more transparent tactics was to point up how much older I was than her and Sheba. She once asked me, with a straight face, if I had fond memories of 'the Jazz Age'. On another occasion she paused in mid-sentence to explain to me that Bob Marley was 'a famous Jamaican singer'. Really, though, she played the game all wrong. Her tactics were so crude that she only did herself harm. Sheba couldn't help but see how jealous she was. I sat back and kept quiet, content to watch while Sue dug her own grave.

∞

According to my notes, Sheba had no further contact with Connolly after the disastrous HC encounter until a couple of weeks into the spring term. She was in her studio one after-noon, tidying up the mess that had been left by her last class of the day, when he slouched in with his sketch pad. Sheba glanced up and then continued what she was doing.

Connolly stood hesitantly in the doorway, watching her. 'Miss?' he said, after a few moments. 'I brought some stuff to show you, Miss.'

Sheba turned and stared at him. 'And why would I bother looking at your work,' she asked, 'when you have been so rude and unpleasant to me?'

Connolly groaned and rolled his eyes. 'Oh go on, Mii-iss,' he said in a sing-song. 'I was only having a laugh.'

Sheba shook her head. That was not good enough, she told him. He could not expect her to treat him like a grown-up – to devote her precious time to him – if he behaved like a child. 'And I'm not sure what you've told your friend Jackie about me,' she added angrily, 'but I didn't like his attitude either.'

'I haven't told him nothing!' Connolly exclaimed.

Sheba was taken aback by the way this sounded. She wanted to object that there was 'nothing' to tell. And yet she was relieved – there was no denying it – to hear him assure her of his discretion.

Connolly began to say something more and then stopped.

'What?' Sheba asked.

'It's just . . . I can't be nice to you in front of the other kids,' he told her. 'They'd think I was a poof.'

Sheba laughed and Connolly stared at her, pleased to have been funny without trying.

'You're nutty, Miss,' he said approvingly.

After that, things became easier between them. Connolly suggested that he help her clear up the classroom and Sheba accepted the offer. The boy had as good as apologized, she told herself; it would be childish of her to hold a grudge. Connolly proceeded to race about the room, picking up bits of paper and clay with great energy. When the room was tidy, he sat down at her desk and began looking through a book of paintings by Manet. Sheba directed him to a double-spread reproduction of *Le Déjeuner sur l'herbe*. It was a very famous painting, she told him, and had caused a great scandal when it was first shown. She half expected him to giggle at the naked lady, she says. But when she looked at him, his expression was one of reverent attention.

'The physical ideal for women was quite different in those days,' she observed. 'These ladies wouldn't make it into *Playboy*, I don't think.' She was gabbling slightly, she noticed. She did not want there to be silence in the room.

Connolly nodded and continued to look at the picture without saying anything. Sheba gazed at his studious profile. From this angle, with his drooping eyes and his swerving, flattened nose, he had something of an old prize fighter about him, she thought. Except, of course, that his skin was so golden and impeccable. She had a powerful urge to put her hand to his cheek.

'What kind of woman . . .' she began.

Connolly turned to her. 'What, Miss?'

'Nothing,' she said, quickly. 'It's gone out of my head.' She had been going to ask him what sort of woman he liked. What kind of female figure he found most attractive. But recognizing the gross impropriety of the question, she had stopped herself just in time.

Soon afterwards, she told him he'd have to push off. She had a pile of work to get through before she went home, she said. Connolly was reluctant to go and asked whether he might stay and sit quietly while she worked. But Sheba was anxious to be rid of him now. She told him firmly that she needed to be on her own. He shrugged then, and said he would be back on Friday. They parted amicably.

An hour and a half later, as she was wheeling her bike out

of the school car park, she found him waiting for her on the street. It was six o'clock and the main road that runs along the west side of the school grounds was busy with rush-hour traffic. All the children, even Homework Club attendees, had gone home. Sweet wrappers and crisp packets – remnants of the afternoon exodus – were skittering about the pavement in the yellowish light of the street lamps. Sheba smiled hello to Connolly and asked what he was doing there. He winced, as if it pained him to say it: 'Waiting for you.'

She knew right then what was going to happen, she says. It came to her, as these things sometimes do, in a perfect and fully formed revelation. He had a crush on her, he had been developing this crush for some time. She had encouraged it, or, at the very least, failed to discourage it. Now, he was going to declare himself, and she – because she could think of no other feasible reaction – was going to affect amazement and horror.

'What did you want to see me about?' she asked him. 'You know, Steven, if you need to talk to me about anything, you can do it in school.'

She started walking fast, wheeling her bicycle beside her. Connolly trotted to keep up.

No, he said, shaking his head, he couldn't tell her in school.

'Well, then,' Sheba said, 'you have to arrange a –'

'I really like you,' he interrupted.

She was silent.

'I think about you all the time. I was –' He gazed at her unhappily.

Sheba smiled. 'I'm glad you like me,' she said, maintaining her tone of teacherly brusqueness, 'but I can't talk to you now. I have to get home.'

'It's more than liking,' Connolly objected impatiently.

They had reached an intersection. Sheba hesitated. Her way

home was to the left, down a long shopping street called Grafton Lane. She needed to get rid of the boy – she couldn't have him trailing her all the way to her house – yet it seemed callous to abandon him there on the street corner. After a moment, she made the left turn and continued to walk with him, past the cheap shoe shop with wire baskets of cut-price slippers crowding its forecourt; past Dee-Dar, the tatty Indian where St George's teachers held their staff dinners; past the post office and the chip shop and the ancient chemist's with dusty boxes of Radox in the window.

Connolly was quiet for a while. And then, in a sudden rush, as if he had been holding his breath, he said, 'I'm really into you, Miss.'

Something in his voice made Sheba think that he was about to cry. She couldn't be sure, because he had his head down. 'Steven,' she said. 'This isn't . . .' She paused, uncertain of how to go on. 'This just . . . it won't do!' She straddled her bike, preparing to mount it.

'I can't help it,' Connolly said, looking up. 'I swear, I can't help myself.' Sheba had been right. There were tears in his eyes.

'Oh, Steven,' she said. She was about to reach out her hand and pat his shoulder when his face suddenly came pressing in at hers.

Sheba says I couldn't possibly understand what it feels like, after twenty years of faithful marriage, to be kissed by someone other than your husband; to feel the pressure of a stranger's mouth on yours. 'Things fall asleep in a marriage,' she told me once. 'They have to. You have to lose that mad sexual alertness you had when you were out in the world on your own. All these years with Richard, I don't think I've ever consciously suppressed anything. I've always been so *grateful* to be married – so relieved that I would never have to be

70

naked in front of a stranger again. But I'd forgotten how exhilarating it is to expose yourself . . . to be a little scared. As soon as Steven kissed me, it all came back in an instant. The, you know, *high* of it. I was amazed at how I could have lived without that all those years.'

It must have been a pretty comic sight – the little suitor reaching on tippy-toe for his middle-aged mistress, the bike smashing to the ground. But the farcical element of their first embrace seems never to have occurred to Sheba. If it has, she has never mentioned it. She has spoken about the warmth of Connolly, the soap smell of him, the bristle at the back of his neck, the texture of his jumper and any number of other tedious details connected with this first embrace. But never about how immensely *silly* the whole thing must have looked.

In the immediate aftermath of the bicycle's collapse, there was confusion and speechless embarrassment. Connolly tried to help Sheba up but she waved him away. She remembers looking around to see who might have witnessed their kiss. An elderly woman with a wicker shopping basket on wheels was staring at them rather malevolently as she hobbled by. But that was all.

'Can I see you properly?' Connolly asked, even as she was still righting herself.

'No,' Sheba said. She held her bike in front of her, defensively. 'No. Look . . . Stop it now, please.' She got on her bike.

'Miss,' Connolly pleaded. But she only shook her head and rode away.

That night, as she was preparing the evening meal and giving Ben his bath, she kept up a low, terrified murmuring. *Oh no, oh no, oh no. What am I doing? What am I doing?* She was still trying to convince herself that she was blameless. She wanted to believe that she had done nothing wrong, that she had not yet gone beyond the pale. When she glimpsed herself in a mirror, she was amazed to see how flushed and happy she looked. 'Did you go for a run today?' her husband asked her at dinner that night. 'You seem awfully rosy.'

It was somewhere around this time that a Chemistry teacher called Heidi Greening mentioned to a few staff members having seen one of the Year Ten boys slipping into Sheba's studio on several occasions at the end of the school day. Heidi was an unpopular woman, with a reputation for sucking up to Pabblem. No one was particularly interested in her information. Marian Simmons did mention something about it to Sheba, I believe, but Sheba responded with such innocent and good-natured ease – made it so clear that there was nothing untoward in Connolly's visits – that the matter was quickly forgotten.

Five

I'm writing this late on Saturday night. I should be in bed, but I haven't been able to get any writing done all week and if I don't put in a few good hours of work now, I'm going to get horribly behind in my schedule. I was planning to grab a few quiet hours this morning when Ben came to the house for his weekly visit. But Sheba got it into her head at the last minute to take him to the pictures and, since it was raining, I ended up being roped in to driving them. We had a rather jolly time, actually. The film was some old Disney rot, but Ben loved it. And that made Sheba happy, which made me happy. Ben really is a dear little boy. Everybody has been very concerned about how he would deal with the current situation. But, touch wood, he seems to be coping amazingly well. He misses his mother, of course. He still doesn't completely understand why she has gone to live in Uncle Eddie's house and there are often tearful scenes when Richard comes to pick him up. But, generally speaking, he's a cheerful old sausage.

Sheba and Richard have always been keen not to baby Ben and in the present instance they have tried to be as honest and straightforward with him as possible. He hasn't been told *everything*. But he's been told a surprising amount. He knows that his mummy is in trouble for being friends with one of her pupils. Today, in fact, he was asking Sheba some rather tricky questions about why he wasn't allowed to meet her friend. Sheba, perhaps stretching the honesty policy too far, said that even *she* wasn't allowed to see her friend any more. 'Oh,' Ben said. 'Does it make you sad?' Yes, Sheba said. It did make her sad. There was a long, thoughtful pause. And then Ben said, 'Do you like your friend more than Daddy?' Sheba hesitated for a moment, but in the end, to my relief, she said no.

After Ben had gone home, Sheba went into a bit of a decline. She often does after his visits. I tried to comfort her, but she quickly grew impatient with my efforts. 'You don't understand,' she said to me. 'You don't understand what it is to be a parent of a child like Ben. He has so much against him in life, as it is. And now he doesn't even have his mother.'

It *is* irritating when Sheba talks this way – as if she were a passive victim of fate, rather than the principal architect of her own suffering. It's a little late in the day for her to start acting the stricken mother. She ought to have been thinking of Ben's welfare back when she was first batting her eyelids at Connolly. I resisted the impulse to say as much, however, and contented myself with urging her to get an early night.

∞

The day after Connolly kissed Sheba for the first time, he came to her hut. As soon as he entered, she stood up from her desk and ordered him to leave. There was nothing more to say, she told him. She was flattered that he liked her but she could have nothing more to do with him. Connolly pleaded. At one point, she says, he suggested that they meet outside school.

'I won't lay a finger on you if you don't want me to,' he promised.

Sheba bridled at this. 'Of course I don't want you to, Steven. For goodness' sake.' She strode over to the doorway where Connolly was standing.

'Miss, please . . .' he whined.

'*No*,' Sheba said and shut the door in his face.

There was something thrilling about doing that, she recalls. She had never played the *belle dame sans merci* before.

For several minutes, Connolly remained outside knocking and pleading to be let in. Sheba grew anxious that someone would walk by and see him. She was just about to give in and open the door when the knocking stopped. Through the window, she saw Connolly trudging away, hunched over against the wind. She sank down into a chair and congratulated herself on her fortitude.

Connolly returned the next day. Sheba had taken the precaution of locking the door and she did not respond when he called out her name. 'I'm going to keep coming back until you let me in,' he shouted before he retreated. And he did come back. He came every day that week. Sheba took to placing chairs against the door for added protection but, in truth, there seemed little danger that Connolly would try to break in. He appeared quite content to stand outside bleating for her and by the beginning of the next week his appetite for even this modest show of dedication had waned. On Monday, Sheba waited for the scuffling and sighing at the door, but it never came. She was amused by the boy's lack of endurance and, at the same time, slightly offended. Later, when they had become lovers, she would tease him about his poor performance as a suitor. 'Oh yes, you were dying for love of me,' she would say. 'Five whole days in a row.'

At first, I think she was relieved to have got rid of Connolly. She speaks of having been 'elated' – of feeling as though she had stepped back at the last minute from a dangerous precipice. But as time went on and she grew used to being safe again, a certain listlessness seems to have set in. She had been at St George's for five months by then. To the rest of the staff, it looked as if she were finally getting into the swing of things. She was dressing more sensibly. She seemed to be much more effective in controlling the children. But Sheba was growing increasingly disconsolate. *She* did not feel that she had become a more competent teacher. On the contrary, she felt that she had surrendered to the 'complacency' of the rest of the staff. Her classes had become more peaceful, it was true, but only because she had given up on trying to make the children learn. She had stopped fighting them. She let them wear their personal stereos and read comics in her classes. And if she was no longer even *attempting* to impart knowledge, what, she wondered, was the point? Connolly had been her one talisman against the drear of St George's. Now that she had sent him away, she wasn't sure why she was bothering with the job at all.

One afternoon, three weeks or so after Connolly had stopped pursuing Sheba, she was walking through the playground when she came upon him and some other Year Ten boys playing soccer. He stopped running when he saw her. His face reddened and he turned away. Sheba walked on quickly, but she was much affected by this surprise encounter. Connolly had looked awful, she thought. Really tormented. She wondered whether she had not treated him unfairly. What had he done, after all, but confess a schoolboy crush?

Over the following days, she began working out possible compromises on what she called 'the Connolly situation'. She would allow Connolly to visit her, on a strictly platonic basis, once a week. No, once a fortnight. Perhaps there would be no limit on the number of times he could visit her but she would restrict their conversation to matters relating to art. Then one day – I've been unable to ascertain the exact date, but it seems to have been in early March – Connolly came to her again. She was just leaving her studio when he ran up to her and thrust a note into her gloved hand. Without uttering a word, he rushed away again. Inside the tightly folded square of paper, Sheba found a terse, handwritten plea to meet him on Hampstead Heath the following night at seven o'clock.

She studied the note for a long time. Despite its brevity, it had evidently cost Connolly much effort. He wrote in a kind of agonized scrawl – upper and lower cases mixed together. In various places, he had torn the paper with the pressure of his pen. She found herself curiously agitated by his bad penmanship. How, she wondered, was he ever going to survive out in the world?

For the next twenty-four hours, Sheba debated whether or not to go to the heath. On the afternoon of the proposed meeting, she had made up her mind against. Clearly, the boy still had romantic designs on her. The only sensible thing to do, she told herself, was to stay away. But as soon as Richard arrived home that evening, she heard herself telling him that her old school friend Caitlin was up from Devon for the night and that she had made plans to see her. She felt she *had* to see Connolly, she says; she had to explain to him, in person, why their friendship could not continue. Readers will have to judge the credibility of this rationale for themselves. To me, it has always seemed a little suspect. Surely Sheba had provided the boy with quite enough explanation by this point? I am hard-pressed to believe that any woman – even one with Sheba's highly advanced capacity for self-deception – could have set off for such a meeting truly believing that her sole mission was to deliver a refusal.

She rode to the heath on her bicycle. The country was undergoing quite a cold snap that month, but she pedalled so furiously that by the time she reached the park entrance, she was perspiring beneath her sweater. She chained her bike to the railings and walked up the path to the pond. It was a large place for such an assignation, and she felt sure that she and Connolly would miss each other. She remembers being struck by the depth of her own disappointment. Then, without warning, Connolly appeared before her. He seemed younger and smaller than usual that evening, she says. As always, he was insufficiently dressed for the weather. He expressed surprise that she had turned up. He had been sure, he said, that she would 'chicken out'. Sheba explained gravely that she was there only because she had been worried by the tone of his note. There was no hope of anything happening between the two of them, she said.

Connolly responded to this with unexpected equanimity. He nodded, understandingly, and suggested that they walk together for a bit. Sheba refused. That wouldn't be a good idea, she said. Then a man with a dog appeared on the path and glanced at the two of them curiously. Sheba changed her mind. There was no harm in a stroll, she thought. Connolly was behaving so sensibly, it was bound to be all right.

As they set off up the path, Connolly promised not to 'try anything on'.

'I should hope not!' Sheba said, amused by his presumption.

But even as she spoke, it occurred to her that perhaps he *would* try something on. Perhaps, she thought, he had plans to rape her. She kept walking anyway. She had begun to feel strangely detached from the proceedings.

'I was sort of watching myself,' she recalls. 'Smiling at what a silly I was being. It was as if I had become my own rather heartless biographer.'

As they approached an area of the heath that was more densely wooded, Connolly turned to her, clasped her hands in his, and began walking backwards, into the trees, pulling her along with him. 'Come on. In here,' he said.

'What are you doing?' Sheba asked. There was indignation in her voice, but she allowed herself to be pulled. It was much darker than it had been on the path and she could barely see Connolly's face. A fairy-tale image came to her of a goblin dragging a princess back to his forest lair.

They continued to walk for another minute or so, and then, just as Sheba was about to protest again, Connolly stopped and released her from his grip. They were standing in a little clearing. He grinned at her. 'We can be private here,' he said. He sat down on the ground and took off his jacket. 'Here,' he said, spreading it out next to him, 'you can sit on this.'

'You'll freeze,' Sheba objected. But he didn't reply; he just sat, looking at her.

'This is ridiculous,' she said. 'I'm not going to sit down. It's just not on.' Connolly made a 'suit yourself' gesture and lay back on the ground. 'Come on, Steven, you're going to catch pneumonia like that,' Sheba said. He was silent. His eyes were shut. She looked down at him, feeling sillier and sillier.

After a while, he opened his eyes. 'Fuck, it *is* cold, isn't it?' he said. This made her laugh.

'I'm afraid I shouldn't have come,' she said. 'I'm going to go back now.'

'No you're not.' Connolly sat up. There was a twig in his hair.

She remembers smiling at him, knocking her arms against her sides like a little girl.

Finally, with a hopeless shrug, she sat down.

They did not have sex on this occasion. It was far too cold, according to Sheba, and she was far too anxious. I know that they kissed. And Connolly must have lain on top of her at some point because, in speaking of this encounter, Sheba has mentioned having been astonished by how 'light and narrow' he was. (She was accustomed, no doubt, to her husband's more substantial girth.) I also know that at a certain point in the proceedings, Sheba asked something woe-struck and rhetorical along the lines of 'What are we doing?' To which Connolly responded with a terse reassurance in the vein of

'Don't worry about it.' Sheba thought he sounded terribly grown-up and capable. She knew he was neither, of course. But she seems to have taken comfort in the illusion.

∞

Going home that night, Sheba was convinced that she would not be able to face Richard without presenting some physical manifestation of her sin. She pictured herself dissolving in tears. Fainting. Spontaneously combusting. But when she arrived at her house, she surprised herself with how expertly she dissembled.

Richard had waited up for her. He was lying on the sofa, watching *Arts Tonight*. He held up his hand in greeting when she entered the living room, but continued squinting at the television. I've seen Richard watching television once or twice. He has a particular way of turning his head away from the screen and peering at it, sidelong. Sheba says that this has something to do with his bad eyesight. But to me it's always seemed a fitting manifestation of Richard's generally superior attitude: it is as if he is trying, in his pompous way, not to let the telly know that he's interested.

'God, you won't believe what crap these people are talking,' he said. They were quiet for a moment, watching the panel discussion. After a while he turned to her. 'Did you have a nice time?' he asked.

Sheba pretended to inspect split ends in the mirror. 'No, not really,' she replied. 'It was pretty dull, actually.' She hadn't planned to say that, but somehow, when it came to it, grumpiness seemed easier to pull off than enthusiasm.

'Oh dear,' Richard said. He was only half listening.

'I think I'm going to go to bed,' Sheba said.

He humphed absently. Then, just as she grasped the door handle, he looked up again. 'So how's Caitlin?' he asked.

'Oh, okay. A bit lumpy and mumsy these days.' Sheba beamed out silent apologies to her innocent friend.

'Well,' Richard said, yawning, 'that's what life in the provinces does to a person.'

'Yes. Probably.' She paused a moment and then, when Richard did not reply, she opened the door. 'Okay, I'm off upstairs,' she said. 'I'm knackered.'

When Richard came up to the bedroom half an hour later, Sheba kept her eyes shut and concentrated on breathing like a sleeping person. He got undressed and then he read for fifteen minutes. When at last the book slipped from his hand and he began to snore, she remembers feeling strangely let down. Aggrieved almost. She hadn't wanted to arouse his suspicion, of course. But she couldn't help feeling that an evening of the sort she had just experienced deserved a less muted conclusion. It would have been nice, she remembers thinking tipsily, as she drifted into sleep, if she could have confided in her husband about her adventure.

The next day, at the end of school, Connolly came to her studio again. There was a brief, awkward struggle when he first walked in. And then Sheba changed her mind and let him kiss her.

'You know, Steven,' she said, after a while, 'it's very, very important – *incredibly* important – that we keep this secret. You haven't said anything to anybody, have you?'

He assured her, indignantly, that he had not. 'I mean,' he added, 'apart from my mates and that.'

Sheba looked at him, thunderstruck.

He looked back at her for a long moment. Then he laughed. 'Fooled ya,' he said.

Sheba was quiet. She put her hands on his shoulders and studied his grinning face. She told him never to joke about this. She told him that it could be very difficult keeping a secret and that one of these days he might feel tempted to confide in someone, but that even if he thought the person trustworthy – even if they swore on their mother's grave not to tell – he was never to say anything.

'I'm not like that,' he protested. 'I wouldn't grass on you.'

'Grass on *us*,' Sheba corrected him. 'You would be in a lot of trouble, too, you know.' She knew this was probably untrue, but she thought it best to give him as much incentive as possible for keeping quiet.

Connolly stood before her, twisting his head from side to side just as he had done the first time they met. 'Come on,' he said gruffly, 'let me kiss you.'

Shortly after that, they repaired to the far end of the room and there, behind the kiln, they engaged in their first act of sexual intercourse.

'Everyone's always asking, "How could she? What made her take the risk?" ', Sheba said to me once. 'But doing that kind of thing is *easy*. You know how you sometimes have another drink even though you know you're going to have a hangover tomorrow? Or, or, you take a bite of a doughnut, even though it's going to give you fat thighs? Well, it's like that, Barbara. You keep saying, *No, no, no* – until the moment when you say, *Oh bugger it. Yes*.'

Connolly kept whispering something in her ear that first time behind the kiln. It was something urgent but muffled and Sheba had to ask him to repeat himself several times. It was only when he reared back from her impatiently and almost shouted, that his words finally made sense. 'Miss,' he was saying, 'is it all right if I come in you, Miss?'

When I first heard this anecdote, it rather confirmed my sceptical assumptions about the kind of sex one might expect to have with a fifteen-year-old. But Sheba didn't intend it that way. She was offering the story as an illustration of Connolly's charming, rough-edged gallantry. She has not furnished me with many details regarding the mechanics of her and Connolly's intimacy, but often, when referring to their love-making, she rolls her eyes coyly or makes little gasping noises. I think it is safe to say that she found the physical side of their relationship satisfactory. I once asked her, rather irritably, how a boy of Connolly's age and limited experience could possibly have known what he was about, sexually speaking. But she only smiled and wagged her finger at me. 'Ah, that's what is so marvellous about the young,' she said. 'They make such quick studies, don't they?'

∽

I might as well admit here and now that any notional damage done to Connolly's psyche by his affair with Sheba has never been of much concern to me. I don't argue with the necessity of there being a law against teachers doing what Sheba did. Clearly, it is not good for any institution's morale to have staff members fraternizing – fornicating – with their juniors. But I certainly don't subscribe to any sentimental notion about the innocence of everyone under the arbitrarily imposed age bar of sixteen years. The people of Britain danced in the streets when the thirty-two-year-old heir to the British throne became engaged to a nineteen-year-old. Is there so much difference between nineteen and fifteen – between thirty-two and forty-one – to warrant the profoundly different reaction in this case? The sort of young person who becomes involved in this kind of imbroglio is usually pretty wily about sexual matters. I don't mean just that they're sexually experienced – although that is often the case. I mean that they possess some instinct, some natural talent, for sexual power play. For various reasons, our society has chosen to classify people under the age of sixteen as children. In most of the rest of the world, boys and girls are

83

understood to become adults somewhere around the age of twelve. They enter puberty and then start doing whatever the adults in their part of the world happen to do – work in factories, hunt bears, kill people, have sex. We may have very good reasons for choosing to prolong the privileges and protections of childhood. But let us at least acknowledge what we are up against when attempting to enforce that extension. Connolly was officially a 'minor' and Sheba's actions were officially speaking 'exploitative'; yet any honest assessment of their relationship would have to acknowledge not only that Connolly was acting of his own volition, but that he actually wielded more power in the relationship than Sheba. I don't think for a minute that he has suffered lasting hurt from his experiences with an older woman. On the contrary, I believe that he's had a rather thrilling ride. Heresy, I know. But there. It's what I think.

When Sheba's story first broke, a chap from the *Evening Standard* wrote an article in which he alluded to unsubstantiated rumours of Connolly's sexual experience prior to his affair with Sheba. He went on to pose the question, 'What red-blooded fifteen-year-old wouldn't welcome a roll in the hay with Sheba Hart?' It was a brave, honest piece, I thought, but it brought forth a glut of sanctimonious articles protesting against the journalist's supposedly frivolous treatment of a serious matter. The Press Council ended up issuing a rebuke and, by way of apology, the *Standard* published a response piece by Connolly's mother. The article, which I have kept, had the headline, 'Boys Need Our Protection Too'. This was its first paragraph:

Sheba Hart's alleged sexual affair with my son – who was fifteen years old when it began – was recently described in these pages as 'a stroke of good luck for Master Connolly' (*Every Schoolboy's Fantasy*,

20 January 1998). As Steven's mother, I am deeply offended by this sort of light-hearted attitude to Mrs Hart's alleged crime. I find it mind-boggling that anyone should consider the sexual abuse of a minor a laughing matter. I can only suppose that Mrs Hart is benefiting from society's double standards when it comes to sex. If Steven had been a girl, I don't think anyone would have been making jokes and I don't think anyone would have had the cheek to question his innocence.

Here, I'm afraid, I must take issue with Ma Connolly. I would have had the cheek. Had the genders of the principals in this affair been reversed – had Sheba been a man engaging in an illicit affair with a fifteen-year-old girl – I would have been just as wary of apportioning simple 'predator' and 'victim' labels to the two parties. Goodness knows, I have seen quite enough concupiscent girls in my time to be familiar with the sexual manipulation of which young females are capable.

But as regards the general public view on these matters, Mrs Connolly is surely right – there *is* a discrepancy in the way that the public judges the sexual misbehaviour of men and women. Oh, the official response to Sheba is very severe. They all say that she has committed a 'despicable' crime. But behind their hands, they're smirking. When I was in the pub the other night, buying cigarettes, Sheba's face appeared on the television screen for a second; immediately, a great roar of salacious laughter went up around the bar. 'Dirty girl,' I heard one man say to his friend. 'Wouldn't mind a bit of that myself.' It's hard to imagine Sheba's male equivalent eliciting such a ribald reaction.

Male sex offenders are never funny. They get all the right-eous rage – the hatchet-faced housewives baying for blood outside the court; the politicians competing for who can be most sickened. Which is odd really, given that paler versions of their despised urges are so ubiquitous, so cheerfully sanctioned, in the male population at large. Don't the scientists now go so far as to suggest that the attraction of older men for younger women is an evolutionary instinct – a reflex encoded in male biology? When a lecherous middle-aged man ogles a teenager's bottom, are we not now encouraged to believe that he is actually doing his bit for the species – responding to the physical symptoms of fecundity, as nature has programmed him to do?

But perhaps that's it. Perhaps the vehemence with which we respond to men's sexual transgressions is proportionate to how discomfortingly common we know those transgressive urges to be. A woman who interferes with a minor is not a symptom of an underlying tendency. She is an aberration. People don't see themselves, or their own furtive desires in her. According to evolutionary science, an affair like Sheba's is nothing more than a freakish lay-by on the grand motorway of human survival. That's why men in pubs can afford to laugh at her.

Is it so much better, though, to be laughed at than to be feared? Being a public monster must be – well, monstrous. But becoming the punchline of a smutty joke is no pleasure, either. And evil at least has some heft. Mrs Connolly is anxious lest Sheba 'benefit' from the double standard. But I doubt very much that Sheba's comic oddity will actually earn her more lenience from the court. In all likelihood, she'll receive exactly the same punishment as a man. The guardians of gender equality won't stand for anything else. In the end, I suspect, being female will do nothing for Sheba, except deny her the grandeur of genuine villainy.

Six

The third Friday in March marked something of a turning point in my relations with Sheba. I have given the date one gold star. The lunch hour was extended that day by half an hour so that the staff could assemble in the headmaster's garden to have their photograph taken. This annual staff portrait is one of the traditions instated under Pabblem's rule. Pabblem, who likes to have evidence – faked up, if necessary – of what a cheerful, raucous ship he runs, uses the portrait on the front cover of the school newsletter. In order to offset the expense of the photographer, he also 'strongly encourages' each staff member to buy a minimum of two souvenir prints at a grossly inflated price.

Friday was a white-skied, drizzly day and there was quite a bit of muttering from the teachers as they began trailing down the path to Pabblem's enclosure. 'Fuck this for a game of soldiers,' Bill Rumer said, prompting a round of appreciative titters from his cronies. 'Ooh, this is so bloody *boring*,' Elaine Clifford whined a little later, as she pushed a grubby pink comb through her hair. (Staff complaint at St George's is never very fiery or subversive. On the contrary, it tends to suggest a certain pleasure in the cosy predictability of things being unsatisfactory.)

Pabblem finally put in an appearance at 12.30. He was closely pursued by Phelps and Jenkins, both of whom were carrying benches borrowed from the gym. It is one of Pabblem's many vanities to believe that he is a 'visual person' and every year he has a new concept for how the staff should be posed. One time, he had us all lie down on the grass while the photographer clambered onto the playground shed for an aerial shot. Another time, he tried in vain to get everyone to jump in the air at the same time. Mrs Freeble, who teaches Domestic Science, landed awkwardly and had to be sent to the A & E with a fractured toe. This year, Pabblem had hit upon the idea of drafting in a few of the younger and more photogenic children from the lower school. The staff was to perch on the gym benches, while Pabblem stood in the foreground with the children clinging to him in attitudes of spontaneous affection and delight.

To no one but Pabblem's surprise, the children proved to be a terrible drag on the proceedings. For a good fifteen minutes the assembled staff sat on the cold benches, pressing their blue hands between their clenched thighs, while the three little girls and one boy who had been chosen expressed their entirely reasonable objections to sitting on Pabblem's shoulders, or crouching behind him with their heads poking through his legs.

After a while, a break was called. Pabblem and the children went off to one side with the photographer to rehearse poses and we were allowed to get up and stretch our legs. I stood with a few other teachers watching Pabblem yank the children about with increasingly terse commands: 'Stand here! Like this! Hold my hand!' At one point, I made a facetious remark. Sheba, who was standing behind me, responded with a loud hoot of laughter and Pabblem looked up angrily. I gazed innocently at the sky. I was in particularly bad odour with Pabblem at this time, having recently handed in a revised version of the St Albans report that he had deemed even less satisfactory than the first. At our last, fraught meeting, he had informed me of his decision to scrap my report and to incorporate some of my 'less contentious material' into a longer paper that he would author himself. This paper, he told me, was going to be a far-reaching examination of all discipline issues currently facing St George's. It would be a big project but he hoped to have it finished in time for the summer term staff conference. Its provisional title was 'Where We Go Wrong'.

The photo session resumed and after some more unpleasant wrangling the children were eventually pressed into service, but by the time we were released we had only three-quarters of an hour left before afternoon classes began. As the teachers started to leave, Sheba came over to me. She apologized for causing trouble with her noisy laughter and then she invited me to join her and Sue at La Traviata for a quick bite. The three of us walked over together.

'I have something to announce,' Sue said, when we were sitting down in the restaurant.

'You're leaving St George's,' I said.

'No,' Sue said, glancing at me sourly. 'Come on, Sheba, can you guess?'

'Oh Sue, I'm terrible at guessing,' Sheba said. 'What is it?'

'Well, you must promise not to tell anyone else, because I'm still, you know, keeping it quiet, until –'

'You're pregnant,' I interrupted.

Sue's fat face fell. 'How did you know?'

'You are?' Sheba said. 'Oh that's wonderful news, Sue!'

Sue began beaming again. 'Not quite three months yet, so it's still a secret. But you must have noticed how chunky I'm getting!'

Sheba paused, diplomatically. In truth, the early stages of pregnancy had made no discernible difference to Sue's Pantagruelian bulk. 'You look terrific,' Sheba said. 'Incredibly well!'

Sue proceeded to prattle on at some length about baby

names and nursery decoration plans and other maternity-related matters. I tuned out for a while. When I tuned back in, she was discussing labour. 'Listen to this,' she said in a scandalized voice. 'Ted is against me having a natural delivery.'

'Well,' said Sheba, 'good for Ted.'

Sue blinked. 'No, I mean, he's got a point. Obviously. I bet *you* were sensible and took the epiwhatisit the first time they offered.'

'No, actually,' Sheba said. 'When Polly was born, I was in labour for twenty-four hours without anything. I'd read all the books about the unnecessary interventions of modern medicine. And there was an element of keeping up with Richard's first wife, Marcia, who had delivered both her girls with a midwife in a birthing pool. I was slightly letting the side down even being in hospital. I wanted to cave in during the final stretch and have the drugs, but by then it was too late. They said it would harm the baby, so I had to bloody well go through with it.'

'And how –' Sue was speaking now in the hushed tones she reserved for sensitive issues ' – how was it with Ben?' She shot me a look. Clearly, she had heard accounts of my staffroom *faux pas* regarding Sheba's son.

'Oh, Ben was an incredibly easy birth,' Sheba said. 'I was determined to have the epidural that time round. I went into the hospital at three in the afternoon and at ten I was playing Scrabble with Richard in the main ward when one of the nurses came up and took a look at me and said, "Oh my God, you're ten centimetres dilated. That baby's coming!" They whisked me straight into the labour room and about twenty minutes later, he was born. So no epidural that time either.'

'Well –' Sue began, but Sheba carried on talking.

'As soon as he came out, they took him off to the side, like they do, to wash him and whatever. They were talking away – how lovely he was, what a pretty boy. And then they all started whispering. I was saying, What? What is it? But they wouldn't answer. And then the doctor went over and there was a lot more murmuring. I started screaming, What is it? And eventually, the doctor came to me and said, "Sheba, I'm afraid your baby has Down's Syndrome."'

I glanced at Sue. Her mouth was a crinkly line of distress. She looked as if she were on the verge of blubbing.

'Afterwards,' Sheba continued, 'Richard said he had been almost relieved, because by that point he'd been convinced the baby was seriously deformed – a Cyclops or something. I wasn't relieved at all. I kept saying there had to be a mistake. We hadn't had the amnio. I wasn't a high risk for that sort of thing and we always said the amnio was a bad idea because what were we going to do if they did find a defect? Exterminate the child because it wasn't up to scratch?'

She paused and looked around the restaurant.

'I mean,' she went on, 'I *still* think that. But, at the time, I don't think I'd considered the full . . . I was just so confident that there *wouldn't* be any problem. I kept saying to them, No, you're wrong. But obviously they weren't. And when they gave him to me, I could see immediately that he was different. I was sort of disgusted with him, actually . . . Isn't that terrible? But I was. I just kept thinking, He's a mistake. He shouldn't have been born. I was terribly depressed for the first month. And then I went the other way. At about ten weeks I became quite euphoric. He was smiling all the time, and I convinced myself that he was actually cleverer – quicker – than other babies . . .'

She looked up at Sue and me, now. 'Oh God!' she cried. 'Don't look so glum! Please! This is a happy day! I didn't mean to be a downer.' Both of us grinned obediently.

'Don't stop,' Sue said. 'Please. You're not being a downer at all.'

But Sheba shook her head. 'Enough childbirth for one day, I think,' she said.

On the way back to school, Sue popped into the chemist's leaving me and Sheba to walk the last five hundred yards to the school gates on our own. The morning grey had given way, in the sudden English fashion, to a brilliant, gelid afternoon. On the patches of street that weren't in shadow, you could feel the sun warming your hair.

'I hope it didn't upset you, talking about Ben and . . . everything,' I said.

'No, no, not at all.'

'It's just, I feel embarrassed about that topic because of, you know, what I said to you that time in the staffroom . . .'

Sheba stopped and squinted at me in the sunlight. 'Oh Barbara, that was much worse for you than for me. You fret too much. How were you to know? Listen, I once told a joke about a one-legged man to a colleague of my husband's who really had only one leg. He was sitting down at a table when I first walked in so I didn't realize.'

'God,' I said. We both laughed.

After our laughter had faded, we walked for a while in silence. I was just beginning to worry about not having anything to say, when Sheba held out her arms, flung back her head and made a happy, stretching sound. 'Ohhhh, how lovely to have the weekend,' she said. She shut her eyes for a moment and when I glanced at her, I saw her amazing lashes lapping like fronds at her cheeks.

'Are you going away?' I asked tentatively.

'Noooo,' she said, opening her eyes. 'Not going away. Not getting out of bed unless I absolutely have to. I've told Richard I'm determined to do absolutely nothing.'

'Oh, that sounds marvellous,' I said. It did sound marvellous – having a life so busy and full that doing nothing was an aspiration. But Sheba misinterpreted the envy in my tone.

'Oh dear, are you going to be very hectic?' she asked.

I considered an array of possible answers, opting at last for what I told myself was medium truth. 'Not especially,' I said. 'Bits and bobs, you know . . .'

We lapsed into silence again. I could hear the prim tip-tap of my heels on the pavement. I ordered myself to talk: *For God's sake, say something, you catatonic bitch*. But nothing came.

Then Sheba spoke. 'Listen, would you like to come to dinner on Sunday?'

Surprise made me stupid. 'What, with you?'

She laughed, although not unkindly. 'Yes, me and Richard and Ben. And Polly too. She's got the day off from school on Monday, so she's coming down for the weekend.'

Had she asked Sue too, I wondered? She had to have. It was impossible that she would invite me without her. 'Oh, but you just said how you were dying to do nothing,' I objected. 'You can't be cooking for me.'

She shook her head. 'It's only dinner. I'd be making it anyway. Believe me, it won't be anything grand. And I'd love you to meet Ben and Polly.'

'Well I . . .'

'Come on, Barbara, I insist.'

'All right then. That sounds lovely.'

'Sunday night is good?'

I wondered if I ought to make some nod to the notion of having to consult my diary. But I thought better of it. I didn't want to risk her glimpsing the white wastelands of my appointmentless weeks.

'Sounds fine,' I said. 'Will Sue be coming?' I blushed. It had slipped out before I could stop myself.

Sheba didn't seem to notice. 'No, actually,' she said. 'She can't. She's going to be in Abergavenny with Ted.'

'Oh I see.' Had I been considered only after Sue turned the offer down? There was a short silence as I pondered the indignity of being Sue's understudy.

'You know, I could have both of you over another time when she's free, if you'd prefer,' Sheba offered.

'Oh, no!' I said.

'That's what I thought.' Sheba smiled. 'I mean, it's not as if we're an unbreakable triumvirate, is it?'

We were at the school gates now.

'Okay, look.' She rummaged in her bag and produced a piece of paper and a pen. 'Here's where I live. And here's my number. You'll be driving, right? So you should call if you need directions.'

She handed the piece of paper to me and I gazed dumbly at it in my hand.

'We're on?' she said.

'Yes, absolutely. We're on.'

'See you on Sunday, then.'

I stood watching her as she walked away. Her long green cardigan was flapping around her in the breeze and her skirt was clinging to her woollen tights, getting caught up between her legs. She was fiddling, as usual, with her unruly hair. 'Damn,' I heard her mutter softly, as she bent to retrieve a hairgrip from the ground. I folded the piece of paper on which she had written her address, placed it carefully in the inner pocket of my handbag and headed slowly towards Old Hall. I kept my head down as I walked, partly so that I could concentrate on replaying the conversation that had just taken place and partly to avoid advertising the foolish smile on my face.

∞

I woke up on the morning of my dinner appointment with Sheba and solemnly promised myself not to start doing anything preparatory until midday. It is a great challenge for me not to place inordinate emphasis on this sort of occasion. Any break in my routine – any small variation in the sequence of work and grocery shopping and telly and so on – tends to take on a disproportionate significance. I'm a child in that respect: able to live, psychically speaking, on a crumb of anticipation for weeks at a time, but always in danger of crushing the waited-for event with the freight of my excessive hope.

By 9 a.m., in spite of my vows, I had twice taken my new sandals out of their box to check that they weren't too tarty. The rest of my outfit, which I had laid out the night before, presented no problems. I had spray-starched my white blouse so it was nice and crisp, and my grey suit from BHS looked almost as good as new. (It had not left its dry-cleaning wrapper since a staff function two years earlier.) The sandals were a worry, though. I had bought them on Saturday at a local boutique in Archway. They were lilac, with tiny bows on the front and a higher heel than I generally wear. Jolly? I asked myself as I stared at them from different angles. Or just cheap? Would they look silly with tights? And if so, could I get away with bare legs?

At 3 p.m. I took a bath. Afterwards, while my hair was drying, I tried getting a fresh perspective on the sandals by walking quickly into the bedroom and catching them, as it were, by surprise. The first time I did this, they looked all right. Pretty. Dainty. Entirely appropriate for a single woman attending a spring supper. Then I did it again. And this time when I walked into the room, they seemed to sit up and roar *mutton dressed as lamb*. In an effort to get off the footwear topic, I tried on my grey skirt. But it seemed that I had put on weight since last wearing it and as I strained to fasten the waistband, one of the buttons pinged off and rolled into the dark, dusty space beneath my dresser. There followed a rather shameful interlude of female madness, which involved me tearing off the skirt and standing on a wobbly chair in the front room, trying to get a full-length view of my naked form in the mirror that hangs over the gas fire.

It's always a disappointing business confronting my own reflection. My body isn't bad. It's a perfectly nice, serviceable body. It's just that the external me – the sturdy, lightly wrinkled, handbagged me – does so little credit to the stuff that's inside. Sometimes, when I lie in bed at night, I can lose all sense of my body, my age. In the darkness, I could be twenty years old. I could be ten. It's a lovely sensation to slough off one's battered old casing for a moment or two. But then, I always wonder, what must it be to have a *beautiful* body? A body that you don't want to escape? Several years ago, when Jennifer and I went to Paris together for a weekend break, we saw a woman dancing on the bar at a little bistro in Montmartre. She was very pretty and very, very young. All the men in the place were dribbling slightly. It was a silly thing really, but just for a moment as I watched them watch her, I remember feeling that I would give *anything* – be stupid, be poor, be fatally ill – to have a little of her sort of power.

I must have made quite a bit of noise during my personal appearance crisis because, at some point, the woman who lives above me began banging on her floor. I stopped crying then, got down from the chair and made a cup of tea. While I sat sipping and sniffling, Portia, my cat, who had been watching my ravings with great, feline contempt, relented and came over to rub herself against my legs.

Slowly, I grew calm. The sandals were all right. I was getting myself in a state over nothing. The skirt was a bother, but it could be safety-pinned. If not, my black one with an elasticated waist would suffice. I would not wear tights.

I left the house with enough time to buy some flowers for Sheba. The flower stall outside the underground station had a rather depleted selection and I agonized over having left it so late. I ended up plumping for a mixed bunch of carnations and sweetheart roses and then, more or less the minute I got into the car, I remembered reading somewhere that multi-coloured flower arrangements were in poor taste. Miraculously, I managed to restrain myself from going back to exchange them.

Sheba lived in a large Victorian house in Boise Lane: three storeys, a big bay window on the ground floor and a front garden with a cherry tree. I got a little bit lost on the way and then could only find a parking space two streets away. By the time I arrived on the doorstep, I was rather tense and pink and the straps of my sandals had begun to chafe.

'Barbara!' Sheba cried when she opened the door. 'How lovely you look!' She hugged me. 'And what lovely flowers!' She took the bouquet that I held out. 'Come in. Come in. Let's get you a drink.'

We walked down a long hallway into a living room that occupied roughly the same square footage as my entire flat. Everything in it was very large – the carpets covering the wooden floorboards, the slabs of worn furniture, the cavernous fireplace. I sat down, at Sheba's urging, in a leather armchair, but the seat was so deep that as I leaned back, my feet lost contact with the floor and I found myself semi-recumbent. When I attempted to haul myself up into a less ridiculous position, my hand grasped a child's sock that was stuck down the side of the chair cushion.

'Oh God, what slobs we are!' Sheba said, clutching her forehead.

She was only playing at being embarrassed, though. When I handed the sock to her, she threw it in a wooden bowl on the coffee table. 'Hang on,' she said, 'let me go and put your flowers in some water. Richard and the children should be down any minute . . .'

The first time Jennifer came to my flat, I cleaned the place scrupulously in preparation for her arrival; I even groomed Portia, for God's sake. And still, I had the most terrible feeling of exposure when she walked in. It was as if my dirty linen basket, rather than my unexceptionable sitting room, were on display. But the awkwardness of having a professional colleague observe her living arrangements had not occurred to Sheba. She wasn't thinking about what I was thinking. She had that absolute, bourgeois confidence in the rightness of her living room, her tatty, gigantic furniture, her children's stray underwear.

Left on my own, I swivelled about at the tip of my chair, taking the opportunity to inspect my surroundings with a less inhibited curiosity. Hanging on the wall were several paintings – the sort of gimmicky modern abstracts that aren't my cup of tea – and a primitive wooden instrument, possibly African, which looked as if it might be rather smelly if one got too close to it. The bookshelves housed a decent but not very inspired collection of fiction, suggesting the strong influence of newspaper 'Books of the Year' lists. You could tell there weren't any *real* literature lovers in the family. The mantel-piece was a gathering point for household flotsam. A child's drawing. A hunk of pink Play-Doh. A passport. One elderly-looking banana.

There was a level of disorder in the place that I doubt I could ever tolerate. And yet, there was something in the disarray that was enviable. When you live alone, your furnish-ings, your possessions, are always confronting you with the thinness of your existence. You know with painful accuracy the provenance of everything you touch and the last time you touched it. The five little cushions on your sofa stay plumped and leaning at their jaunty angle for months at a time unless you theatrically muss them. The level of the salt in your shaker decreases at the same excruciating rate, day after day. Sitting in Sheba's house – studying the mingled detritus of its several inhabitants – I could see what a relief it might be to let your own meagre effects be joined with other people's.

'You're Barbara,' a voice said. I looked up and saw a tall man with a lot of crazy grey hair standing in the doorway, peering at me through thick spectacles. 'Hello,' he said. 'I'm Richard.' Sheba had mentioned that her husband was older than her; I was taken aback to discover by how much. Richard was not yet what you could call elderly, but middle age was no longer a plausible category for him either. His shoulders had begun to slope in the manner of overburdened coathangers. The backs of his hands had a shiny, yellowish look.

'Sheba has spoken so fondly of you,' he said, coming over to shake my hand. His belt was cinched a little too tightly beneath his pot belly and there was art, I saw now, in the tousling of his hair. He was not going unprotestingly into his dotage. 'I gather you're one of the few civilized people at St George's.'

'Oh, I don't know . . .' I began.

'Now!' he said, ignoring my demurral. 'I see my wife has abandoned you without even giving you a drink. Monstrous woman! What can I get you?' He rubbed his hands and grinned. His eyes, behind the spectacles, had a bulbous, insectoid look. A rogue image swam into my head, of his pruney old mouth pursed at Sheba's breast.

'Whatever you . . . what do you have?' I said.

Richard waved his arms expansively. 'Everything! We're very dedicated boozers in this house.'

'Well then . . . . a sherry would be lovely.'

'Sherry?' The ghost of a smirk passed across his face. 'Really? Goodness, I think you may have hit upon the one thing we *don't* have.'

He went over to the drinks cupboard and began rootling around.

Sheba came back, carrying my flowers in a vase. 'Oh you've met!' she said. She looked anxiously at Richard and then back at me. 'The children will be down any minute.' She spoke with a strange, ersatz cheerfulness. She had probably had to do some wheedling to get her husband to agree to my visit, I thought. This would explain the self-conscious saintliness with which Richard was attending to me. In the little economy of the marriage, my invitation to dinner had posted a substantial credit in his column.

'Darling,' Richard said, removing his head from the interior of the drinks cupboard, 'do we have any sherry that you know of ? Barbara wants sherry.'

'No, honestly,' I protested. 'I'll be perfectly happy with something else. White wine . . .'

'I know!' Sheba said. 'I've got some Marsala in the kitchen. I use it for cooking. Would Marsala do, Barbara?'

'Absolutely. But please, don't go to any trouble . . .'

'Oh!' Sheba cried, pointing at my feet. 'You've hurt yourself.'

I looked down and, sure enough, blood was trickling down my left ankle; the strap of my stupid shoe had bitten into the skin.

'Poor you,' Sheba said. 'Are they new shoes? Let me go and get you a plaster . . .'

'No, no, don't worry . . .'

'Don't be silly. I won't be a sec.' She disappeared.

Richard smiled at me, embarrassed. 'You ladies and your stilettos,' he said.

'They're hardly stilettos . . .' I protested.

'Bash used to insist on wearing high heels,' he went on. 'And then one time she fractured her ankle running for a bus. After that I put my foot down . . . Ha! As it were. I made her buy a pair of clogs.'

There was a short silence.

'I've never seen the point of high heels myself,' Richard continued. 'It's all about creating a sexually provocative posture, isn't it? Bending the spine, forcing the bottom out. Like those marvellous, purple-arsed orang-utans . . .' He paused. 'I think I'll make myself a drink while we're waiting for your sherry.'

Sheba came back now with the Marsala and the plasters. She was accompanied by her daughter, Polly – a sulky, rather beautiful seventeen-year-old, with her father's curly hair and her mother's long, thin body. 'Polly, this is Barbara, my friend from school,' Sheba said.

'Hello,' Polly said curtly, casting a quick glance in my direction. She gestured at the box of plasters in her mother's hand. 'What are they for?'

'Barbara cut her foot,' Sheba said.

Polly turned to look at my bleeding heel. 'Oh, gross,' she said.

'Polly!' Richard murmured in a tone of vague reproof.

Sheba came over and handed me a plaster with a bundle of toilet paper to clean my wound.

Polly slumped on the sofa with a gusty sigh. 'Can I have a vodka with a twist, Dad?' she asked.

'Oh, all right,' her father said, in a twinkly tone of indulgence. He smiled at me and shook his head. 'My daughter the alcoholic.'

'So, Polly,' I said, as I tended to my ankle. 'You must be doing your A Levels now. How are your courses going?' The blood soaked through the first toilet paper tourniquet with no sign of staunching.

'*Fine*,' Polly said in a bored voice, pulling at the hairs on her arm.

'Polly!' Sheba said.

'What?' Polly said. 'What was I meant to say?'

This riposte evidently stumped Sheba, or perhaps she was trying to avoid a scene. In any case, she didn't pursue it. I chuckled, to indicate that I had not taken offence. Although of course I had. It sounds mad for a woman who has spent her life in the teaching profession to say so, but the truth is, I am not very good with young people. I am perfectly confident in a classroom, where the rules – regardless of whether or not they are respected – are clearly defined. But in other contexts I find myself at a loss. I cannot affect the casual, knock-about style of conversing with the younger generation that seems to be *de rigueur* these days. I am not a casual person. Horse-play and nonsense jokes do not sit well on me. I tend to become stiff and awkward in young company – and then, when I see that my companions are bored by me, I grow pre-emptively cold and forbidding.

Richard brought me my drink. 'There you go, my dear,' he said, in a jocular imitation of a north country accent.

'Is there somewhere I can put this?' I asked, holding the plaster wrapping and the tissue in my fist.

'Give it here,' Sheba said, taking the little bloodied bundle from me. 'I'm just going to check on dinner.'

Just then, there was the noise of someone running very heavily down the stairs and a chubby, fair-haired boy burst into the room.

'Hoola! Hoola!' Richard shouted, crouching down and opening his arms wide. 'Ben's here! Hoola! Hoola!' The child rushed at him, giggling. Richard grasped him and held him upside down. 'What's it like down there, Benno?' he asked playfully.

Sheba stood smiling at the tomfoolery. Polly, who was sipping at the vodka that her father had given her, did not look up.

'Hmm, have you got any pocket money for me, Benno?' Richard said, swinging the upside-down child from side to side. Ben squealed with excitement as coins fell from his pockets.

'Okay,' Sheba said. 'Let's not get too manic right before dinner.'

Richard put the child down. 'Okay, Benno McBenjaboo, time to behave now. This lady here is called Barbara. She's come to dinner with us.'

'Hello,' Ben said, stepping forward and shaking my hand. 'My name is Ben.' I had been dreading this moment in case I said something silly, or failed to understand what he was saying. But it went off okay. He had that slightly strangled, adenoidal voice of the handicapped, but he was perfectly comprehensible. 'Did you know I have a girlfriend already?' he went on. 'I'm only eleven.'

'No, I didn't,' I said.

'Her name is Sarah. She's going to come to tea next week.'

'Goodness,' I said.

'Sarah is a friend from Ben's school,' Sheba explained.

'Not just a friend, Mum,' Ben objected. 'She's my girlfriend. We're going to do slow-dancing together.'

'Well, we'll see about that.' Sheba raised her eyebrows at me. 'Hormones seem to be kicking in earlier and earlier these days.'

Ben watched her carefully as she spoke. 'What do you mean, Mum?' he said. 'What are hormones, Mum?'

We ate dinner all together at a round table in the large ground-floor kitchen. Sheba had made shepherd's pie and salad. Richard opened a bottle of Rioja. 'Bash is the chef in this house,' he said as he poured wine for me, 'and I am the sommelier.'

The dinner conversation was lively. Ben talked about a recent visit he had made with his school to the London zoo and we all marvelled at his renderings of various animal noises. Sheba got me to describe for Richard the recent St Albans debacle and Richard roared with laughter. He raised his eyebrows when I described Pabblem as a north London version of Turgenev's Matthew Ilich.

'Turgenev, eh? Very good, very good,' he said, as if he were putting a little tick in the margin of my essay. Then, by way of rewarding me for not being a completely ignorant person, he went on to talk for quite a long while about the book he was writing. It seemed to be about right-wing bias in the media, but when I suggested as much he yelped and said that he hoped it was 'slightly more subtle' than that. He spent ages trying to get me to understand this one particular point about the insidious way in which newsreaders use verbs. It sounded pretty silly to me. But for the sake of harmony, I feigned credulity.

There was only one sticky moment during dinner and that had nothing to do with me. It arose when Sheba tried to get Polly to eat a little more and Polly shrieked at her mother to leave her alone.

'Polly, your manners are appalling. I will not have you speak to me that way,' Sheba said, quietly.

'Well then, don't go on at me about what I eat,' Polly replied in a defiantly loud voice.

'I was not going on at you,' Sheba objected. 'I was trying to make sure you don't starve yourself.'

'Oh please leave it, Bash,' Richard said.

There was a tense silence for a moment or so, which was broken by Richard saying, 'It's difficult isn't it, Barbara? One pretends that manners are the formalization of basic kindness and consideration, but a great deal of the time, they're simply aesthetics dressed up as moral principles, aren't they?'

'Oh Richard . . .' Sheba said.

'No, I'm serious. I mean, it's clear that politeness to one's elders can't always be justified on the basis of the elder's superior wisdom. It's just that it's not *attractive* to see a young person answering an older person back. Isn't that it? What do you think, Barbara?'

I rather thought that he was a pretentious fool, but I kept that to myself. 'Well, I'm not sure . . .' I began, but Richard's attention had wandered already.

'Pudding time!' he shouted now, in his jokey baritone. 'Come on, Bash, what's for pud?'

Pudding was vanilla ice cream and shop-bought chocolate cake. 'We're immediate-gratification people, I'm afraid, Barbara,' Richard said, sounding not at all afraid, as he cut wedges of cake for the table. I resented his constant explications of family culture. In the guise of welcoming me in, they seemed only to push me further out. *You couldn't be expected to understand our colourful, posh ways.*

After pudding, Sheba took me to see her pottery studio in the basement. 'Richard's terribly impressed with you,' she said, as she led me down the stairs. 'He never talks to anyone about his book.' I struggled to look honoured.

We were standing now in a large, slightly damp-smelling room. It was painted primrose yellow and outfitted with a kiln and a pottery wheel. Along one wall, there were shelves displaying Sheba's work. I had never seen anything that she had produced before. For some reason, whenever she had mentioned her work to me, I had always envisaged earthenware – those clumpy, grey-beige objects that they sell in gift shops. But the pieces on the shelves were not like that at all. They were delicate, romantic things – bowls with lacy, latticework rims; urns with handles in the shape of animals and birds. Rows and rows of rainbow-coloured plates.

'My goodness, Sheba, your work is so . . . sweet,' I said.

'Oh dear.'

'No, not sweet. These things are *lovely*. I mean, when I think of pottery, I think of . . . not lovely things like these.' I pointed to a large bowl trimmed with a winding trail of yellow roses and plump, blue sparrows. '*Look* at this. I do envy you being able to make things. May I?'

She nodded. 'Go ahead.'

I picked it up carefully. 'How did you *do* it? These colours . . . so clever. I *love* these birds.'

'Have it,' she said.

I put the bowl down. 'Oh God, absolutely not. Please, Sheba, I wasn't fishing, I promise . . .'

'No, I know. I'd just like you to have it.'

'Oh, but I –'

'Barbara, don't be tiresome about this,' she said smiling. 'Take the bloody bowl.'

It is always difficult, the transition from noisy refusal to humble acceptance. 'Are you sure?' I said.

'Absolutely.'

'Well, thank you,' I said. 'I'm terribly touched. I haven't received such a lovely gift in a very long time. It's beautiful.' I paused, aware that I was being a bore. 'Polly's a very pretty girl,' I added, to change the subject.

'Yes,' Sheba murmured. She unfolded two chairs that were stacked against the wall and gestured at me to sit down on one of them.

I thought that was all she was going to say about Polly, so I began looking for other topics. But just as I opened my mouth to remark on how peaceful it was in the basement, she started speaking again. 'No one ever expected Polly to turn out so nicely,' she said. 'She became beautiful quite suddenly, at the age of eight. Before that, she was an ugly little thing. A little rat of a girl. People were always telling me tactfully that she was very *robust*. I never cared. Her ugliness made me love her more. For the first two years of her life, I could hardly put her down. I carried her everywhere, as if I were bearing the infant Boudicca on her triumphal litter.' She paused. 'It's probably a good thing that your kids turn into difficult adolescents,' she said. 'The feelings you have for them as infants are much too intense, too enervating, to sustain.'

'Polly's a bit difficult, is she, then?' I said.

Sheba looked at me wryly. 'You needn't pretend, Barbara. Yes, Polly is an absolute pain in the arse. She's got a lot of "positions" on things. Vegetarianism. Feminism. All that. And she doesn't like it at all if you happen not to share them with her.'

I smiled.

'She's always rejecting boys on the basis that they're not political enough, or that they're "sexist",' Sheba went on. 'Don't you think there's something a bit hard, or just a bit *unimaginative*, about a young woman who can turn down a suitor on those grounds? I mean, surely at seventeen, you're allowed to just fancy people?'

I shrugged. 'Each to her own.'

'I was a lot sillier and more innocent at her age, I know,' Sheba said. 'And infinitely more woundable. But I had more fun, I think. I was so excited by things! So looking forward to becoming an adult! I used to practise rolling around in bed at night with my future boyfriends. I had a whole collection of fantasy lovers. The cowboy, the doctor, the Arab sheikh. I was the proud, rebellious one in the sheikh's harem. The one with "spirit" . . .' She laughed. 'When I think back to all that, I feel almost sorry for Polly. You know? I mean, what men does she dream of ? The district leaders of Animal Rights Now?' She stopped abruptly, as if embarrassed at how passionate she had allowed herself to become on this subject.

'Well, anyway,' she said after a moment, 'that's it. Teenagers are hard work. You know that.'

I nodded. 'So now, where did you learn to do this?' I asked, gesturing at her work. 'Did you study art somewhere?'

She smiled a little wanly. 'Not really. I took a foundation course at St Martin's. But then I met Richard – he was one of my lecturers – and we got married.'

'Oh! You must have been so young!'

'Yes, twenty. And I wasn't even pregnant. He asked me and it seemed like something to do.' She laughed. 'I was always a bit of a scaredy cat about the big wide world. I told myself that it was subversive of me to be doing something so conventional.'

'What did your parents say?'

'Oh, they were appalled – Daddy especially. He said he hadn't raised me to be a ninny housewife. After we were married he was always on at me to get a job. I did try various things to please him. I took a typing course and temped for a bit. I got a job with one of his friends, working at a charity for the homeless, but I got sacked for not being efficient enough. After that, I did a teacher training course. And then I got pregnant. My starting salary in teaching wouldn't have covered the cost of the nanny, so that was that. I always said I'd go to work when Polly was five. But just after her fifth birthday, I found out I was pregnant again. And then Ben turned out to be . . . Ben. It was only last year, when we finally got him settled into a good school, that the question of work came up again.' She stuck out her chin. 'There. Now you know how I find myself so hopelessly without achievement.'

'How can you say such a thing?' I protested. 'You have two beautiful children. Ben is so marvellous. You can't possibly regret devoting your energies to him. To have brought up two children – one with handicaps – I mean, that's huge, a huge achievement. Certainly bigger than anything you could have done by having a career.'

Sheba nodded impatiently. 'Oh yes, I know. I know all that. And believe me I allow myself plenty of private gloating about my selfless parenting. But raising kids is not the same as what I'm ... It can't possibly offer the same satisfactions as doing things out in the world. I don't care what you say, it's a terrible bore to have never made or done anything noteworthy, to have laboured in such absolute obscurity.'

I was just stuttering a protest when she interrupted: 'Barbara – sorry, I don't mean to impose on you, but could I ask your advice about something? I need very badly to talk to someone at the moment. I've got a little problem. At school.'

I nodded earnestly, trying to look worthy of her confidence. 'What is the ...'

'Well.' She patted nervously at her hair. 'It's about one of the pupils. Actually it's that boy, you know, the one you helped me deal with last term.'

'Which boy?'

'The very blond one? Steven Connolly?'

'Ah, yes.'

She went on to give me a heavily bowdlerized account of their relationship. They were friends, she said. He had an interest in art and he often came to see her out of school hours, to discuss his drawings. She had been teaching him about pottery. But lately, she had sensed that he was developing some sort of crush on her and she was concerned about how to proceed. When I asked her what cause she had to suspect a crush, she hesitated, as if embarrassed. Then she explained that the previous week, as she was leaving school, Connolly had approached her on the street, and tried to kiss her.

For all its omissions, it was a long narrative, which she told with many fastidious digressions. Listening to her, I had the impression that she was trying to be very, very scrupulous and accurate. Several times, she stopped to correct herself on tiny points relating to the exact time that a conversation had taken place or precisely what salutation she had used on a specific occasion. It was almost as if she were giving a police report.

'What day was it again, that he actually attacked you?' I asked, when she had finished.

'Oh no, it wasn't an attack . . .' she said.

'All right, whatever it was. When was it?'

'Um, last Thursday.'

'Have you seen him or spoken to him since the incident?'

'He's come to my studio a couple of times, but I sent him away.'

I thought for a while. 'If the situation is really as you have described it,' I said, 'your course of action seems to me quite clear-cut. The boy has been harassing you and needs to be stopped. You must inform the headmaster straightaway and have the boy disciplined.'

Sheba looked at me, horrified. 'Oh no!' she said. 'No, no. I couldn't possibly . . .'

'But the boy tried to kiss you. It's very serious.'

'No, no, Barbara,' she said. 'I've given you quite the wrong impression. He's the most harmless boy. When I say "kiss", you have to understand, it was a terribly sweet, romantic thing – not at all aggressive – and the moment I protested, he stopped. He's got a crush, you see. It would do nobody any good to make it a discipline issue.'

We were both quiet for a moment.

'Sheba, I have to ask you this. Do you have feelings for this boy?'

She blushed. 'Well, yes. What – you mean, do I fancy him or something? God, *no*. Absolutely not. I'm fond of him. He's a sweetie. I just, you know, need to know how to handle this, without hurting his feelings.'

I nodded. 'I'm going to tell you something now, that you're not going to like,' I said. 'You're new to this game and you have a lot of worthy, completely impractical ideas about what your role as teacher should be. The fact is, it isn't your job to be a friend to your pupils. When you blur the lines of the teacher–pupil contract – when you try to be soft and chummy and "one of them" – you are actually doing your pupils a disservice. I don't pretend to know exactly what ails this boy, but it would seem fairly obvious that he has formed an intense attachment to you. I strongly advise you to refer this to the Head. If you won't do that, you must at least make it clear to the boy that you're prepared to do so. You have to tell him, firmly, that there is to be no further contact between the two of you.'

Sheba had been nodding vigorously as I was talking. When I was done, she said, with great fervour and determination, 'You're right, you're right. I know you're right. Oh Barbara, I'm going to do just as you say. I've been a terrible silly. But I'm going to be very, very tough from now on. I promise.'

She went to a cupboard, took out some old newspaper and began wrapping my bowl. I took this as a signal that our conference was at an end and I got up from my chair.

'I'm so glad I spoke to you about this, Barbara,' she said, handing me the bowl. 'It's been preying on my mind all week.

I knew you'd put me right. You must think me awfully foolish . . .'

I shook my head and then – a little tentatively, because casual affection is not my forte – I patted her on the shoulder. 'Not at all. Not at all. These are difficult matters for a new teacher to deal with. I'm very glad you spoke to me about it.'

At the foot of the stairs, I turned to her. 'Forgive me for asking, but have you told anyone else about any of this?'

'No. No, I haven't,' she said.

'Not even Sue?'

'No. Why?'

'Well, no, I was just thinking it would probably serve you best *not* to tell Sue. She's not a bad person. But she's not . . .' I chuckled. 'She can be a bit of a goose, can't she?'

Sheba nodded. 'You're quite right. I shan't tell anyone else.'

Much later on, when Sheba finally told me the truth about her relationship with Connolly, when I found out all that she had omitted from this first, bizarre faux-confession, I was very angry. I couldn't understand why she had gone to the bother of telling such a radically compromised truth. Just two nights before she had me over to her house, she had been rutting with Connolly in a public park. Had it given her a thrill to play at confessing to me? Or had she offered this innocent version of their relationship, in order to counter any suspicions among the staff of something worse?

In the beginning, I was willing to attribute the worst possible motives to her deceit. But as time went on, the more melo-dramatic theories lost credibility. It is mad to describe a middle-aged adulteress as innocent and yet there *is* something fundamentally innocent about Sheba. It goes without saying that she is capable of all kinds of sin. But she is not one of life's schemers. She does not have the cunning that is required to connive and plot – at least not in any sustained, committed way. I am more inclined at this point to see her first account as the sort of quasi-confidence that young children impart when they want relief from the burden of a secret but are unwilling to face the ramifications of full disclosure. Down in that basement studio, I believe that she *wanted* to tell all. Her courage simply failed her. The queasy look that I mistook at the time for general anxiety was, in fact, a thwarted desire for absolution.

Upstairs, the children had disappeared to their rooms and Richard was in the kitchen making coffee. Sheba and I went to sit in the living room and shortly afterwards Richard came in with the coffee tray. He made a great song and dance about it – tootling a fanfare and wearing a tea cosy on his head. From this and from the extravagant gratitude with which Sheba thanked him, I gathered that Richard's contributions to the domestic commonweal were rather infrequent.

The three of us sat and talked for forty-five minutes or so. The conversation was mainly about our plans for the summer holiday. Richard and Sheba were going to be in Provence for a month. 'We go every year,' Sheba said. 'My family has a house – well, more of a shack, actually – that my father bought a hundred years ago for tuppence halfpenny. It's completely primitive but very pretty. Near Avignon, if that means anything.' I mentioned a tentative plan to travel to Madrid and Richard, who had spent some time in Spain as a young man, had a great deal of advice about what I ought to do and see while I was there. Then it was ten thirty and time for me to leave.

On the way home, I stopped in at LoPrice, the supermarket at the end of my road, to get a pint of milk and some bread for the next morning. The man in front of me at the checkout laid his purchases on the conveyor belt with a terrible, shy precision: a jar of instant coffee; a single Kaiser roll with a smudge of dirt on its hard crust; a tin of tuna; a large jar of mayonnaise; two boxes of Kleenex. I thought of the casually extravagant meal that I had just eaten at the Harts. *They* surely never shopped at overpriced, unhygienic little supermarkets like this one. No, they would take advantage of their economies of scale and make jolly family expeditions to the flagship Sainsbury's in West Hampstead. I could just picture them bouncing along the aisles, throwing economy packs of toilet paper into their trolleys and shouting, 'What's the rice situation, darling?' at each other. The man at the checkout watched his things being rung up with careful attention. Back home, he would make his grim tuna sandwich and his cup of sawdust coffee. He would eat in front of the television, as single people do. And then he would turn to his bounteous supply of tissues . . . for what? Tears? Sneezes? Masturbation?

There was a small confusion when the girl at the till mistakenly included my milk and bread as part of the man's basket. 'No, no,' the man murmured angrily. Shooting me a nasty look, he grabbed the little metal divider and slammed it down on the conveyor belt to section off my things from his. Lonely people are terrible snobs about one another, I've found. They're afraid that consorting with their own kind will compound their freakishness. The time that Jennifer and I went to Paris together, we saw an airline employee at Heathrow ask two very fat people in the check-in line where they were both off to. The fat people were not a couple as it happened, and the suggestion that they were, panicked them. Leaping apart, they both shouted in unison, 'We're not together!'

I understood their horror. Even Jennifer and I were prey on occasion to a certain self-consciousness about the impression we made as a twosome. Alone, each of us was safely unremarkable – invisible, actually – as plain women over the age of forty are to the world. Together, though, I always suspected that we were faintly comic: two screamingly unhusbanded ladies on a day out. A music-hall act of spinsterhood.

For a second, I had an impulse to shout at the man in LoPrice – to tell him that I was not like him at all, that I had friends. That I had just come from a warm and delightful family dinner at someone's house. But of course I didn't. I merely lowered my head and pretended to look for something in my handbag until he was safely out on the street.

Later, in bed with a cup of tea and Portia, I reflected on the evening with some satisfaction. Notwithstanding the bloody ankle, I had made a good showing, I felt. I had been mannerly and appropriate with the children. I had got along well with the husband. And when asked by Sheba for advice, I had responded with wisdom and sympathy. Sheba had clearly been very grateful.

How deluded I was! But how happy!

Seven

Location, I believe, was the predominant concern of the lovers in the early days of their romance. Where to meet. Where to do it. For want of any more agreeable alternative they returned to Hampstead Heath many times. (Sheba is uncertain of the exact number, but she estimates at least twenty.) The alfresco aspect of their sexual relations has greatly exercised the press but, contrary to all the reporters' salacious innuendo, Sheba and Connolly did not feel that there was any erotic bonus to their trysting outdoors. It is quite difficult, apparently, to disport oneself with convincing abandon on sodden London parkland. In early April, the evenings were so cold that Sheba would often lose all feeling in her lips and hands. And even in more clement weather, fear of insects and of dog shit made complete relaxation an impossibility. Once a man stumbled into the clearing where Sheba and Connolly were huddled together. Sheba panicked and screamed, causing the man to scream himself and run away. Afterwards, Connolly tried to soothe Sheba – assure her that the man wasn't coming back. But she could not be convinced and the evening was ruined.

Later, she discovered that she and Connolly had unknowingly set up camp in the area of the heath frequented by homosexuals. The man who disturbed them had been not a Peeping Tom but a queer Lothario in search of a conquest. Still, Sheba remained sufficiently unsettled by the episode to arrange her next meeting with Connolly back in her school studio. She locked the door and drew the curtains, of course, but the school cleaners, who kept uncertain hours, had keys to the room. The risk of being caught was high.

It is hard, I tell her, to interpret such drastically incautious behaviour as anything other than sexual obsession. But Sheba objects to that phrase. She says that it places undue emphasis on the carnal aspect of her relations with Connolly. The remorseless vulgarity of the press coverage has made her defensively high-minded. She wants it to be known that she and Connolly were not merely engaged in 'illicit romps' and 'sex sessions'. They were *in love*. Just after the scandal broke, a *Sunday Express* reporter ambushed Connolly outside his house and asked him what had drawn him to his teacher. Connolly, in what is his sole public statement about the affair to date, replied, 'I fancied her, didn't I?' before being whisked by his mother into his father's waiting cab. The line is now famous. I understand it has become a kind of humorous catch-phrase in the media. For Sheba, though, it is a terrible humiliation. When she first read what Connolly had said, it seemed to her that he was wilfully belittling their romance – disowning his true feelings in order to gratify the coarse expectations of the tabloids. She has since forgiven him. (He didn't know how it would sound, she says.) But the quotation itself – and the widespread perception that their relationship was the smutty stuff of Carry On films – remains a very sore point.

There were a few occasions, she will acknowledge, when the two of them only had time to make love hurriedly before parting again. But such encounters were unsatisfactory to both of them, she says. They were always looking for opportunities to spend 'real' time with one another. Connolly had a pager and whenever Sheba found herself with an unforeseen spare moment, she would call him. It was difficult to arrange proper outings without arousing the suspicion of their respective families, but they managed it at least three times.

Once they went to the National Portrait Gallery. Another time, they went to a West Indian restaurant in Hammersmith. (Sheba made Connolly eat goat for the first time.) Once, for reasons that history does not relate, they visited Hampton Court. On each of these trips, they took taxi cabs, she says, and always laughed with slightly hysterical relief when the cab drivers pulled up, revealing themselves *not* to be Connolly's father. Inside, they would press themselves into a corner and pretend that the driver could not see them while they groped and panted at each other all the way to their destination.

I sense from what Sheba has told me that these dates, beneath their surface larkiness, were rather tense for her. In the classroom or on the heath with Connolly she could believe that theirs was a beautiful, forbidden love – something sweet and healthy and, if only the circumstances were tweaked, infinitely viable. Out in the world, she was forced to recognize their radical oddness as a couple. Once, as they were walking down St Martin's Lane together – this was their National Portrait Gallery trip – she caught a glimpse of their rippling reflection in a shop window. It was a long moment before she made the connection and understood that the bony, middle-aged housewife clutching the hand of a teenaged son was *her*.

At the restaurant in Hammersmith, Connolly apparently requested a sickly cocktail to go with his curry. Sheba suggested he have a soft drink instead, or a lager, but he was insistent: he wanted his rum and Coke. She did not press the matter. She could hardly hector the boy about the dangers of strong drink, she felt, when she was about to take him to the park for sex.

Early on in the affair, Sheba started buying underwear for herself – nylon flowery things intended for girls of Polly's age. She kept them at the back of her underwear drawer and put them on only when she knew she would be seeing Connolly.

Once, she says, while she was picking through a bin of thongs in the noisy basement of an Oxford Street boutique, she looked up to see Diana Selwood, the wife of one of Richard's colleagues, approaching her. Diana was with her teenaged daughter, Tessa. Sheba stepped back from the bin and folded her arms. She greeted Diana and they chatted for a while about their children and husbands. Then Diana looked down at the bin.

'Golly, Sheba,' she said. 'I take my hat off to you. I stopped bothering with fancy underwear years ago. How the hell do you wear these things?'

'God, no idea,' Sheba said, staring blankly at the floral scraps. 'I thought they were headscarves to tell you the truth.'

Connolly was always cooing over her beauty in those first months – stroking her hair, placing his beefy little arm around her waist and marvelling at its narrowness. Encouraged by his worshipfulness, Sheba took to wearing more cosmetics. Richard had never cared for make-up, but Connolly responded in the most gratifying way to the artifice. The first time that Sheba arrived for one of their assignations sporting red, glossy lips and kohl around her eyes, his mouth opened in wonderment.

'What?' she asked. 'Is it the war-paint?'

'You look just like a model,' Connolly whispered.

The affair did not have any immediate adverse effect on her marriage, she claims. Her relationship with her husband actually benefited at first. The nights on which she came home late from being with Connolly, she remembers being struck by how warmly affectionate she felt towards Richard. Picking up the underpants that he had abandoned on the bathroom floor, or gently retrieving a container of dental floss from his sleeping hand, she felt neither resentful nor guilty: just grateful for the cosy fact of her husband's existence. It was comforting, after her strange, chilly assignations on the heath, to climb into the warmed marriage bed – to feel Richard's body shift sleepily to clasp hers. When he wanted to make love, she always submitted without protest. It didn't seem so awful at the time, she says, to go from her lover to her husband in the same evening. It seemed quite natural. She always showered before she got into bed. And she still liked Richard that way. These things don't just switch off, she says.

Eight

It's Saturday morning, and I'm in the house on my own. If I'm disciplined and don't go out to buy the papers, I should be able to put in a good three or four hours on the book before Sheba comes back. Today is her day for seeing Ben. For the last couple of weeks, Richard has insisted that she conduct her 'visitations', as he calls them, at the Hampstead home of the Beckwiths – old friends of Sheba's parents. The official reason for this arrangement is that it's more convenient for Richard to drop Ben off there, but the real reason, I suspect, is that it spares Richard unpleasant confrontations with Sheba. He always makes sure to be long gone from the Beckwiths by the time that Sheba arrives.

Now, to work. I should have started long ago, but I had to call Sheba's mother to ask for money and that little chore ended up taking forty-five minutes. Since Sheba stopped living with Richard and stopped working, the monthly sum she receives from the Taylor family trust has become her sole source of income. It's a pittance: barely enough to cover the grocery bill, let alone extras. Sheba badly needs a new pair of shoes at the moment. And sooner or later, she's also going to have to buy some new clothes for court. She can hardly be wafting in before a magistrate in one of her transparent, hippy get-ups.

But Mrs Taylor isn't too bothered about any of this. When I had finished explaining the reason for my call, she gave a nasty laugh. 'Does Sheba know you're calling me?' she asked. 'Because she'll tell you, dear, I'm not in the habit of subsidizing her wardrobe.'

'Look,' I replied, 'Sheba is walking around with holes in her shoes. It's not as if I'm asking for frivolities. You are still her mother, you know.'

'Oh,' she said, tittering. 'Thank you for reminding me. So, let me get this straight. You're handling Sheba's budget, now? Well, that's handy. Will you be wanting me to buy *you* a new pair of shoes also?'

'Mrs Taylor,' I said, 'I am perfectly capable of supporting myself, thank you very much. I have worked for forty years as a teacher and I can assure you that my retirement pension, while by no means generous, is perfectly adequate for my needs.'

That shut her up a bit. After a lot of hemming and hawing, she finally said she'd put a cheque in the post next week.

It's hard to believe that it's come to this. Sheba going about like a bag-lady, her mother and Richard treating her like Typhoid Mary. Back when I was first getting to know her, Sheba seemed to me invincibly happy; a modern wonder of contentment. Her life with Richard – the dinner parties, the French holidays, the house buzzing with colleagues and children and ex-wives and family friends – was the stuff of newspaper 'Living' sections. There was always a noisy group excursion in the offing: a picnic in Regent's Park, a walk through Highgate Cemetery, a trip to the Bethnal Green Children's Museum. It was rare for me to see Sheba alone. Once, when Richard took Ben to the swimming baths for the afternoon, Sheba and I went to a Dürer exhibition together. And another time, she drew my portrait in the studio while Ben and Richard were playing Monopoly upstairs. (Radio 4 was on, I remember, and Sheba told me, as she stared frowningly over the easel, that I had 'tremendous bones'.) Most of the time, though, I was obliged to share her.

Early on in our friendship, I remember, she invited me to

Ben's twelfth birthday party. I went, anticipating something along the lines of the pin-the-tail-on-the-donkey affairs of my youth, but when I got there, the front door was wide open and the house was filled with parents reclining on sofas, drinking wine and listening to Richard's jazz records. 'Oh, helleh,' they drawled when I wandered in. A small crowd had gathered around the kitchen door and when I looked in, I saw Richard laid out on the kitchen table. Sheba was standing over him, dressed in surgical scrubs and mask. She was 'operating' on him for the entertainment of the ten excited little boys and girls sitting in front of her. 'Now,' she was saying in a heavy German accent, 'vee hev extracted ze eyeballs! I shall allow each of you a short time to examine zem. Please to pass zem on to your neighbour promptly ven you hev finished.' The children wriggled and squealed as two large, peeled grapes were passed among them. 'I do hope you hev all vashed your hands,' Sheba said. 'Oh, you heven't? Ah vell, not to mind . . . Oh my! Look, my assistant Doctor Barbara Babinski has arrived. Come along now, Barbara, I need you to help me pull zis liver out.'

It was intoxicating to be included in this raucous domesticity. Not perfect happiness. Perfect happiness would have been something else. But still, such fun! Jennifer once told me about a Hindu temple in a remote part of southern India that she had visited in her student days. It had seemed fantastic to her – impossible – that such exotic scenes of worship took place on the same planet as her own prosaic life in Barnstaple. Back in England, whenever she thought of the sari-clad women dipping themselves in the murky temple pool and lighting incense for Ganesh, she was half persuaded that she had made them up. That was how I felt about Sheba's household. When I walked to my car at the end of an evening spent there, I would have to fight the childish instinct to whirl around and check that the house was still standing – that it hadn't disappeared into the ether, like some fairy illusion. Later, as I lay in bed, I would try to imagine the Harts settling down for the night: each family member journeying to and from the bathroom – the swosh of toothbrushes, the shouts up and down the staircase, the yelps of laughter, and then the noise slowly dying out until the only sounds in the house were the murmur of bed-sheets and the *flup flup* of book pages being turned. Sooner or later, I always grew incredulous. This was all make-believe, wasn't it? Surely the family ceased to exist when I wasn't there?

I would have bet everything I owned that Sheba was faithful to Richard. The marriage was not perfect by any means. Richard condescended to Sheba, as he condescended to everybody. And whenever he got a little tired, or felt the spotlight shift momentarily from himself, or had one of his opinions challenged too vigorously, he tended to lapse into petulant babyishness. (He was like the king in the A.A. Milne rhyme: not a fussy man but he *did* like a little bit of butter on his bread.) Sheba was too observant not to see these failings. But for her, Richard's pettiness and vanity were necessary components of his intelligence – the fault lines in his character that gave him pathos and made him 'human'. She had grown up with Ronald Taylor for a father. The rules for being a hand maiden to a great, pompous man were more or less instinctive to her. It seemed genuinely to pain her when Richard's behaviour inspired hostile reactions in others.

Once, after a dinner at which he had been particularly obnoxious and garrulous, she took me aside in the kitchen. 'Oh please don't hate him, Barbara!' she whispered. She was slightly drunk.

'I don't hate him,' I said.

'I *know* he can be a bore,' she went on, 'but underneath,

he's so sweet. He's had a very tough life. Did you know that without his glasses he's legally blind? His mother was an awful woman and she never got him the glasses he needed when he was little, and when the hospital gave him a patch for his left eye she didn't make him wear it . . . Oh, it's not funny!'

I had been smiling at the thought of Richard's self-pitying diatribes against his mother. 'I don't think it's funny,' I said.

'No, well you shouldn't,' Sheba said. '*Please* forgive him when he behaves like a buffoon. He's very dear, really.'

A few times, I recall her saying something a little wistful about having got married so early. But she was always careful not to blame Richard for this. If she had missed out on opportunities, it was nobody's fault but her own, she insisted. Richard was the reason their marriage worked so well, she said. He had made her 'a much nicer person'. He had helped her 'grow up'. 'Richard's been through it once before,' she told me, 'so he's much wiser about married life than I am.'

Once, I suggested to her that she ought to turn her pottery into a proper commercial enterprise. 'You could sell your stuff to department stores,' I told her. 'It'd go for a bomb.'

'No, no,' she said, waving the suggestion away, 'if I'd been going to do something like that – start my own business – I should have started earlier.'

'Well, it's not too late,' I argued. 'You're hardly an old lady, you know.'

She shook her head. 'No, I know I'm not old. But it *is* too late. It always was. A few years back, I became terribly right-eous and angry about everything I thought I'd sacrificed for my family. I had this idea that if only I hadn't met Richard, and buried myself in marriage so young, I would have done brilliant things, made great sculpture, travelled the world, or whatever. One night I even told Richard that he had "deadened my imagination". God! And eventually, Richard got so bored with my complaining that he renovated the basement and turned it into a studio for me. He worked out a new timetable with the babysitter and everything, just so that I could have three afternoons a week without Ben. He took a lot of trouble and it cost a lot of money which we couldn't afford . . . And you know what? After all that, I *still* didn't do anything really. I mean, I made some very pretty plates. I even made a few sculptures. But they weren't any good. Mostly, I watched daytime soap opera and took naps.' She laughed. 'It turns out that Richard and the kids hadn't been stopping me from doing anything. Quite the reverse. Marriage, for me, has been a wonderful cover-up for my fundamental lack of drive.'

'You're terribly hard on yourself,' I said. 'You don't know how things would have turned out if you hadn't married. The fact is, you *did* miss out on your youth.'

Sheba shook her head again. 'No, no, no. If anything, I think I've artificially prolonged my youth by being with Richard. I've been allowed to stay a child, don't you see? All my adult life, I've been the younger person, the baby in the group. Our friends, our social life has been with Richard's generation and not mine. I got old without knowing it, still imagining myself Daddy's best girl. A few years ago, I suddenly looked around and realized that all those people I was mentally dismissing as older people – Richard people – were in fact my age. Younger, in a lot of cases. Richard had been protecting me from confronting my own middle age.'

And when she said this – when she said all the other nice, loving things about Richard and her family and her charming, sun-dappled life in Highgate – she and the boy were carrying on together. It's dumbfounding. After that first conversation in her basement, Connolly's name came up again only once. I asked if she had sorted out her problem with him and she told me cheerfully that she had done as I had advised. She had 'nipped the thing in the bud', she said. In retrospect, it seems silly of me to have accepted this account so readily. Why did I never bother to ask *how* she had got rid of him? But Connolly was a very peripheral figure in my consciousness back then. If I thought about him at all, it was as an irrelevancy – a tiny mote that had swum mistakenly into Sheba's charmed atmosphere and been duly expelled. Sheba never *behaved* like a woman who was having an affair. Perhaps she was some-times a little giddier than the immediate circumstances would seem to warrant. But at the time I rather imagined – I dared, that is, to hope – that this high-spiritedness had something to do with *me*.

∽

Just after I wrote that last sentence, Sheba rang me from the Beckwiths shouting unintelligible things about Richard and asking me to come and help her. I tried for several minutes, without success, to find out what was upsetting her. Then I gave up, got into the car and drove over to Downshire Hill, where the Beckwiths live. When I arrived, Sheba was standing outside on the street, her face mottled by crying. Lila Beckwith was hovering next to her, looking embarrassed.

'He's got, he's got . . . some *woman* in there,' Sheba said, 'and, and he says she has to come with us if I go out anywhere.'

'Sheba, it's not as bad as all that,' Lila said.

'Ben says this?' I asked.

'*No*,' Sheba shook her head in frustration. 'Of course not. *Richard.*'

'What woman? What do you mean?'

'She's actually a nice girl –' Lila began.

'Megan somebody or other,' Sheba interrupted. 'Some post-graduate of his. He says I have to have a chaperone if I take Ben out. It's because last week I took him out for tea at the patisserie on the High Street and didn't tell anyone where I was going. Lila and Hugh thought I'd run away with him.' She glanced at Lila reproachfully. Lila studied the pavement. 'I've told Richard it's ridiculous,' Sheba said, 'but he won't listen. He says I can either accept the chaperone or spend the day indoors with Ben.' She began to cry again.

'This is outrageous,' I said. 'Come on, you and I are going back to sort this out.'

'Oh,' Lila said, 'I don't know, Barbara. He's not in a good mood. Let's not have a blow-up.'

Sheba looked at me uncertainly.

'Do you want to be escorted everywhere by this friend of Richard's?' I asked.

'*No.*'

'Come on then.'

I took her hand and led her across the street, back up to the house. Lila loped along reluctantly behind us.

In the hallway, we met Hugh Beckwith. He was wearing his gardening jeans and carrying secateurs. He looked mortified at having his house hijacked by someone else's marital drama. 'Hello, hello!' he shouted with slightly batty good humour as he galloped up the stairs. Then Richard emerged from the kitchen.

I hadn't seen Richard in a while. He seems gaunter and greyer these days. Adversity has lent some dignity to his fatuous features.

'What's she doing here?' he asked, pointing at me.

'I called her,' Sheba said.

He tossed his head. 'Oh for God's sake! This is difficult enough.'

'Look, Richard. I don't want to make trouble,' I said. 'If you think that Ben and Sheba need a chaperone, perhaps *I* can be of . . .'

Richard snorted. 'You? I don't think so.'

I sharpened my tone. 'Sheba does have a right to see her son, you know.'

'And I have a right to insist that she is chaperoned by someone I trust,' Richard said. 'Last week, she went missing with him for more than two hours. Lila and Hugh were absolutely freaked out.'

'We were, yes,' Lila murmured, sheepishly.

'I've taken legal advice on this, Barbara,' Richard said, 'so don't try it, okay? Frankly, I would have a very good case for denying her any contact with Ben.'

'Where is he now?' Sheba asked.

'Upstairs, playing,' Richard said. He couldn't seem to bring himself to look directly at his wife.

'You're punishing her, Richard,' I said. 'You can't really believe she would abscond with Ben . . .'

Richard gave an angry smirk. 'There are very few things I consider impossible any more. I would have thought it was obvious why I might doubt Sheba's fitness to be in sole charge of a little boy.'

Sheba gasped and grabbed at Richard's hand. 'Oh, Richard, please! What are you implying? You don't . . .'

Richard flinched from her touch. 'For Christ's sake! I don't need to justify myself to you!'

'Perhaps,' I said, 'we should come in and discuss this?'

Richard shook his head. 'This isn't a negotiation. She accepts Megan, or she cannot leave the house with Ben. Simple as that.'

Sheba was crying noisily now and for a moment all of us – Richard, Lila and I – stood looking at her.

'Can she at least talk to this Megan, before she makes her decision?' I asked Richard.

Richard hesitated. Then he seemed to relent. He glanced at Lila. 'I'm sorry . . . would it be all right? Do you mind?'

Lila shook her head. 'No, no, of course not.'

We followed her through the doorway into a large kitchen.

At the table, a young woman with her hair in a plait was sitting reading the newspaper. She regarded us with cool curiosity, as we trooped in.

'Megan, Sheba wants to talk to you before deciding on whether she'll take Ben out today,' Richard said.

'Sure,' Megan chirped magnanimously, as if her permission had been asked.

'Please. Sit down,' Lila said. 'There's coffee on the stove. I'll just go and check on Ben and Polly. Do call if you need me.'

'Polly's here?' Sheba asked, as Lila hastened from the room.

'Yes,' Richard said.

'Well, maybe *she* could be the chaperone –' Sheba said, suddenly excited.

'She doesn't want to see you,' Richard cut in.

Sheba looked as if she had been smacked.

I pulled out a chair. 'Come on, Sheba.' She sat down obediently, facing Megan.

I sat next to her. Megan smiled brightly. At the time, I thought she was anxious to show that she wasn't afraid. In retrospect, I think she was just slightly dense.

'So, come on,' Richard said impatiently, after a while, 'what do you want to ask her?'

Sheba opened her mouth and then closed it again. She turned to me, helplessly.

'Have you met Ben before today?' I asked Megan.

She glanced at Richard. He nodded. 'Yes,' she said, 'I've been helping Richard out here and there, for the last month or so.'

'Oh! How nice for Richard. Doing what?'

'Just, you know, keeping the house tidy, making sure Ben's okay . . .'

'You're one of Richard's students?' I asked.

'Well, sort of,' she replied. 'Richard's my thesis supervisor.'

At this, I felt Sheba's knee pressing heavily against mine.

'How old are you?'

'Twenty-five.'

'None of your fucking business!' Richard shouted. 'I won't have this. I'm not letting you interrogate her. *She* hasn't done anything wrong, you know.'

'Excuse me,' I said. 'You told me I could ask her questions. This is hardly the third degree . . .'

'Keep your bloody nose out of this, okay Barbara? This has absolutely nothing to –'

'Okay!' Sheba interrupted. 'Okay!' She raised her hands in a gesture of surrender. 'I'll take her. I'll take her. Only no more shouting. Please, let's just go.'

After that, Richard went upstairs to fetch Ben and for a few minutes, we three women were left alone at the kitchen table.

Megan continued smiling at us in her vapid way.

'So,' I said, 'Richard's your thesis supervisor, eh?' She nodded. 'I see. And what's your thesis about, then?'

She smiled. 'The modern romantic novel, actually. Mills & Boon books and bodice-rippers and all that. It's sort of about reading reactionary texts in a subversive way.'

There was a silence and then Sheba let out a great yelp of laughter. Megan and I both jumped.

Before anyone could say anything more, Ben burst into the room. 'Hoola! Hoola! Mummy! Mummy! Mummy!'

Following him in, Richard shot me a nasty glance. 'I think you can go now, Barbara,' he said.

Pompous bastard.

Nine

Sheba is very morose this morning. She ate hardly anything at breakfast and immediately afterwards she went off and secreted herself in her bedroom 'to do some work'. She's been complaining about missing her studio lately, so the other day I brought home an enormous sack of modelling clay for her. She was rather snooty about it at first, despite the fact that I'd nearly broken my back getting it in and out of the car. It isn't the stuff she's used to working with, apparently. But she has started using it. When she left her bedroom this morning to go for a pee, I had a quick glance in, to see what it is she's working on. It looked as if it were a model of a mother and child, but I couldn't be sure. I didn't have much of a chance to inspect it before Sheba came charging back from the loo and slammed the door in my face.

Sheba has often told me that she thinks there's a rhythm to married life, an ebb and flow in the pleasure that a couple take in one another. The rhythm varies from couple to couple, she says. For some couples, the see-saw of affections takes place over a week. For others, the cycle is lunar. But all couples sense this about their life together – the way in which their interest in one another builds up and recedes. The happiest couples are the ones whose cycles interact in such a way that when one of them is feeling jaded, the other is ardent, and there is never a vacuum. Now that Sheba and I are living together, I wonder whether this theory might apply to us. If Sheba is being moody and difficult at the moment, perhaps that's just because it's her turn to be. Perhaps the shifts will change soon and it will be *my* time for some attention.

According to my notes, the next big gold star event on Sheba's timeline occurs at the beginning of June. This was when Polly got thrown out of school. I was over at Sheba's on the evening they got the news. We had just finished an early dinner and Richard was trying to persuade Sheba that they should buy a warehouse he'd seen for sale in the East End. 'No!' Sheba protested in pretend horror. 'Darling, we'll end up in the poorhouse!'

'But it's a marvellous investment, Sheba,' Richard said. 'We could take out a second mortgage on this place to finance renovations and we'd end up with a beautiful loft for peanuts.'

Richard's real estate ambitions were a frequent source of semi-joking debate in the Hart household. Richard saw himself as a frustrated entrepreneur. He was always champing at the bit to get into the housing market – to buy low, sell high, make easy money. It maddened him that he and Sheba had sat on the sidelines throughout the real estate boom of the nineties. But the Highgate house, for which Sheba's father had provided the down-payment, represented their only equity and Sheba adamantly refused to gamble with it.

'If you hadn't been such a Nervous Nelly, we could have made millions by now,' Richard told her that night. He looked at me. 'Isn't that right, Barbara?'

'Well, maybe it's a good thing that Sheba is careful,' I said. 'She probably knows a thing or two about handling the purse strings. She is an economist's daughter, after all.'

'Pfah!' Richard made an impatient gesture. 'Sheba doesn't know a thing about money. Her caution stems from ignorance.'

The phone rang and Sheba left the room to answer it. Richard continued to talk. 'If Sheba had her way, we'd keep all our money in wads of five-pound notes in the biscuit tin. The thing is, Sheba is *scared* of money, because she's never learned how it works . . .'

As he went on, I found myself distracted by Sheba's voice wafting in from the next room.

'No . . . look,' she was saying, in an agitated tone, 'I'm just sure you've got this wrong . . . Right . . . right, no, I understand. But isn't that rather an extreme measure?'

Richard smiled complacently. 'Uh-oh. Sounds like Sheba's mother . . . What can I offer you for pud, Barbara? We have some lovely tangerines.'

As I was about to reply, Sheba began shouting. 'Oh, for goodness' sake! No, *no*, I'm sure she's being absolutely beastly . . . *Yes*, but I'm just . . . She is only seventeen, you know.'

Richard's amused expression faded. 'What is it, Bash?' he called out. 'Is something wrong?'

Sheba didn't reply. 'I understand that,' she was saying to the person on the phone. 'I'm not talking about tolerance . . .'

I got up to clear the plates from the table but Richard held up a hand to shush me. He was scrunching his eyes in an effort to hear Sheba.

'Isn't it your job to help her through this?' she was asking now. 'It doesn't sound to me as if you've made any attempt to help her at all . . .'

I sat down again.

'Bathsheba!' Richard shouted. He got up and went into the other room. 'What the hell is going on?' I heard him ask angrily.

The two of them spoke to one another for a moment or two in low tones. Then I heard Sheba say, in a shrill tone of exasperation, 'For God's sake, Richard! Could you let me talk to the man, please?'

Richard came walking back, very quickly, into the dining

room and began to clear the dinner plates with a lot of clang and slam. He didn't look at me.

After a minute or so, Sheba hung up the phone and followed him in.

'Bloody school,' she said.

'How did you leave it?' Richard asked.

'They want us to go down and get her tomorrow.'

'Such nonsense!' Richard said.

'Is there anything I can do?' I asked.

'No, no. Oh God, I'm sorry,' Sheba said, swinging round and smiling at me. 'It's just Polly's got herself in trouble at school. They're expelling her.'

'What's the problem?'

'She's bullying, they say,' Sheba said.

'Bloody ridiculous.' Richard huffed.

'What sort of bullying is she accused of ?' I asked.

'You name it,' Sheba said. 'Terrorizing girls in the lower forms. Extorting money. They say she's a real little gangster.'

'It's all sooo silly,' Richard said.

'Why do you keep saying that?' Sheba snapped at him.

Richard looked affronted. But he only said quietly, 'Because it is.'

I stood up. 'I should go. If there's anything I can do . . .'

Sheba smiled and patted my shoulder. 'Thanks, Barbara. It's awfully nice of you, but there's nothing to be done.'

Richard and Sheba drove down to Brighton the next day. They saw the headmistress first and then the school counsellor. These interviews were long and tedious, but Sheba didn't mind. She was happy to have the confrontation with her daughter delayed. The school counsellor, Mr Oakeshott, was a nice, rather dim man. He told her and Richard that Polly's bullying was a behaviour indicating low self-worth and that it was a mistake to take a girl like Polly at face value. Not very far below her rough surface, he said, they would find a lot of 'anxiety and self-doubt'.

I laughed out loud when Sheba recounted this for me. It's always fascinating to hear bleeding hearts give their soppy rationalizations for delinquency. As far as I can tell, teachers have been congratulating Sheba and Richard for years on having a daughter who is full of grit and spunk, and whatever else it is that modern little girls are meant to be made of. Then, the minute Polly is found guilty of anti-social behaviour, they're falling over themselves to say that her toughness is merely bravado. Polly is 'vulnerable', they say. She is 'anxious'. Well, excuse me – *everyone* is anxious. What counts, surely, is what you do with your anxiety. The fact that Polly administers Chinese burns to twelve-year-olds in order to get them to surrender their Mars Bars, isn't 'a behaviour'. It's a mark of her character, for goodness' sake.

When at last it was time to go and collect their daughter, Sheba and Richard were directed to the school sick bay. Polly had been withdrawn from her dormitory and given temporary quarters in the school nurse's examination room. 'So this is where the miscreant lives!' Richard cried cheerfully when Polly came to the door, eating a pear. In defiance of the cold weather, she was wearing a pair of tiny shorts and a T-shirt with the words BITCH GODDESS printed across the chest. Sheba picked up a ball of socks that was lying underneath the nurse's desk and handed them to her. 'You'd better put on some more clothes and hurry up,' she said, with a sternness that she automatically regretted. 'I don't want to be late for Ben.' Polly scowled and began wandering about the room, gathering up her things in a desultory fashion. Sheba thought she looked tired and thin and very beautiful. Her legs appeared to have grown several inches since Sheba had last seen them.

It has been difficult for Sheba, I think, watching Polly blossom. The way she looks at her daughter sometimes, it's not entirely friendly. She struggles against the envy. She knows she had her time. But it's never easy to hand over the crown, is it? I've seen her close to tears on a number of occasions, describing the withering of her buttocks or a new knobble of varicose she's found on the back of her knee. She feels, she says, as if her insides are slowly pushing outward – demanding to be noticed, finally, after all their years of patient service. Welcome to the club, I say. But she doesn't want to be in the club. She wears a bra to bed every night because when she was a girl, one of her friends' mothers told her that was the way to stop your breasts from falling. Every night! I've told her it's useless. I've told her she could spend her entire life horizontal, with her breasts in steel reinforced slings, and they're still going to end up looking like empty purses. But she won't take the bra off.

On the way back to London, it began to rain. Sheba, Richard and Polly stopped at a motorway service station to get some late lunch. Sheba baulked at the idea of eating *in* the place – too depressing, she said – so Richard left her and Polly in the car and went to get takeaways. Sheba and Polly watched him run through the slanted downpour in a defensive crouch. Polly asked to have the radio on but Sheba told her she wasn't in the mood for radio din. After that, the two of them sat looking out at the car park, listening to the rain and each other's breathing.

Sheba told me a story once about going to visit her mother just after her father had died. The two of them had devilled eggs for lunch in the dining room of the Primrose Hill house. They were trying very hard to be gentle and kind with one another, but it was awkward. After a while, Mrs Taylor put her fork down and said, 'Oh dear, this isn't much fun, is it?'

Sheba began to protest, but Mrs Taylor shook her head. No, it was a fact, she said. Even when Ronald had been alive, she had always found it harder to get along with her children when he wasn't there. It was so much easier being a parent when one was performing for another adult. Sheba was terribly shocked by this at the time. 'You mean,' she said to her mother, 'you were only ever nice to me to show off to Daddy?' But since her own daughter became a teenager, she says she has become increasingly sympathetic to the point that Mrs Taylor was trying to make. Dealing with her daughter is never easy, but it's pretty much impossible without the motivation of an audience. If there's no one about to witness her patience and kindness, she finds herself too weary to tackle Polly's sullen mystery: 'I sit there,' she says, 'summoning up the energy to make some jolly assay at conversation and then I just slump, thinking, *Bugger it. Let her stew.*'

At last, they saw Richard running back across the car park, polystyrene cartons bulking out his jacket. When he opened the car door, he brought with him a whoosh of rain and French-fry smell. 'Hoof!' he said as he climbed in. 'It's completely bloody out there.' He started pulling out his purchases: 'I got super-duper cheese burgers for everyone.'

Polly groaned. 'I don't eat McDonald's,' she said.

Richard looked at her, confused. 'But I thought you'd given up being a veggy . . .'

Polly put her face in her hands and made one of her irritation-noises. 'Yurrrrrr. I did, Dad. I just don't eat McDonald's.'

Sheba was relieved to see some exasperation finally showing itself on her husband's face.

As soon as they got back home, Sheba made an excuse to go down to her studio. She locked the door behind her and then she rang Connolly's pager. 'Listen,' she said when he called back a few minutes later, 'can we meet tonight?' After making an arrangement, she quietly replaced the receiver and bounded upstairs to say hello to her son.

Ten

By summer, my connection to Sheba was well established. Hardly a week went by when we didn't see each other outside of school hours. Sue Hodge had not yet been utterly vanquished; she was still hanging in there, waddling with us to lunches at La Traviata. But her days were definitely numbered. Now, on afternoons when it rained, it was I – not Sue – who heaved Sheba's bicycle into the back of my car and drove her home. (Sheba, I was amazed to discover, had never learned to drive. 'I always get lifts,' she told me cheerily. 'I know it sounds terribly conceited, but I'm the sort of person people like to do things for.') Sue had fought a valiant battle but, in the end, she simply wasn't able to put the sort of work into Sheba that I was. She had her impending Sue-spawn, her ghastly little love nest with Ted, to worry about. Try as she might, she couldn't keep her eye on the ball.

Shortly after Sue caught on to the fact that I had leap-frogged her in Sheba's affections, it became apparent that she was saying things about Sheba and me to other members of staff. Sheba and I were a bit *too* fond of one another, she told people; a bit *too* close. The implication was that Sheba and I were engaged in some sort of Sapphic love affair. I was not distressed on my account. I have been on the receiving end of this sort of malicious gossip more than once in my career and I am quite accustomed to it by now. Vulgar speculation about sexual proclivity would seem to be an occupational hazard for a single woman like myself, particularly one who insists on maintaining a certain discretion about her private life. I know who I am. If people wish to make up lurid stories about me, that is their affair. I could not be sure, however, that Sheba would be capable of matching my indifference. I feared that she would be offended, or enraged, or else horribly embarrassed. After considering the matter carefully, I decided it was best not to tell her about the rumours.

It wasn't easy keeping quiet. It was immensely irritating, in fact, not to be able to expose Sue's rank hypocrisy. Sheba was always so generous to Sue. She would allow her to sit there, sucking up to her for hours, and never let on for a second that she was bored. She wouldn't even tolerate me making jokes at Sue's expense. Once, when Sue left our table at La Traviata, to go to the toilet, I made the mistake of calling her a 'fat fool'. Sheba just frowned at me and said quietly, 'What energy you spend on hating people!'

Sheba was always very upfront that way – never afraid to express her disapproval when she thought I was being bitchy. Once or twice, when we were on the phone together, she actually slammed the receiver down in protest at my being 'too negative'. The first time that it happened, I was in mid-sentence and it was a few moments before I realized that I was alone on the line. I called back, assuming that we'd been cut off but, no, she told me, she'd simply grown tired of hearing me drone on.

It was a new experience, being told off like that. In my other friendships over the years, I have tended to dominate. I've never made any conscious bid for power; it has always come about quite naturally that I should be the one to lead. But I can see now that my imposing personality has caused problems. It has created inequality and that inequality has bred resentment. Jennifer always *seemed* perfectly happy for me to be in charge. She never uttered a critical word against me until the very end. (And then, of course, criticism was the *only* thing that came out of her mouth.) But after we had parted ways, I came to understand that there had been something subtly aggressive in all her meek compliance. There is, I see now, such a thing as the tyranny of the humble person – the person who nods and watches quietly while you babble and show off and shout too loudly and generally make a fool of yourself. How much healthier to have a friend who isn't afraid to take you on, to tell you what's what! It is never pleasant to be upbraided. There were many times, I don't mind saying, when I badly wanted to give Sheba a shove. Yet, even in my anger, I always knew that her forthrightness was an asset for our relationship – something that could only strengthen our bond.

And certainly, I felt, there was still some strengthening to be done. Loving and attentive as Sheba was when I was with her, I did not yet have the sense that I could truly count on her. She had a strong tendency to scattiness. She was often elusive. There were times when she did not return my calls all weekend; times when having made arrangements for an outing with me, she would forget having made them. I tried not to take these slights personally. Sheba had a family, I told myself. She had little Ben to look after. And her time management skills were not all they might have been. But even after I had made such allowances, it was hard not to conclude that I occupied a very low place on Sheba's list of priorities. I was confident that she valued me. But as what? An amusing colleague? A good listener?

When school broke up for summer in July, we had made no specific plans for meeting during the vacation, but there was, as far as I was concerned, an implicit understanding that we would be seeing each other shortly. As it turned out, I didn't see or hear from Sheba for six whole weeks. I knew that she was spending a month of the vacation in France with her family. I myself spent ten days touring in Spain. But it had not occurred to me that she would let *six weeks* go by without being in contact. There were phones in France, after all.

My trip to Spain was pleasant enough. I saw some pretty things. But the food was greasy and I was rather miserable. This was the first trip abroad I had taken since falling out with Jennifer and I had forgotten how mortifying it can be for a woman to dine alone in a foreign hotel restaurant. On my return to London, I left a few messages at Sheba's home, thinking she might ring in from France for them. But I still didn't hear from her. I became worried that she might ring while I was out on an errand and I invested in my first answering machine – a cream-coloured device with an electronic voice that made announcements in the slightly surprised, pre-war tones of Joyce Grenfell. This purchase introduced a new and not unwelcome degree of suspense to my homecomings. Every time I returned to my flat, I would rush to see if the little red light was blinking. But only once was my anticipation rewarded that summer. And then it was just a message from my landlord, returning a call I'd made earlier about a leak from upstairs. Sheba never did get in touch. I had learned by now a little something about how these things are played. I knew it was important not to overstep the mark, not to appear too clingy, so I left only a few more messages at her house before I stopped ringing her altogether. Then I waited.

I am good at waiting. It is one of my great skills. Richard described the Harts as immediate-gratification people. Well, I come from deferred-gratification stock. In my family, when I was growing up, taking what you wanted at the moment you wanted it was regarded as in very bad taste. My sister and I were taught to look down on the children at our school who had new clothes each week. Their parents didn't know how to save, our mother explained to us. 'They have new jackets now,' she liked to say, 'but they'll have run out of coal by the end of the month.' Saving was the ultimate virtue in our household, for it was only by saving – by putting off anything desirable for as long as humanly possible – that the terrible fate of being 'common' was to be escaped. We ate bread and lard for tea all week so that, even though my father earned his living selling stationery to shop-owners out of a little van, we always had proper jam and scones on Sunday when our relatives came to visit.

My mother had an 'everyday' and a 'best' of everything. She saw it as a mark of her good, English sense that by making me wear a frayed crochet cap every day of my life for five years until the thing disintegrated on my head, she was able, during the same period, to maintain my 'best hat' – a glazed straw meringue decorated with three paper roses – looking as pristine as the day she had purchased it. On those occasions that she broke down and let me wear the best hat, she insisted on my wearing a bag over it until I was safely at my destination. So strong was the pleasure-deferral instinct in my mother that she would rather have me walk down the high street with a brown paper bag standing high on my head like a papal crown than risk exposing the sacred meringue to the dirty air.

So you see, I know all about biding my time. Those early days when Sheba was keeping herself tantalizingly remote, I never became irate or flustered. I simply went on with my life – reading my books, preparing my meals, changing my sheets – quietly certain all the while that, sooner or later, she would wake up to my importance in her life.

Although Sheba didn't find time for *me* that summer, I know now that she managed to put in several calls to Connolly. She rang him once, breathlessly, from a pay phone at a super-market in Avignon. (He was away from his pager and by the time he picked up the message, she had had to dash off to meet Richard and the children.) And when she came back to London in August, she rang him again. This time he got back to her straightaway. He was very excited to hear from her, apparently. He had missed her; thought about her constantly. They both agreed that it was impossible to wait until term began before seeing each other again.

Connolly proposed a plan. He was meant to be going with his parents to the family caravan in Maldon for the last week of August. When he got there, he would tell them that a soccer match had come up and that he needed to get back to town early. His mother would probably insist on his staying at a friend's. But on Saturday afternoon he would meet Sheba somewhere, and together they would sneak back to his parents' empty house.

When the Saturday came, Sheba put on a white sundress that showed off her French tan and took the tube down to Warren Street. Ben was spending the afternoon at a friend's house. Richard was at home, working on his book. Polly, who was not in the habit of revealing her social plans, was simply out. Sheba had told them all, with as much casualness as she could muster, that she was going to the West End to do some clothes shopping.

She had arranged to meet Connolly at a bus stop near the women's hospital on Hampstead Road. He was late. When she finally spotted him, hurrying towards her from the direction of Mornington Crescent, she began to wave madly. He was still about a hundred yards off when he caught sight of her. As he made his self-conscious, gangling approach, he put his hands in his pockets and avoided her gaze by pretending to be interested in passing cars.

When he got to her he squinted and nodded hello. They had agreed previously not to engage in any public embraces, but unable to contain herself, Sheba playfully feinted a punch to his belly. 'We'll go round the back, through the garages,' he told her and Sheba laughed – partly with nerves, she says, and partly at the way he pronounced 'garage' to rhyme with 'marriage'. They set off.

The little square where Connolly lives is at the centre of a sprawling council estate that occupies half a square mile or so of land between Hampstead Road and Albany Way. Connolly had chosen to enter his house by the back way in order to avoid any difficult encounters with friends or neighbours. But as they walked up the rear alley where the local tenants keep their cars, a young man emerged from one of the lock-ups and nodded at Connolly. Connolly responded with an almost negligible twitch of his eyebrow, and kept moving. When they got to Connolly's door, Sheba glanced back, and saw that the man was staring at the two of them.

'Who was that?' she asked Connolly.

'Just the brother of my sister's mate,' he answered.

'Still,' Sheba said, 'you should probably have something prepared. Just in case he asks you who I was. Don't you think?'

'Don't worry about it,' Connolly muttered – slightly irritably, she thought. He had opened the door now. He led the way through a small laundry room into the house's front hall and on into the kitchen.

Sheba recalls being very impressed by the cleanness and order of everything. The wood-look Formica counters were completely bare. The white backsplash tiles gleamed. Even the grout between the tiles was without spot or stain. The only indication that the kitchen had been recently used, she says, was a neatly folded, pink cloth that hung over the sink's shining steel faucet.

Connolly offered her a cup of tea. Sheba said she'd rather have a glass of water. He had a distracted air. When she leaned forward to kiss him, he appeared not to notice and turned away. She remarked on the tidiness of the house. His mother's kitchen put her own to shame, she told him. Connolly didn't say anything but it seemed to Sheba that he was vaguely displeased by this comment.

'Seriously,' Sheba persisted, 'your mum must spend her entire life scrubbing.'

'Not really,' Connolly said, frowning. 'She just likes it neat.'

After a bit, Sheba asked to see the rest of the house. Connolly nodded. They climbed the stairs to the first floor in silence.

'This is the front room,' Connolly said, opening a door. Inside the air was sickly with air freshener, Sheba recalls. There was a nylon, patterned carpet, a display case containing several framed school pictures of Connolly and his sister, and a large three-piece suite in beige and cream stripes. Sheba had never actually seen a three-piece suite before, she says. Not 'in real life'. The sighting amused her. 'It was like meeting a crying clown,' she says, 'or a sailor with an anchor tattooed on his forearm.'

The other room on the first floor was his parents' bedroom. Connolly hesitated before opening the door and Sheba, sensing that her breezy comments were only adding to his unease, remained silent as they gazed briefly at his parents' neatly made double bed. As they climbed the final flight of stairs, Sheba enquired about the family caravan in Maldon. Was it nice there? 'It's all right,' Connolly said. Then he added, in a sulky tone, '*You* probably wouldn't like it.'

Now they had arrived at the top floor of the house where Connolly and his sister slept. Whenever Sheba had tried to picture Connolly's bedroom, she had imagined something along the lines of her brother Eddie's childhood room. A fusty den, with a skull and crossbones on the door; a chaotic carpet of cricket bats and chess sets and other Boys' Own jumble. But

Connolly's room was nothing like Eddie's. It was absolutely square and white and it bore the same signs of fastidious housekeeping as the rest of the house. The curtains and eiderdown were made of crackly nylon, imprinted with images of Grand Prix racing cars. On the wall facing the bed, there was a large, almost life-size poster of an American actress whom Sheba recognized but could not identify. The actress was standing with her hips thrust forward and her wet lips slightly open. Sheba felt suddenly dowdy and middle-aged, she says. Not wanting to have Connolly catch her looking, she averted her eyes from the poster, but, as she did so, she noticed the legend printed beneath the actress's feet in squiggly blue script: *Foxy Lady*. She had always wondered where Connolly had got that queer, antiquated phrase. She felt sad for a moment, picturing him in his little room, painstakingly copying out the lettering. Then she told herself that she was being pompous and decided to be amused.

'May I?' she asked, motioning to the bed. She walked over and sat down on it with a cheerful, deliberate bounce. 'Well!' she said. 'This is nice.'

Connolly smiled sheepishly and remained standing. Sheba asked to use his bathroom. Even though it was just across the hall, Connolly insisted on taking her there himself. On the way, she caught a glimpse of his sister's bedroom: a tantalizing pink wedge of eiderdown and frilled doodads and stuffed toys. She would have liked to have seen more, but she sensed that this would make Connolly uncomfortable. At the door to the bathroom, he moved aside at the same time as she moved to get round him. They both laughed awkwardly.

This is madness, she remembers thinking when she was finally inside, alone. *Complete bloody madness*. But she had muttered this, or something similar, to herself so many times in recent months that the sentiment no longer held much conviction. She sat on the toilet, trying to work out why Connolly was being so difficult. But that was silly, she decided. He didn't have to have a reason. He was a teenager. She felt suddenly scared – although of what exactly, she was unsure. Connolly's house was alarming to her in the way that a foreign country is alarming when you first arrive. The bathroom door had been much lighter than she had expected and when she closed it, it had slammed, causing the walls to shudder slightly. *The place is made of cardboard*, she said to herself. She thought, with a mixture of satisfaction and guilt, of her solid, Victorian walls in Highgate.

When she got back to Connolly's bedroom, he was sitting on the bed, waiting for her. He stood up as soon as he saw her and began undressing. She made an exclamation of joking surprise – a little, startled 'Oh!' But Connolly didn't smile, or stop. And after watching him for a moment or two, she too began to disrobe.

They made love rather quickly and – at Connolly's behest – on the floor. Sheba was fearful of carpet burns, but not wanting to spoil Connolly's youthful fantasy of sexual abandon she went along with the idea. When he got up abruptly to fetch a towel to lay beneath them, she eagerly suggested that they could move to the bed if he was uncomfortable. But Connolly shook his head. He wasn't uncomfortable, he said. He just didn't want to stain the carpet.

Afterwards, they did get into the bed, which was dressed with the sort of quick-dry, poly-cotton sheets that gave Sheba the shivers. Connolly propped himself up with pillows. And then he got up again and began fumbling in the dresser next to his bed. At length, he produced a single, slightly flattened cigarette, and a box of matches. 'Nothing like one afterwards, is there?' he said. Sheba remembers having to suppress a smile at this studied, post-coital nonchalance.

They lay quietly for a bit, listening to the tiny noises Connolly made as he blew smoke rings. Sheba remarked that her daughter liked to do the same thing when she was smoking and Connolly seemed interested by this. He began asking questions about Polly. Did Sheba let her smoke in the house? Did they argue a lot? Why was she at boarding school? At a certain point, Sheba interrupted his questioning to kiss him and tell him how handsome he was. Connolly grimaced. 'All right, all right. Calm down,' he muttered. He never responded well to compliments, Sheba says. They brought out something mean in him. A scornful look of satisfaction would cross his face, as if he had tricked her into giving up something that she hadn't intended to.

Connolly wanted to ask more questions about Polly, but Sheba, growing impatient with the subject, suggested he tell her about *his* family. Did he think that his mother and father were happy together?

'They're all right,' Connolly said. The terse defensiveness with which he had spoken when they first entered the house had now returned.

'"All right"?' Sheba teased him. 'What does *that* mean?'

He choked slightly on his cigarette and then, still coughing, he said stubbornly, 'I mean, all right. They get on okay.'

'Do you think they still have sex?'

He paused. Something happened around his mouth, Sheba recalls. 'Don't ask me to say bad things about my parents,' he said.

Sheba began to protest, but then stopped. 'Bad things' were precisely what she had been angling for, she realized. It was no use trying to coax him into that sort of conversation. He didn't have the vocabulary for it. It offended some atavistic, working-class code of family loyalty.

They were both silent for a time and then Sheba began to

ask Connolly about his previous sexual experience. She had an idea that this lubricious topic would lighten the mood.

Connolly put her off at first, saying things like, 'That's for me to know and you to find out.'

But she persisted. 'No, come on,' she said. 'Have you slept with many girls? Women?'

He paused and then held up a palm.

'Five?' she asked.

'Yeah. Not including you. And none of them as sexy as you.'

Sheba asked what ages his five lovers had been. Again, Connolly resisted answering her. Again, she pressed. At length, he said, 'You're my first old lady if that's what you mean.'

She poked at him in protest. 'Oi. Enough of that.'

'And I'm your first lickle boy, aren't I?' he went on.

Sheba was repulsed by his baby voice. 'Yes, you are,' she murmured.

He laughed and licked at her arm. 'Don't like that, do you?'

'What?' She was trying, she says, not to show him how much he was irritating her.

'Talking about your age and that . . .' he said. He paused, apparently weighing up whether he dared to utter what he had in mind. He giggled again. 'You're worried your vadge has gone loose.'

She had heard him say ugly things before, she says – things about people at school that had taken her aback with their angry vulgarity. But she had always dismissed these comments as experimental swagger. He had never before aimed his hatefulness at her.

'What a disgusting remark,' she said. She gave him a strong kick that sent him sprawling half off the bed. From the look on his face as he clambered back in, she thought at first that he was going to strike her. But he didn't. He just lay down and gave an odd sigh. She wanted to say something else to him. She was still furious. But she could think of nothing impressive enough, so she turned on her side, with her back to him. The bed was really too small for this sort of gesture, and in order not to let any part of her body touch his, she had to press herself against the cold, exterior wall.

It is a mark, I suppose, of how enslaved Sheba had become to the boy or, at least, to some idea of the boy, that this ugly incident did not lead to the relationship's demise. She did not leave his house. She did not tell him that she was unable to continue a relationship with a foul-mouthed, foul-minded child. She stayed and sulked and threatened to leave. And then, presently, when he roused himself to make a grudging apology for his behaviour, she forgave him. He begged her not to 'have the hump', she recalls. He told her that she was beautiful, that she was the 'best girlfriend' he'd had. And this, it seems, was enough.

'It was the way he had been taught to speak,' she says now. 'He didn't mean to offend me. He was trying to be funny. It was awful, I know. I'm not defending it. There *are* drawbacks to having a relationship with a boy like Steven. But he was so remorseful. And, and . . . I would have felt so *silly*, ending the whole thing over a figure of speech.'

Eleven

I found out about Sheba's affair in November. It had been going on for a little over eight months at that point and, though Sheba was not aware of it, it was already in its decline. The occasion for the revelation – which I have marked with two gold stars on the timeline – was Guy Fawkes night. Sheba had invited me to join her family for dinner. Afterwards, the plan was to go to Primrose Hill to see the fireworks. Never having been much of a firework fan, I expressed some reservations about participating in the second part of the evening, but Sheba was insistent. 'Oh *please*, Barbara,' she begged. 'I need the moral support.'

The Hart household was under some stress. Richard and Sheba's efforts to place Polly in a new school had been unsuccessful. The schools that Polly deemed acceptable didn't want her and vice versa. As a stop-gap measure, a tutor had been hired. Sheba's mother was paying. Richard made hearty jokes about Polly being 'home schooled'. But it was not a very satisfactory situation. The tutor came for three hours a day, and for the rest of the time Polly lounged about the house making her parents miserable. Sheba had lost almost half a stone in weight.

Guy Fawkes fell on a Wednesday night. As Sheba had requested, I went over to the house early. Polly let me in. 'Hi,' she said languidly before walking away. I followed her into the living room where she and Ben were lying on the floor, watching television.

'What's this then?' I said, gesturing at the cartoon that was on. Ben grunted a response that I couldn't hear. 'What?' I asked.

Polly glanced up at me. 'Mum's in the kitchen,' she said.

I found Sheba leaning on the kitchen counter, gazing hopelessly at the steaks she had bought for dinner. 'They look awful, don't they?' she said. 'I only bought them yesterday. Do you think they're off?'

The meat laid out on the butcher's block did look awful. It was slimy and had a dreary purple hue – the kind you get when you mash all the plasticine colours together. I sniffed at it gingerly. 'I can't tell.'

Sheba groaned. 'Great. I've got the ex coming and I'm serving rotten steak . . .' She went to the kitchen door. 'Polly!' she shouted. 'Darling, could you lay the table, please? Marcia and the girls will be here soon.'

She turned back to me. 'Richard invited them without asking me. And now, of course, Marcia's car isn't working, so she's summoned Richard to go and collect them. Why she couldn't take a taxi . . .' She trailed off as Polly slouched into the kitchen.

'Are you slagging off Marcia again?' Polly asked rhetorically.

Sheba, standing with her back to her daughter, gritted her teeth and said nothing.

'What were you screaming at me about?' Polly asked.

'I wasn't screaming, darling,' Sheba said. 'I was just asking you to lay the table. Dad is going to be back soon.'

'*Ew*,' Polly said, pointing at the steaks. 'Is that what we're eating tonight?'

'I haven't decided yet,' Sheba said. 'Come on, Polly. Be a love and lay the table.'

'Not now. After the cartoons are over,' Polly said.

'No, now, please, Polly.'

Polly rolled her eyes theatrically as she flounced out of the kitchen. 'I'm not your bloody maid, you know.'

Sheba looked at me and made a face. 'Oh, Barbara, you can't *imagine* what she's being like,' she whispered.

Actually, I felt that I probably could.

'She is beastly to everybody,' Sheba went on. 'Even to Richard. When she's not hitting him up for money. With me, she is breathtakingly rude – treats me as if I were some slightly embarrassing maiden aunt. Her two new phrases are "charming", uttered with great sarcasm, whenever either of us dares to get angry with her, and "fucking A".' Sheba paused, searching for more evidence of her daughter's awfulness. 'Oh,' she said, 'and she's smoking joints in her bedroom at night.'

I shook my head sympathetically.

'We've forbidden it,' she continued, 'but it's useless. We have no authority over her at all any more. Richard's tried to compromise – he made this rule that she could only smoke pot outside in the garden. But she ignores that too. Her room stinks of the stuff, Barbara. I get high just walking in there. She has a bong sitting in the middle of the carpet, for God's sake. I'm convinced that the whole house is going to go up in flames one of these nights . . .'

She stopped and looked back down at the steaks. 'Oh bloody hell, we can't use these. We'll all end up with botulism.' She picked up the chopping board and slid the meat into the bin. 'All right,' she said with a sigh as she opened the larder door, 'I suppose it'll have to be pasta for dinner.'

Richard came back half an hour later with his ex-wife, Marcia, and his eldest daughter, Saskia. The younger daughter, Claire, had decided at the last minute to stay at home. 'Hello, Barbara! Hello, Bash!' Marcia cried when she hobbled into the kitchen. She was wearing a flowing purple gown, the hem of which dragged on the kitchen floor, picking up the spill from Sheba's messy chopping. 'Oh marvellous! Pasta!' she trilled, peering into the pots on the stove. 'That's just what I feel like – something simple and homey.'

'Well, I had planned to give you steak . . .' Sheba began.

'Oh no!' Marcia said. 'Pasta is just the thing! Carbohydrates. Yummy yum!'

Sheba smiled thinly.

Sheba's official line on Marcia is that she adores her, that they're great friends. She is terribly lucky, she says, to have picked a husband with such a nice ex-wife. But there's something excessive in these protestations of goodwill. Beneath the showy sisterhood, I detect an unacknowledged enmity. If truth be told, Marcia is an awful pain – what with her dimbo daughters and her witchy dresses and her 'early onset rheumatoid arthritis'. When Sheba and Richard were newly married, Marcia took Sheba out for coffee and assured her that there were absolutely no hard feelings. 'It's not about families any more. It's about tribes,' she said. 'I mean, if we were in Africa, Richard would probably be on his *fifth* wife by now.' Sheba appears to have bought into this tribe nonsense, along with the idea that Marcia is some sort of indispensable clan matriarch. But come on! The woman has been divorced from Richard for over twenty years. Why is she still hanging around him like a bad smell? If Sheba could ever get rid of this duty she feels to *like* everybody, I dare say she'd discover that she really quite detests Marcia.

Richard came into the kitchen now with wine for everybody. 'Darling,' Sheba said brightly, 'why don't you take Marcia and Saskia into the living room so they can sit down? And could you ask Polly to lay the table?'

Richard trooped off with his ex-wife and daughter in tow.

A few moments later, we heard him angrily telling Polly to turn the television off.

'Stir your stumps, Polly!'

Then came Polly's high-pitched retort: 'Why am I the fucking Kunta Kinte around here?'

Dinner was a fraught affair. Saskia announced when the pasta arrived on her plate that it was inconsistent with her diet. Marcia praised Sheba for her lack of pretension in using supermarket cheddar instead of Parmesan. Sheba snapped at Ben for wiping his face on his jumper. The only blessing was that Polly remained silent. Afterwards, the group split into two – one lot in my car, the other in Richard's – and we drove to Primrose Hill.

As I say, I have never been a big fan of firework displays. All that brightness falling, the sad, smoke smell, the finale that is never quite as magnificent as it should be. And then there's the dispiriting, figurative tendency in modern fireworks. To stand in the cold, watching coloured sparks momentarily take the ragged shape of a smiley face or a drunken script that spells 'Happy Holidays' would seem, by any objective standard, to be a very low form of entertainment indeed. Yet appreciating fireworks is one of those things by which one is judged on one's child-like delight in life. It is perfectly acceptable to hate the circus. But to admit that one finds fireworks tiresome is to render oneself a pariah. I suspect that only the tiniest fraction of the crowd gathered on the top of Primrose Hill was genuinely invested in the spectacle, but we all stayed there for a full frigid hour, dutifully manufacturing sharp intakes of breath and other symptoms of ingenuous wonderment. All, that is, except Polly, who grasped at the opportunity to press home her alienation by chain-smoking cigarettes and kicking holes in the muddy ground with her boots.

At the end of the display there was a terrible crush as the crowd surged towards the park exits. Richard got panicky and tried to get us to stay at the top of the hill until the crowd had dispersed. But it had grown extremely cold by then and everyone was eager to get home, so he was overruled. We descended the path on the north side of the hill without too much trouble, but when we got to the flat where the people on the paths were attempting to move in two directions, the congestion was a lot worse. 'Where's Mum?' Polly said at one point. I looked around. Sheba had disappeared. 'Shit!' Richard said. 'Look, everyone must hold hands – form a chain – so we don't lose anyone else.' There was a girlish note of panic in his voice and, out of pity, I briefly considered obeying his command. But I was walking between Polly and Marcia and both of them seemed as disinclined to hold my hand as I was to hold theirs, so thankfully we all remained detached.

The long snaky line moved slowly. We were about two hundred yards from the Regent's Park Road exit when off to my left, beneath the trees, I glimpsed Sheba. She was standing with a young male. I couldn't see his face – his back was turned to me – but I could see hers; she was talking with great energy. People got in the way and I lost her for a few seconds. When I found her again, she was alone, walking towards me. I waved to attract her attention: 'Sheba!' Catching sight of me she smiled, and at that moment the boy turned and glanced back at her. He had floppy, blond hair, and sad, drooping eyes. Connolly.

Sheba must have registered my startled expression because she instinctively turned to see what had provoked it. For a split second we both looked at the boy. Then she looked back at me. There was fear in her expression but also something else – a kind of glee or amusement. 'Mum!' Ben called out from further up the line. 'Where've you been, Mum?' Sheba ran to him. I couldn't hear her reply to his question. I only saw her laughing and shaking her head as she pulled Ben into an embrace.

Sheba was in my car for the trip back home, but so were

Ben and Polly. Sheba spent the drive chattering with Ben. Polly and I said nothing. When we arrived back at Highgate, I made noises about going straight home, but Sheba put her hand on mine and urged me to come in. Richard had still not returned from dropping Marcia and Saskia back in Muswell Hill. Polly went straight to the living room and turned on the television. Sheba sent Ben upstairs to bed and told him she would be up in a bit to tuck him in. Then she suggested that we go down to her studio.

Neither of us spoke until we were in the basement and sitting on her fold-up chairs. I had hoped that Sheba would spare me the indignity of having to ask questions, but after a few moments of silence, during which she stared at the floor, I could bear it no longer.

'That was the Connolly boy I saw you with just now, at the park, wasn't it?' I said.

'Yes, yes it was.' She looked up at me coyly, from beneath her eyelashes.

'What's going on, exactly?'

'With Steven, you mean?'

'Yes.'

She looked down at her hands. 'It's difficult to say . . .'

'Just tell me. Is he still bothering you?'

'No, not bothering me. He . . . I . . .'

'Please, Sheba. Spit it out. What is your relationship with him?'

She looked at her hands again. 'I suppose you'd have to say we're involved. I mean . . . we're having an affair.'

Like an idiot, I gasped. 'Are you telling me the truth?'

She nodded.

'How long has it been going on?'

'Oh I don't know. A long time.'

'Approximately.'

'Pretty much since that time I told you about the kiss on Grafton Lane . . .'

'But that . . . you said . . .'

'No, we kissed then. I wasn't being entirely truthful when I said he only tried.'

'Sheba, this is very, very serious. Do you understand how serious?'

'Yes. Oh, yes.'

'No, Sheba, I mean this is something you could be sent to prison for.'

'I know.' She looked frightened for a moment and then she laughed. It was quite unlike her usual expression of mirth: a strange, slightly hysterical honking.

'For God's sake, Sheba,' I said. 'I mean, he's a . . . I don't have to say it. He's a *boy*.'

'Well, not completely,' Sheba said. 'I mean, obviously not a man. But in transition, I think you'd have to say.'

I stared at her. 'Whatever you want to call it, Sheba, he's very, very young. And you don't even *like* younger men. You told me yourself, you go for older men.'

'I *know*. It is odd, isn't it?' She spoke with an airy detachment, as if we were discussing a philosophical conundrum quite remote from her own life. 'But then,' she said, 'these labels we give our sexual feelings, they're so silly, aren't they? As if our tastes were that easily categorized or that unchanging. It's like men saying they're breast or leg men. I mean . . .' She let the sentence trail off.

'You're right, of course,' she went on after a moment. 'He *is* awfully young. But I can see now that boyhood has a very distinct charm. You know when feminists get angry about older men chasing younger women? I never could get behind all that. I always sympathized with the old goats. And now I'm glad I did, because I see for myself what it is that can drive you mad about a beautiful young body. I can stroke and nuzzle Steven for hours and I've never had quite enough. It's like I want to . . . to . . . penetrate him.'

'No,' I raised my hand. 'Please.'

She laughed, honkingly again. 'I don't mean, you know, *literally*, with one of those ridiculous dildos. The fantasy is more that I would burrow up inside him, somehow. Or be swallowed by him. It's similar to the way you feel cuddling an infant or a kitten, when you want to squeeze it so hard you'd kill it . . .' She folded her arms. 'Oh,' she said with a smile, 'you think me very depraved.'

I shook my head. She was speaking to me as if I were some withered old woman who had forgotten what lust was. She didn't *want* me to understand, I saw now. She was enjoying the idea of being incomprehensible.

'This isn't just about you,' I said. 'You have children. Have you considered them?'

Her face changed then. 'Oh, I know it, Barbara. I know I'm being a terrible person. I think about ending it all the time.'

'Stop thinking and just do it, for God's sake.'

Sheba made a dismissive gesture with her hand. 'Please don't lecture me, Barbara. It won't do any good. Being in love is a condition, isn't it? It's like being depressed. Or like being in a cult. You're basically under water – people can talk to you about life on dry land, but it doesn't really mean anything . . .'

'What are you talking about love for?' I said. 'Don't be a bloody idiot.'

'Why are you talking like that?'

'I'm trying to help you.'

'No, I mean the swearing. You never swear.'

'Look, Sheba, please. Don't start saying you love him. This isn't love.'

'I'm not sure I could categorize *what* this is. People always want to boil these things down, don't they? I want to recapture my lost youth. He wants experience. I'm forcing him into it. He's forcing me into it. He feels sorry for me. I feel sorry for him . . . But it's never that simple, is it?'

I shook my head. 'This is madness. You're making it into something it's not. It's all in your mind.'

Sheba was about to protest and then she laughed. 'But isn't that the worst place it could be?'

I had an urge to slap her, to put my hands about her neck and shake her like a doll. 'Stop it! This is so . . . I mean, do you have a single shared interest? Beyond the sex, I mean?'

'Oh, I can't be doing with all that,' Sheba said. 'I've read the women's magazine quizzes too, you know – "The Confusion of Sex and Love", and "Are You Mistaking Your Orgasm For The Real Thing?" I know about all that stuff and I'm telling you, I think it's *nonsense*. I don't even know what it means. I mean, who invented the distinction? Isn't it arbitrary? Can't we just say I feel something very *powerful* for Steven?'

'More powerful than you feel for Richard? For your family?' I was shouting now.

'Yes!' Sheba shouted back. 'No! I mean . . . yes, actually. Yes.'

We sat in silence for a moment, absorbing this admission.

'*As* powerful, in any case,' she added, quietly, after a bit. 'Right now. I mean, *of course* it's physical. And no, we don't have "shared interests". What do you think? He's *sixteen*. Our shared interest is us. Why shouldn't that be enough? I'm not planning to marry him.'

'Well, I'm grateful for that small residue of clear-sightedness . . . You've considered the fact that he is probably boasting about this to his friends?'

'Yes, I've considered it. But he's not.'

'How can you possibly be so sure?'

Sheba shrugged. 'I'm not always. But mostly I am. It's complicated. In some ways, I trust him more than anybody. He has a hardness about him, but also this enormous vulnerability . . . I can't bear – literally *can't bear* – to think of him in pain of any sort. I *weep* with rage at the thought. I think I feel more of what people call maternal instinct for him than I do for Polly.'

'But, Sheba . . .'

'I know this is indefensible behaviour, Barbara. I just have to do it. I *want* to do it.'

'Do you want to be caught? Is that it? The danger of the thing?'

'No!' she exclaimed, wringing her hands in exasperation. 'No. I can't tell you why I'm doing this. That's what I'm saying. I don't know. That's sort of the point of these kinds of experience, isn't it? That they can't be reduced? There have to be some mysteries – I don't mean holy-moly ones, but mysteries of human behaviour – that *can't* be fathomed.'

When I left, an hour or so later, Sheba embraced me warmly on the front doorstep and we agreed to speak further the next day. I was friendly enough. But the moment I was in the car, anger began to seep out like acid from a battery. It wasn't just the dreadful folly of Sheba's actions – the squalor of what she was now involved in – that upset me; it was the immense duplicity that she had so casually revealed. We had spoken of the deceit that she had been practising on Richard, on her children, on the school, even. But nothing had been said by either of us about her deceit of *me*. It hadn't occurred to her to apologize for *that*. Did our friendship mean anything to her? Or had it been a diversion device all along – a way of throwing the staff off the scent of the real scandal? All those months, when I had imagined we were so close, she had been making a mockery of me.

At a traffic light on Highgate Hill, I noticed that the little girl in the back seat of the car in front of mine was staring at me with very round eyes. For the last minute or so, I realized, I had been smacking my steering wheel repeatedly. When I looked down, there was a large, shiny red indentation on the heel of my palm.

Back at my flat, I sat in the living room, eating a Swiss Roll and chain-smoking while I considered the evening's revelations. For upwards of an hour, I was fully determined to go into school the next day and tell Pabblem everything. I had no great concern for Connolly's moral welfare. My assumption then – as now – was that the boy was quite capable of fending for himself. My desire to tell Pabblem was entirely motivated by fury.

Slowly, however, as the cigarettes and the Swiss Roll dwindled, my rage began to evaporate. Of course I was not going to tell Pabblem. Sheba had behaved very poorly towards me, that was certain. But she hadn't meant to hurt me. She had evidently *wanted* to tell me from the start. She had not been operating with a clear mind. She was having a sexual affair with a pupil, for goodness' sake. Obviously, she was undergoing some manner of breakdown.

It was 2 a.m. when I got up to prepare myself for bed. My face looked tired and green in the bathroom mirror. *Sheba is my friend*, I told my reflection. *She needs me now*. Portia sat on the side of the tub, observing my teeth-brushing with her usual hauteur. I spat and rinsed, and put on my cold cream. *Who else will help her, if I don't?* In the bedroom, I slipped on my nightdress and removed the decorative pillows from my bed. The landlord's dog was whining in the back yard. From one of the neighbouring streets, I could hear the drunken shouts of young people. Portia had followed me in now and was winding herself around my legs. I peeled back the counterpane and climbed into bed. *Come on. Buck up. True friendship weathers this sort of crisis.* Portia jumped up and stalked about for a bit, testing out potential sleeping spots with her claws. She committed, finally, to lying heavily – and hotly – across my calves. I set my alarm and turned out the light. Through a gap in the curtains, a moonbeam shone glamorously on Portia, like a spotlight. *Sheba contra mundum*, I announced to the still, dark room.

Twelve

It is Easter and Sheba and I have come down to the seaside to spend a few days with my sister's family. The Harts usually have a lot of people over to their house at this time of year; Sheba does a big baked ham and there's an egg hunt in the garden. This year, for obvious reasons, that was out of the question, so Richard has taken Polly and Ben to stay with friends in Shropshire. Sheba was terribly distraught when she found out that she would not be spending Easter with her son and I did try intervening with Richard on her behalf, but he was in one of his vindictive moods and wouldn't hear of altering his plans. Sheba became very low after that and spent hours and hours locked in her room, working on her sculpture. In a slightly desperate effort to cheer her up and take her mind off things, I decided to bring her to Eastbourne.

Marjorie took some persuading. She and Dave are not accustomed to entertaining celebrity deviants in their home. When I first rang to propose the visit, she said she'd have to 'pray on it' before giving me an answer and I didn't hold out much hope. But she ended up consulting with her pastor, Des, and he was of the opinion that God would want Marjorie to hold out the hand of friendship to a sinner. The night we arrived, Marjorie got me in the hallway and assured me in an urgent whisper, 'Jesus is very pleased that Sheba is here.'

Marjorie and I were both brought up in the Church of England, but neither of our parents was remotely pious, so it's a mystery where Marjorie got her religious gene. She was introduced to the Seventh Dayers in her late teens by Ray, a chap she was dating at the time. Ray ended up going off to Saudi Arabia to work for an oil company, but Marjorie stayed with the church after he left and eventually she started going with Dave, another member of the congregation. They've been married for almost thirty years now and their life is entirely church-centred. Every room in their house is crammed with religious bric-a-brac. They own at least twenty plaster models of Jesus Christ (beatific infant Jesus in porcelain nappies; he-man Jesus with biceps knocking over stalls in the Temple; thirty-something Jesus lolling gloomily in Gethsemane and so on). Over the dresser in their bedroom, there's a deliciously bad rendering of the Last Supper with all the disciples sporting pompadours and levitating slightly. And in the front room, where Sheba and I are sleeping, there's a six-by-four-foot poster of a harbour at sunset, captioned with a quotation from Matthew: '"Come, follow me," Jesus said, "and I will make you fishers of men."' In honour of Easter, my sister has improvised a Passion tableau on top of the telly: a gilt crucifix, encircled by ten china Easter bunnies wearing tam o'shanters.

This is my sister's real attachment to God, I think: the accessories. Years ago, before she married Dave, we travelled to Europe together one summer and paid a visit to Lourdes. I don't think I've ever seen her as happy as when she was trolling through the Lourdes gift shops. She liked the amputees and spastics lining up to be dangled in puddles of holy water. She enjoyed the singalongs and the torch-lit processions. But it was the trinkets, the T-shirts, the gewgaws, that really popped her cork. It's a shame, I often think, that Marjorie didn't end up a Catholic. She would have got such a charge out of rosary beads.

I've been slightly worried about how Sheba would react to the set-up down here. I can't imagine that she's had much interaction with believers before now. But, so far, everything seems to be going smoothly. She professes to be enchanted by my sister and brother-in-law. 'How happy you are,' she keeps telling them, as she floats about the house in her nightie. And while I may detect a tinge of *de haut en bas* in the pronouncement, Marjorie and Dave are terribly flattered. 'Isn't she pretty?' Marje stage-whispers whenever Sheba turns her back. 'Doesn't she talk nicely?' Even Dave, a man of legendarily few words, has conceded gruffly that the pictures of Sheba in the paper 'don't do her justice'.

Yesterday morning Sheba further ingratiated herself by making a special request to join the family at the Good Friday morning service. Marjorie nearly wet herself with excitement. I didn't go, of course. I was careful to remain 'asleep' until they were all safely out of the house. Then, when I was quite sure that no one was coming back for a forgotten pair of gloves, I got up and gave the front room a bit of a tidy. It was while I was sprucing things up that I came across Sheba's handbag.

I had no intention of going through Sheba's stuff, but when I caught a glimpse of the chaos inside the bag, I couldn't resist giving it a little spring-clean. The rubbish that Sheba hangs on to! Fistfuls of loose coins. A blemish-covering stick that has lost its top and is now covered with bits of fluff. Several grubby-looking Polo mints. A couple of tampons that have begun to mushroom out from their torn plastic wrapping. Right at the bottom, poking out from the bag's torn lining, I found an envelope containing a sheaf of battered photographs.

Naturally, I hesitated to look at them. I take no pleasure in violating Sheba's privacy. But as Sheba's unofficial guardian, I have certain obligations that I cannot shirk. The photographs were of Sheba and Connolly as it turned out – all of them taken on a single evening on Hampstead Heath. There were a few not very flattering shots of Sheba sitting on the grass. There were many shots of Connolly clowning about: flexing his muscles in the style of Charles Atlas, sticking out his tongue, turning his upper eyelids inside out. The sight of his banal little face made me quite nauseated. But worse was yet to come. At the bottom of the pile four or five slightly wonky shots showed the lovers together. (Connolly had apparently been holding the camera at arm's length.) These pictures were of a distinctly lewd character. In two of them, Sheba was topless. In another particularly revolting image – the memory of which I have tried, but failed, to erase from my mind – Sheba was kneeling before Connolly as he exposed himself.

My hands were shaking as I replaced the photographs in the envelope. Sheba has sworn to me on several occasions that she has destroyed all mementos of her relationship with Connolly. Yet here she is, still hoarding pornographic snapshots of the boy in her handbag. My instinct was to destroy them, but I could not have done so without alerting Sheba to the fact that I had been going through her things. Reluctantly, I put the envelope back in her bag.

Sheba returned from church bursting with excitement. What a rewarding experience it had been! Oh, she couldn't wait to do it again! I kept hoping for a wink or something – some acknowledgement of the absurdity of the situation – but there was nothing. It would be less excruciating somehow, if she were at all sincere about Marjorie's church. But she's in no danger of getting religion. The God business is just a diversion for her – a bit of Marie Antoinettish dabbling in someone else's charming rituals. I dare say if my sister and her family had been devotees of the Santeria cult, she would have joined in just as cheerfully, toasting effigies and sacrificing goats.

Today, partly to please her and partly because the photographs have convinced me that I need to keep a closer eye on her, I accompanied Sheba on her second trip to church. A notice on the bulletin board in the church vestibule referred to the morning service as 'the Good Lord A.M.' When I quietly pointed out this egregious Americanism to Sheba, she didn't so much as crack a smile. Throughout the sermon and the hymns, she had this horrid, holy little grin on her face. Later on, when Pastor Des called congregants to the front for 'the Lord's Supper', I was astonished to see her stand up. I thought at first that she was confused and didn't know what people were lining up for. But she knew, all right. Apparently, she'd taken communion the day before, with my sister.

After the service, Dave and the kids stayed behind at the church to help with the Easter food kitchen. Marjorie, Sheba and I walked back home to get the lunch going. Sheba rattled on about how nice the hymns were and wasn't Pastor Des a super fellow? And then, at a certain point, she started on about love. 'Sometimes, I think I've been in a kind of trance state the whole of this last year,' she said. 'I mean, what is romance, but a mutual pact of delusion? When the pact ends, there's nothing left. That's the thing about people who believe in God, isn't it? The love they have for Him never ends. He never lets them down. I read some writer once, who said that love – he was talking about romantic love – love is a mystery and when the solution is found, it evaporates. It didn't mean anything to me at the time. But now I see how true it is. It's so spot on, isn't it?' She gazed at Marjorie, who smiled and remained silent. Throughout this mad little speech, I had been on tenterhooks lest Sheba should say anything to shock or offend my sister. But I needn't have worried. Poor old Marje had not the slightest clue what Sheba was on about.

★

I come now, with no little reluctance, to the events of December 1997. For me, this period constitutes the most painful part of my narrative – not least because, if I am to be entirely truthful, I must confess some very reprehensible behaviour of my own. Having read the following account, some will be inclined to judge me harshly. To them, I say: no judgement you conceive could possibly be harsher than that I have passed on myself. My remorse for my own lapses is infinite. If I seem to take particular care in describing how I came to act as I did, it is not because I hope to exculpate myself, but rather because I wish to be as rigorously and unsparingly truthful as possible.

December started out a difficult month – for both Sheba and me. Sheba was having problems with Connolly. She sensed that his enthusiasm for the affair was ebbing. His manner with her had grown increasingly offhand, even bored, and on a couple of occasions she had come away from seeing him with the distinct impression that she was being 'handled'. She was reluctant to confess these suspicions at first. She had an idea, I think, that to speak them aloud would confer on them some ineradicably official status. But her anguish was too intense to hide for long.

'He's going off me!' she wailed one evening, as we were leaving school together. 'He's retreating, I can feel it. And the more he does, the more whiny I become.' The affair had begun to create in her a heady, slightly maudlin state of introspection, she told me. She was filled with a sense of the momentousness of things – a sense of attunement to the grand, melancholy truths about life. Being in love had never produced these solemn sensations in her before. Her courtship with Richard had been a happy, carefree business. The nearest she had ever come to her present state of mind, she said, had been during the third trimesters of her pregnancies when, as now, she had found herself moved to tears by the most inconsequential things.

She had started to write Connolly long, lyrical letters, she said – letters filled with gloomy analyses of her feelings and passionate statements of her commitment to him. It was too risky to send them, so she handed them to him at the end of their assignations. (Sometimes, when they next met, he would ask her to explain what certain words meant.) For the first time in her life, she was experiencing sexual jealousy. At their last encounter, Connolly had mentioned that he was going to a party that weekend and she had been agonized. Connolly had rarely spoken of his social activities before; he had always strenuously resisted her proddings on the subject. Did he mean to taunt her now? Sheba had tried to remain cool, but she had kept picturing him at the party, drinking his rum and Coke from a plastic cup, dancing with peachy-skinned girls in slutty dresses.

'Will you get off with someone?' she had asked. It was a stupid question but she couldn't help herself.

Connolly had smiled. 'Dunno,' he'd said. 'I might.'

She was being ridiculous, she knew that. She couldn't possibly expect him to be faithful to her. And yet, the thought of his touching someone else – of someone else touching him – filled her with despair.

Things were also going badly between her and Richard. They had begun to argue over trivial matters, she said. This was galling because she and Richard had always prided themselves on the tranquillity of their domestic relations. Sheba's parents had been terrible fighters. She and Eddie had spent a disproportionate part of their childhoods, she said, banished to the garden in order that their parents might shriek at one another with abandon: 'Sometimes they'd forget about us and we'd be stuck outside for hours. When we were finally summoned back in, my father would have left the house and my mother would be slamming about the kitchen, making not-so-veiled allusions to the misery of her married life. Awful. I swore I would never have that kind of a marriage. Richard and I have always been so good at talking things out.'

Sheba's instinct was to attribute her marital difficulties to Polly's presence in the house. 'She's intolerable, intolerable!' she would say, angrily. 'She's driving the family mad!' But as the weeks went by, she became more inclined to admit that her affair with Connolly was the true source of the trouble. 'The fact is,' she told me one night, 'I feel contempt for Richard. For his not knowing. I can't believe he's so blind! How can he love me and not see it? When I come home from being with Steven, I look at him snoring away and I want to bang a saucepan over his head. I want to shout, "Guess what, you complacent old fart? I've been out on the heath, getting fucked by a sixteen-year-old! What do you think of that?"'

I was unhappy in December too. I was troubled by Sheba's situation, of course. But my main concern was for Portia's failing health. One Friday night in mid November I had arrived home from school to find a puddle of pale pink vomit on my bed. After a series of tests, the vet had diagnosed cancer of the colon and she was now undergoing a rigorous course of radiation therapy. The vet spoke confidently about the prospects of a complete recovery and I badly wanted to believe in his optimism, but the illness, or the treatment, or both, were sucking the life out of Portia with alarming speed. The proud, ironic creature with whom I had shared my life for twelve years was transforming before my eyes into a cringing, humourless moggy. Every day, she grew more desiccated.

I dare say it will seem inappropriate to some people for me to assume a parity between my troubles and Sheba's. They will be hard pressed to believe that an ailing pet could cause a person as much heartache as a wayward lover. Sheba certainly didn't understand this. In fact, it was her failure to respect my grief – to respond with anything like the proper sympathy – that lay at the root of our brief but catastrophic rift.

On Saturday in the first week of December, I picked Portia up from a radiotherapy session at the vet's. She was always somewhat enervated after these treatments, but on this occasion she seemed particularly depleted. I was so distressed by her condition that I drove straight to the Harts' house. I had never before gone to Sheba's home unannounced, but I judged that the circumstances were sufficiently extraordinary to warrant a lapse in etiquette. The house was dark when I arrived. I took the cat's travel-cage out of the car and went up the steps to ring the bell anyway. Portia was sleeping now. I stood on the front step, hoping against hope that Sheba would be in. After a moment or two, I was turning to walk away when I heard running steps and then Sheba opened the door. She had been working down in the studio, she explained. Richard and the children were out. She did not acknowledge Portia's presence.

'Actually,' she said, as we walked down to the basement, 'I'm not *really* working. I'm waiting for a call from Steven. We're meant to be meeting up this afternoon.'

I placed the travel-cage carefully on the floor and sat down on one of Sheba's folding chairs.

Sheba laughed nervously. 'He was supposed to phone an hour ago, but I haven't heard a peep yet. Wretched boy.'

I nodded.

'I expect he's having trouble getting away from his family,' she went on. 'He's normally pretty punctual. His mother sometimes makes him go shopping with her. To carry the bags . . .'

'Portia's in a terrible way,' I said, gesturing at the basket.

Sheba stared. 'Oh dear. Poor Portia. Have you just come from the vet?'

'Yes. She's suffering so much. I can't bear it.' I began to cry.

'Poor Barbara,' Sheba said. 'How awful.' She came over and crouched down in front of me. 'It'll be okay,' she said, patting my knee.

After a bit, she got up and pulled up a chair to sit next to me. 'Please don't cry. The vet will make her better.' The effort at consolation was so cursory – so silly – that I was briefly enraged. I took a tissue from my sleeve and dabbed slowly at my eyes.

Sheba's long arms were lying slackly in her lap. Her skin was so pale that you could see all the veins beneath the surface: long greenish strands, like seaweed glimpsed through water.

'Did you and your friends stroke each other's arms when you were at school?' I asked suddenly.

She laughed. 'What? No.'

'Oh, we did,' I said. 'We used to stroke the insides of each other's forearms during study hall. One girl would do one girl's forearm while another girl did her forearm. We'd form great long chains of arm-stroking. It's one of the loveliest sensations.'

Sheba laughed disbelievingly. 'For sex-starved thirteen-year-old girls perhaps,' she said.

'Oh no, it's nothing sexual,' I said. 'Look, let me show you.'

I took her right forearm and ran the tips of my fingers up and down, from elbow to wrist. It was a bold thing to do. I had never touched Sheba so intimately before.

She giggled, at first. 'It's just tickling!' she said.

'No, no,' I said. 'Shut your eyes. Feel it.'

She shut her eyes and I continued running my fingers lightly across her spindly arm. After a second or two, her mouth fell open. Then she pulled her arm away.

'Just relax,' I told her, pulling her arm back.

'Don't,' she said sharply. 'It creeps me out.' She rolled down her sleeve.

The phone rang and Sheba leaped up to get it. I could tell it was Connolly on the other end by the way she began to whisper and giggle. She carried the telephone into the basement toilet and shut the door.

I sat, angrily swinging my legs, waiting for her to return.

When she came out, she was smiling. 'Gosh, I hate to do this, Barbara,' she said, 'but I'm going to have to go. That was him.'

I watched her as she began hurriedly to gather up her things.

'No,' I said.

Sheba looked round at me, her eyebrows startled into little Chinese hats.

'I mean, please,' I said, somewhat taken aback myself. 'Don't go just yet. Stay with me a bit longer.'

She came over to hug me. 'Everything's going to be all right,' she said. 'You'll see.' Then she stood up and put on her coat.

'Don't go, Sheba,' I said again.

She looked at me curiously. 'Barbara, come on. I *have* to go.'

I wanted to scream. Bloody Connolly. Bloody bloody little boy. 'Sheba . . .' I murmured, grasping at the arm of her coat.

'Please!' she shouted and moved away so abruptly that I lost my balance and fell from the chair, managing to smash my hip on the side of her pottery wheel as I did so.

There was a strange noise from the travel-cage, like a thumb being dragged across a pane of glass. Portia had woken up.

'God, Barbara, are you all right?' Sheba was peering down at me with a nice combination of impatience and alarm.

I sat for a moment, groping at my hip. 'I think so.'

'Are you sure?'

'Yes, yes. It's just my hip.' My hip hurt like damnation as it happened, but I didn't want to make a fuss. I peered into the travel-cage. Portia was huddled down at the far end, with her fur up and claws out. 'Shush. It's all right,' I whispered through the bars.

'Sorry about that,' Sheba said. Then she slung her handbag over her shoulder and put on her hat. Was she still going to leave? Even after knocking me down? I stood up and staggered slightly.

'Do you think you'll be all right driving home?' she asked.

'Oh yes, I'm fine,' I said. Sheba was too preoccupied to notice the frost in my voice.

'Good, good,' she said, heading for the door. I picked up the travel-cage and limped after her.

Out on the street, we embraced stiffly. 'Well, I suppose I'll see you on Monday then,' Sheba said. She was shifting anxiously from foot to foot, like someone in need of the toilet. I nodded and took out my car keys. 'So, now . . .' she said, 'take care of yourself.' She patted my back as I bent to unlock the car.

'Ouf,' I said, rubbing my hip. 'I'll probably have quite a bruise in the morning . . .' But when I turned around, she was already gone – half-running down the street, to catch her lover before he changed his mind.

Thirteen

For the next two weeks I stayed away from Sheba. At school, I kept to my classroom during breaks and when she approached me in the corridors I was polite but remote. Once, she rang me at home and asked me over to her house, but I made a deliberately weak excuse as to why I couldn't go. My mood was defiant. *Enough of her*, I thought. *Let's see how well she gets along without me.* And then, after a while, I became rather depressed. Perhaps more confused than depressed. My life had become incoherent to me. Why did my friends always fall out with me? Why was I always being let down? Was I never to be rewarded for my constancy?

The weather that fortnight was foul. First, there were hailstorms, followed by a few days of sullen, yellow skies. Then came semi-hurricane winds. Four hundred London trees were felled in a single night. I wondered where, if at all, Sheba and Connolly were managing to meet. I was sleeping very badly at the time. Even when I am in good spirits, sleep does not come easily to me. I tend to wander around for ages before I get into bed, trying to put off the moment when I pull the cold sheet to my shoulder and acknowledge the closing of another day. During this period, I frequently roamed my flat until three or even four in the morning. Sometimes, I drifted off in my armchair with Portia on my lap, only to be woken, a few minutes later, by the wind shrieking through the street outside.

Portia's health seemed worse than ever. She was spending most of the time on the sofa now, her face a Kabuki mask of despair. I grew so demoralized at one point that I was even considering taking sick leave from school and going down to my sister's with Portia. At least, I reasoned, I'd have my meals cooked for me.

And then, just before the Christmas break, Bangs, the Maths teacher, invited me on a date. He approached me slyly in the corridor one day and suggested that I join him for lunch that coming Saturday. At a restaurant. This was intriguing. I knew better than to suppose that Bangs had romantic designs on me. But even a platonic interest on his part was a surprise. Bangs had been at St George's for four years and until then, he had never demonstrated the slightest enthusiasm for cultivating my acquaintance outside school. I know now that I should have declined the invitation. But, being at such a low ebb, I was inclined to see his approach as a sign: a message of hope.

Bangs was at least fifteen years younger than me and he was a fool. (Even my most optimistic speculations did not lose sight of those facts.) But he had noticed me. He had chosen *me* to share his Saturday lunchtime. And who was I to pick and choose? For a few days, I'm afraid I let my imagination run away with me. I pictured myself shedding my old, unfortunate self and stepping forth into the light and air of the regular world. I would cease to be the shut-in biddy waiting around for an invitation from my one, married friend. I would become, at last, a person who had easy relations with the world, a person who spent my weekends having dates, who carried photographs in my wallet, documenting scenes from the jolly parties and rowdy barbecues and delightful christenings that I had recently attended. I remember it being of particularly piquant satisfaction to me that I was now in possession of a social plan – a *personal appointment* – of which Sheba knew nothing.

By the time the Saturday of my lunch date rolled around, I had grown very nervous and would probably have spent the morning working myself into one of my stews, had I not been saved from such nonsense by having to rush Portia to the vet's. The poor thing had spent most of the previous night retching all over the living-room floor. At dawn, she had retreated to the sofa, where she lay mewling in the most pitiful way. I rang the vet's answering service at seven o'clock and got an emergency appointment for nine. When I took her over there, the vet gave her a brief examination. Then he said he wanted to run more tests. I looked at my watch. In order to make it back to Archway for my hair appointment, I would have to leave Portia there on her own. I battled with my conscience for a few moments. Then I gave Portia a shame-faced kiss and hastily departed.

I loathe going to the hairdresser's and do so as infrequently as possible, but my unhappiness over the previous fortnight had caused me to neglect my appearance. For a short time I had ceased brushing my hair altogether and I was now badly in need of a set. The people at the salon were exhibiting the rather desperate good cheer that is characteristic of the British workplace at Christmas. All the girls were sporting sprigs of tinsel in their hair and picking, in a not very hygienic way, at a grey-looking Yule log which one of the customers had brought in. They treated me with their usual contempt. As a punishment for being not quite five minutes late, I was made to wait an agonizing half an hour before I was seen to. And then, when I was getting my hair washed, I happened to open my eyes and catch the ghastly girl giggling at me and making faces at one of the other girls over my head. It was lucky for her that I was not in the mood for a fight, otherwise, you can rest assured, she would have caught the sharp edge of my tongue.

After my hair was finished, I had just enough time to rush back to the flat and change my clothes. I wore my black skirt and plain shoes (no silly heels this time). Then I drove down to Camden Town. The restaurant that Bangs had chosen was a new place – well, new to me anyway – called Vingt-et-trois, just off Camden High Street. It was raining quite heavily when I parked the car, but I took an umbrella and made myself walk slowly around the block two times before I went in, to be sure of not being early.

I was still the first to arrive. It was dark inside the restaurant and loud pop music was being played on a stereo system. At the maître d's lectern a young woman was mouthing the words to the music. She wore a T-shirt that stopped several inches above her navel and trousers that began several inches below it. I gave her Bangs's name, but she couldn't find it in her big book (he had failed to make a reservation) and although there were at least six tables vacant, the girl said it was impossible to seat me until all members of my party had arrived. I became stupidly panicked at this point. She must have noticed and taken pity because she gave me a menu and said, quite pleasantly, that I could wait at the bar if I liked. The bar was in another room, through a little arch, and as she was leading me there she hooked her arm around her waist and scratched lazily at the strip of honey-coloured back between her T-shirt and trousers.

The man behind the bar was a very raucous person wearing a red Father Christmas cap and a sprig of mistletoe behind his ear. He kept shouting unintelligible greetings at his fellow employees and the three patrons who were perched on bar stools. 'Y'owl right, Barry?' he was bellowing at a passing waiter as I entered. He had a very enunciated, self-conscious London accent – the accent of someone taking pleasure in the distortions of dialect. When he asked me what I wanted to drink, it was with such booming aggression that, despite being rather thirsty, I shook my head and said I wanted nothing. 'Nothing?' he shouted in pretend outrage. 'Nothing? You sure about that?' He was smiling as he uttered these words and the other people at the bar looked at me and smiled too. I understand now, it was just a joke – well, not a joke exactly, more a sort of aimless good humour. He was a 'character', you see. But at the time, I had the idea that some specific point was being made. That I was being mocked.

'I'm waiting for a friend,' I said, by way of explaining myself. I had to raise my voice to be heard above the pop music.

'A *friend*?' the barman said, maintaining his tone of panto-mime disbelief. 'Friend, eh? That right? Waiting for a friend? You gotta have friends 'aven't ya? *Yusss*, friends are what it's all about, innit?' I nodded, feeling confused and foolish. 'Go *on*,' the barman said. 'Have a drink. Have a *driii-nnnkkkk*. A nice glass of wine, treat yourself . . .' He leaned in across the bar and gave me an ironic, goggle-eyed smile.

'*Please, stop that*,' I said suddenly.

There was a brief moment of silence during which the people on the bar stools swung round to gaze at me. The barman paused for a moment, then laughed and turned away. At that moment, Bangs appeared, stooping slightly, beneath the arch.

Living things out in your mind never prepares you for the reality. My mental preparation for this lunch date – the black-and-white film I had been playing in my head all week – had served only to make the actual, colour version more overwhelming. I found myself stunned and slightly appalled by the corporeal presence of Bangs. He was wearing his red V-neck sweater and a jacket of the sort that American baseball players wear. The back and front were made of thick, felt-like material, but the sleeves were white leather. This was a special weekend garment, I presumed, since I had never seen him wearing it at school. He was clutching anxiously at his left earlobe and even at a distance of a few yards I could see that his shaving rash was in full flower. For a while, it seemed to me that I might black out from the sensory overload of the moment, the sheer Bangsness of Bangs.

'Hiya!' he was saying. 'Sorry I'm late. I hope you haven't been waiting long.' He approached very quickly, and then, without warning, he made a sort of dive at me, like a bird swooping on food. Rearing back, I felt a glance of damp lip on my chin and understood, too late, that he had been aiming to kiss my cheek. A hard knock ensued, his head colliding with mine, and it became clear – again too late – that he had been going for a kiss on both cheeks. He stepped away and I stood up from the bar stool. The immediate introduction of physical intimacy was a horrid misjudgement on his part, I felt. He had never so much as shaken my hand before.

'No, no, you're not late,' I said. (He was, of course. But only by seven minutes or so.) As I rose from my stool, my handbag, which had been resting on my lap, fell to the floor. When I bent to pick it up, I could hear the oceanic roar of my own rushing blood.

'Have you already ordered a drink?' Bangs asked. 'Or, or, shall we sit down?'

'No, I haven't. Let's sit down.'

We returned to the girl with the navel who wanted to know were we smoking or non-smoking.

Bangs looked at me. 'You want smoking don't you?'

'Yes, but I . . . I don't mind not.'

'Oh, all right. No smoking then.'

We sat down and first I, then he, made noisy little exhalations of air – the kind that are meant to indicate the restoration of calm and contentment after a great hubbub: *haaa*. We had been given menus and Bangs said that we ought to look

183

at them straightaway because he was starving. For a few moments, we studied our glazed texts in silence. Then, fearful of letting a pause become an unbridgeable gap, I said, 'That's quite a jacket you have there, Bangs.'

Bangs seemed pleased by my comment and for the next several minutes he became quite enlivened on the subject of his outerwear. The jacket, it turned out, was one of ten similar garments that he owned. He collected them. 'Not because I'm a fan of baseball,' he said. 'They're just cool, aren't they?'

I nodded. 'Yes,' I said. 'Very.'

Looking back on my date with Bangs, I am always particularly excruciated by the memory of this exchange about the jacket. There were other, much starker humiliations to follow. But for some reason, this is the moment to which I keep returning, the moment that makes me clench my fists and hum out loud. Is it my feigning approval of a hideous jacket that offends me? Or my acquiescence to Bangs's use of teeny-bopper terminology? Both those things, I suppose. But even more, I think, the motivation behind them – my desire to have Bangs like me.

We struggled on. Bangs told me about some of the places he had acquired his jackets, and after that we had a frank exchange of views on the 'freedom fighter' mural that Pabblem had recently proposed for the main school playground. (Bangs thought it was quite controversial but might be fun.) Then the waitress came and we ordered our lunch. There was an anxious lull between making and receiving our orders but, happily, I thought to ask Bangs about the new Maths textbooks that had recently arrived for his GCSE classes. This proved a fertile topic for discussion and his opinion of the new books carried us right through our hors d'oeuvres and our main courses. Things went so swimmingly, in fact, that when the waitress came by to ask us if we would like anything else,

Bangs smiled warmly across the table and suggested that we skip dessert and repair to his flat for a coffee. I hesitated only a moment. 'Certainly,' I said. 'Why not?'

We split the bill. Bangs calculated in his head that my half came to £23.45 plus £1.64 tip (or £2.34, if I wanted 'to be generous'). Then he patted his thighs and winked. 'Okay, shall we go?'

Perhaps the wine had befuddled me. Perhaps I was clinging to an idea that things would improve. Perhaps I simply couldn't bear the idea of returning to my flat, with my hair still stiff from the hairdresser's, to lie on my bed and watch horse-racing for the rest of the afternoon. 'Yes,' I said, standing up. 'Let's.'

Sheba and I had an argument about children, once. We were talking about my retirement and I made a jokey remark about how desolate it was going to be.

'Oh, don't say that,' Sheba said. She looked genuinely pained. But somehow, her remark irritated me. I felt that I was being shut up.

'Why shouldn't I?' I asked. 'It's the truth. I am a dried-up old lady with no husband, very few friends, no children. If I'd had just one child . . .'

'Oh nonsense.' Sheba's tone had a surprising sharpness.

'What do you mean, nonsense? You don't even know what I was going to say.'

'Yes I do. You were going to say that a child would have given your life meaning or made it worthwhile or whatever, and that isn't true. It's a myth. Children give you a lot of things, but not meaning.'

'How can they not? Look, when you die, Ben and Polly will be living. When I die, that'll be it – there'll be nothing left.'

Sheba laughed. 'You think my children are my immortality? They're not *me*, you know. And if life is meaningless, bearing children is just giving birth to more meaninglessness . . .'

'But I'm *alone*, Sheba, don't you see?'

She shrugged. Confronting a married person with the irre-ducible fact of one's singleness is usually the trump card that ends the discussion. I was surprised to find that Sheba did not yield. 'Being alone isn't the worst thing in the world,' she said.

'But it's funny, isn't it,' I said, 'how it's always people who *aren't* alone, who say that?' I was quite angry now.

'Not *so* funny,' Sheba replied. 'Maybe they're in the better position to judge.'

'Look, Sheba, the only indisputable purpose humans have on the earth is to reproduce. And I haven't done it. There's no getting round that.'

'Purpose – that's closer to it,' Sheba said. 'Children *do* give you a purpose. In the sense of keeping you busy, in the sense of something to get out of bed and do every morning. But that's not the same as meaning.'

I laughed rather bitterly, I'm afraid. What I thought was: *That is the sort of fine distinction that a married woman with children can afford to make.*

But she was right. Being alone is *not* the most awful thing in the world. You visit your museums and cultivate your interests and remind yourself how lucky you are not to be one of those spindly Sudanese children with flies beading their mouths. You make out To Do lists – reorganize linen cup-board, learn two sonnets. You dole out little treats to yourself – slices of ice-cream cake, concerts at Wigmore Hall. And then, every once in a while, you wake up and gaze out of the window at another bloody daybreak, and think, *I cannot do this any more. I cannot pull myself together again and spend the next fifteen hours of wakefulness fending off the fact of my own misery.*

People like Sheba think that they know what it's like to be lonely. They cast their minds back to the time they broke up with a boyfriend in 1975 and endured a whole month before meeting someone new. Or the week they spent in a Bavarian steel town when they were fifteen years old, visiting their greasy-haired German pen-pal and discovering that her hand-writing was the best thing about her. But about the drip drip of long-haul, no-end-in-sight solitude, they know nothing. They don't know what it is to construct an entire weekend around a visit to the launderette. Or to sit in a darkened flat on Halloween night, because you can't bear to expose your bleak evening to a crowd of jeering trick-or-treaters. Or to have the librarian smile pityingly and say, 'Goodness, you're a quick reader!' when you bring back seven books, read from cover to cover, a week after taking them out. They don't know what it is to be so chronically untouched that the accidental brush of a bus conductor's hand on your shoulder sends a jolt of longing straight to your groin. I have sat on park benches and tubes and schoolroom chairs, feeling the great store of unused, objectless love sitting in my belly like a stone until I was sure I would cry out and fall, flailing, to the ground. About all of this, Sheba and her like have no clue.

'So this is it,' Bangs said, with a little flourish, as he opened the front door of his flat. 'The bachelor pad!' The living room in which we were now standing smelled strongly of old fry-up. There was a gauze-like consistency to the air. An elderly yellow beanbag and a cheap metal chair sat in the middle of the floor facing a television and a shelving unit filled with videos. These four items – beanbag, chair, TV and shelving unit – constituted the sum total of the room's furnishings. 'Not much, but it's home,' Bangs said cheerfully, taking off his jacket and hanging it carefully on the chair.

'Do you think I could use your toilet?' I asked.

To get to Bangs's bathroom, I had to go through his bed-room. Here the fry-up smell gave way to another, equally strong scent of body – a sort of stale, hormonal mugginess. When I used to visit my father after my mother died, his unlaundered dressing gown gave off a similar odour. Bangs didn't have a proper bed, just a mattress on the floor and a very flat, defeated-looking duvet, dressed in a cover of almost sinister ugliness: navy octagons, mustard squiggles. I had a brief vision of Bangs purchasing it – standing clueless in the bed linen department of John Lewis while a dragon-lady assistant with a wire-wool beehive and a vast, iron-clad bra, assured him that it was a very 'masculine' choice.

In Bangs's bathroom he, or perhaps some previous inhabitant of the flat, had adorned the lid of the toilet with a cosy – a grimy, orange fur cover – which proved horribly damp to the touch. The sink had green water stains beneath its taps, and propped up in the bath tub there was a clothes horse hung with a collection of socks and briefs that had gone stiff and crackly as they dried. Adjacent to the tub there was a small, plastic counter. Here, set out with poignant symmetry, were the instruments of Bangs's toilette. A bar of Imperial Leather soap. A small bottle of Silvikrin hairspray. A tub of something called Krazy Hair. And a rather ancient grooming set, each faded-red-plastic item of which was imprinted with the words, *The Burgundy Collection*. It is bizarre, really, that spinsterhood is considered the uniquely pathetic destiny, when bachelors are the ones so fatally ill-equipped for a spouseless life.

On my return to the living room I did my best to appear unshocked, but perhaps my face betrayed something because Bangs, who was making coffee in his galley kitchen, giggled nervously and said, 'Find everything you needed, did you?'

I nodded and sat down on the chair. 'Is it all right for me to smoke in here?'

To my amazement Bangs winced as he came out with coffee cups. 'Oh,' he said in a grudging tone of concession, 'all right, then.' As if cigarette smoke could do anything other than improve his stinky little home. He went back to the kitchen to get me a saucer for my ash.

I noticed as I opened my pack that I was running low on cigarettes. I made a mental promise to ration the remaining ones carefully.

'So now,' Bangs said, handing me my coffee and sitting down opposite me on the beanbag, 'tell me, what kinds of things do you like to do with your spare time?'

I gave him a list of activities that I had engaged in at some time or another over the last five years. Reading, walking, listening to music. And then, because he seemed to be expecting more, I added swimming.

As soon as I said it, he sat up. 'Really?' he said. 'That's great. Where do you go? Local baths? Fabulous.'

The last time I swam, I was a teenager. In point of fact, I don't even own a swimming costume. But I hadn't been counting on Bangs paying attention to my answer. I had assumed that he had only asked the question as a polite route into talking about *his* spare time.

'Well, to tell the truth,' I said, 'I don't go that often . . .'

'What, do you go with Sheba?' Bangs asked.

'No . . .'

'Does she wear a bikini, then? Because I tell you what, she must get quite a lot of attention in a bikini . . .'

He proceeded to guffaw as if he had said something exceedingly witty and louche.

'I go swimming alone,' I said stonily, curiously protective of my lie now.

There was a longish silence, and then I said, 'And what about you, Brian? Do you have hobbies?'

The smile that had remained after his laughing fit, faded. 'Oh yeah, different things,' he said glumly. 'I'm football crazy, of course. Never miss an Arsenal home game. And I like comedy. I try to go to a comedy club fairly regularly.'

I nodded. It was hopeless. All hopeless.

'Oh, and I am completely and utterly bonkers about *Seinfeld*,' he said.

I nodded again.

'*Seinfeld*? You know? The American comedy series?' He gestured at the shelving unit. 'See all those videos there? Most of them are tapes of the show. I'm, like, a major fan. It's great, not one of those normal, corny American shows. All the plots are about silly little things that drive you mad in everyday life . . .' His loud, chirpy voice faltered.

I looked at my watch. 'Goodness . . .' I said, stubbing out my cigarette.

Bangs leaned forward out of his beanbag with sudden urgency. 'Can I tell you something, Barbara? Would you promise to keep it secret?'

'Well, I suppose so,' I said.

'No, I mean you've really got to promise.'

I took out another cigarette. 'Okay, I promise.'

All my life I have been the sort of person in whom people confide. And all my life I have been flattered by this role – grateful for the frisson of importance that comes with receiving privileged information. In recent years, however, I have noticed that my gratification is becoming diluted by a certain weary indignation. Why, I find myself silently asking my confiders, are you telling *me*? Of course, I know why, really. They tell me because they regard me as safe. Sheba, Bangs, all of them, they make their disclosures to me in the same spirit that they might tell a castrato or a priest – with a sense that I am so outside the loop, so remote from the doings of the great world, as to be defused of any possible threat. The number of secrets I receive is in inverse proportion to the number of secrets anyone expects me to have of my own. And this is the real source of my dismay. Being told secrets is not – never has been – a sign that I belong or that I matter. It is quite the opposite: confirmation of my irrelevance.

'The thing is, you see,' Bangs said, 'I've got a crush on someone. Someone at school.' He got up from the beanbag and began striding up and down the room.

I understood immediately. How could I have not seen it before? I did not try to stop him, though. There was something angry in me that wanted to play the thing out. 'Ah,' I said.

'Can you guess who?' he asked. He smiled coquettishly. If he had had a fan, he would have flicked it.

'Ummm . . .' I looked up at the ceiling, blinking. Pretending to think. 'Me?'

His face froze in bewilderment.

'Try not to look so repulsed, Brian,' I said.

He laughed. 'Oh you. You know I didn't mean it that way. As it happens, Barbara, I think you're a very attractive lady. You must have been ever so pretty when you were younger.'

I looked out of the window at the battered trees lining the street. They were bending creakily in the wind. While I was noticing the trees, I was thinking that in another second Bangs would understand how rude he had been and that then I would have to watch the embarrassment dawn on his face. But the moment passed. The trees outside continued their wan exercises.

'No, so come on,' Bangs said, 'shall I tell you?'

'Go ahead.'

'Don't laugh, all right, but the person I've got a crush on is Sheba.' He paused, waiting for a reaction. I gave none. 'Honestly, Barbara, I'm nuts about her,' he went on after a moment. 'I know she's married and everything, but I can't get her out of –'

'Brian,' I broke in, 'you offer me this information as if it were news – rather than a statement of what has been, for some months now, blindingly obvious to the entire staff. There is not a single one of your colleagues who has failed to observe your "crush" as you call it.'

'What?' Bangs said. He was standing directly in front of me now. The blood was rushing into his face – mottling his cheeks, crimsoning his ears, turning the shaving rash purple.

'Yes,' I said. 'The fact is, Brian, you've been making an awful fool of yourself. We've all been having a good laugh about your behaviour. It's bizarre that you didn't notice –'

'All right,' Bangs said in a tight voice. 'Don't go on.'

'Don't get angry,' I said. 'I'm only the messenger . . .'

'All right! Just shut up!' he shouted. 'Shut up, will you?' He stepped towards me. I could see the beadlets of sweat on his nose. 'Sheba likes me,' he said quietly. 'I know she does.'

There are certain people in whom you can detect the seeds of madness – seeds that have remained dormant only because the people in question have lived relatively comfortable, middle-class lives. They function perfectly well in the world, but you can imagine, given a nasty parent, or a prolonged bout of unemployment, how their potential for craziness might have been realized – how their seeds might have sprouted little green shoots of weirdness, or even, with the right sort of anti-nurture, blossomed into full-blown lunacy. It occurred to me now, as I watched him sink down into his beanbag, that Brian Bangs was one of these people.

This realization, if nothing else, ought to have deterred me from saying what I said next. But it didn't. 'Oh Brian,' I cooed, 'don't tell me you have entertained hopes of reciprocation? That's so *sweet*, Brian . . .'

Bangs put his fingers in his ears like a little boy. 'Shut up!' he exclaimed. 'I know she's married. I thought . . .'

'Well . . . But it's not *just* that she's married. I mean – the truth is, Brian, you don't fit her type.'

'Oh, you're wrong there,' he said, shaking his head confidently. 'Sheba's not a snob. She'll talk to anyone, Sheba.'

'I wasn't referring to social class, Brian. It's not that you're not posh enough . . .'

'What then? What do you mean?'

'It's just . . . Oh, nothing.' I chuckled.

'*What?*'

'Well, it's more a question of age. Sheba likes younger men, you know. *Much* younger men.' I paused a moment. 'I mean, you *are* aware of her unusually *close* relationship with one of the Year Eleven boys?'

Bangs's face seemed briefly to inflate before crumpling in on itself. '*No,*' he whispered.

Chance is everything, isn't it? I so nearly didn't go to Bangs's flat and then, when I did, I so nearly left before I said anything damaging. It seems to me that an enormous amount of vice – and virtue for that matter – is a matter of circumstance. It's entirely possible that if my cigarettes had run out sooner, or if Bangs hadn't been quite so provokingly abject, Sheba would never have been betrayed at all. Evil will out, my mother used to say, but I rather think she was wrong about that. Evil can stay in, minding its own business for eternity, if the right situation doesn't arise.

After I left Bangs's flat I stood in the street, trying to collect myself. I wanted to go home – bury myself under my blankets, block out the fact of what I had just done. But then I remembered Portia. Poor Portia! I went to get my car and drove to the vet's dangerously fast.

'She's not at all well, I'm afraid,' the vet said as soon as I was shown into his surgery. 'The radiation doesn't appear to have been as effective as we had hoped.' He looked at me with the principled indifference that people in positions of medical authority often affect when delivering bad news. 'She's a very sick girl.'

'But you said she was going to outlast me . . .' I murmured. I had the momentary, childish hope that I could shame him into reverting to his earlier, cheerier prognosis.

'Well, these things are not always easy to predict,' he said defensively.

'Can you operate?' I asked. 'How long has she got?' (How smoothly we slip into the idiom of hospital melodrama!)

The vet grimaced. 'No, there would be no point in operating. The X-rays show the tumour to be pretty big. In a human, you could cut out a chunk of colon and give the patient a colostomy, but obviously that wouldn't be appropriate here.'

'Cats can't have colostomy bags,' I said dumbly.

'That's right,' the vet said. He was standing in an odd way, as if he'd forgotten his natural stance. He probably thought I was going to make a scene. 'So,' he went on, after a short pause, 'the question is, what do you want to do?'

'I don't know. Is she in a lot of pain?'

'At this point, yes, a fair amount I would say.'

We both looked at Portia. Her chest was rising and falling like the Sleeping Beauty that they used to have in Madame Tussaud's. 'Could you . . . do you think you could give her something for it?' I asked. 'For the pain?'

'Yes, that's possible. I . . . Look, I can give you something but I have to be honest with you, I don't think medicating her is the long-term solution here. To completely cancel the pain, we'd probably have to drug her so much she'd be semi-comatose anyway.'

'I see.' It was possible, I realized, that I would cry after all.

'So you . . . you would advise putting her to sleep right now?'

'Well . . .' The door opened and the vet's assistant looked in. Portia shifted slightly at the sound. 'Give us a minute,' the vet said, and the assistant, shooting me a deferential glance, backed out again. He must have told her.

There was a pause. 'I understand,' I said. 'It wouldn't be fair to keep her hanging on. I know that. I'm just wondering . . . the thing is, I don't want to just, you know . . . put her down now. Would it be all right if I took her home for the night? To say goodbye? You could give her something to soothe her and I'd bring her back in tomorrow. Would that be okay?'

He nodded, relieved. The old bag wasn't going to make a fuss. 'That would be fine,' he said. 'In the meantime, I'll give her some morphine. That should make her more comfortable.' He pressed a little buzzer and the assistant came back in.

While the two of them prepared the injection, I thought of something Sheba had told me once about taking her children for their infant shots. They had always been unheeding up until the very last moment, she said, and then, when the needle pierced their skin, a terrible look of surprised accusation would come over their faces. 'Very grown-up, it was. As if they were saying, "*Et tu*, Mummy?"' Portia was not up to that sort of recrimination. She hardly flinched when the needle went in. And when I picked her up to put her back in her cage, she didn't resist at all; just issued a low, stoned, yowl and allowed herself to be slid in.

On the way back to the flat I picked up some sausages and a half pint of cream at LoPrice, and when I got home I made a little bed of cushions and blankets in the kitchen so that Portia could lie comfortably and watch me while I cooked. I chopped the sausages into very small pieces and then fried them in butter – an old treat. But all of this was more for my benefit than for Portia's. It was obvious that she wasn't well enough for an extravagant last supper. When I laid the sausages before her, she remained motionless, gazing at them dully. I watched her for a bit and then I bent down and picked her up. There was a pale murmur of displeasure here, but no struggle. I took her into the bedroom and tried sitting cross-legged on the bed with her in my lap. She wasn't happy with this, so I let her arrange herself on the counterpane and then I curled myself around her, very gently scratching her under her chin. Her eyelids fell but did not quite close – her customary, slightly creepy expression of pleasure – and presently she began to purr.

Then, at last, I did cry. Although, because mourning – even for dumb animals – is never the focussed, unadulterated business we pretend it to be, my tears were only partly for Portia. Once the engine of grief was revved up, it began ranging, as grief tends to, about the crowded territory of my other discontents and regrets. I cried from guilt and remorse that I had not been a better, kinder pet owner. (All the times I had rubbed Portia's nose in her own mess when she didn't make it to the litter box.) I cried because I had dealt what seemed to me an almost certainly fatal blow to my friendship with Sheba. I cried because I had been desperate enough to consider a liaison with a ludicrous man who collected baseball jackets and even he had rejected me. I cried because I was the sort of woman at whom girls in the hairdresser's giggle. I cried, finally, at the indignity of my crying; the sheer stupidity of being a spinster blubbing in her bedroom on a Saturday night.

It didn't take very long. After about five minutes, the self-consciousness that preys on the lone weeper crept up on me. I began observing the rhythms of my sobs and the damp tracks that my tears had made in Portia's fur. Shortly after that, my commitment to my own misery began to wane and I stopped being able to focus. In the end, I turned on the television and, for half an hour before I fell asleep, I watched the evening news, utterly dry-eyed.

Fourteen

In the days immediately following my lunch date, I went over what I had said to Bangs countless times, trying to calculate the likelihood of his passing the information on to anyone else. The afternoon on which I buried Portia, I returned to my flat and composed at least three confession-letters to Sheba, all of which I ended up burning in the kitchen sink. My depression returned now, freshly invigorated by guilt. I found myself plagued by a slew of minor health problems. At night, when I got into bed, my right leg would twitch and judder uncontrollably for hours at a time, making sleep a greater challenge than usual. I acquired a constant, low-level head-ache. Shortly after I arrived in Eastbourne for the Christmas holidays, my chin broke out in a spotty rash and my toenails became infected with an unsightly fungus. Clearly, these were psychosomatic responses to stress. But, at the time, I was convinced that they were the wages of sin; retribution for my betrayal of Sheba. I was encouraged in this superstitious interpretation by the fact that none of the remedies recom-mended by the local Eastbourne chemist appeared to have the slightest impact on my ailments. On Christmas Day, one of my blackened toenails fell off and I wept hysterically in Marje's downstairs toilet, convinced that I had become leprous.

Polly ran away from home on Boxing Day. I was still down at my sister's at the time and I didn't pick up Sheba's message until I returned to London the next day. As soon as I heard Sheba's voice saying, 'There's a bit of a crisis here,' I assumed the worst. It was something of a relief, I confess, to discover a few moments later that Polly was missing. I rang back immediately.

'Oh, Barbara!' Sheba said when she came to the phone. 'I'm sorry to have alarmed you. Everything's okay. Polly's been found. The silly girl ran away to her grandmother's. I'm flying up to Scotland tomorrow to collect her.'

She was going alone, she said. Richard was staying behind in London to look after Ben. I asked her if she wanted me to accompany her and at first she declined. Her mother was not someone she imposed on friends, she said, unless absolutely necessary. But then we talked a bit more and she began to have second thoughts. It would be nice to have company, she mused. And of course, it *would* be helpful to have my car. Did I really not mind? No, no, of course I didn't.

When I went to pick her up at the house in the morning, she looked rather haggard and puffy-eyed. On the street, before we got into the car, I stopped and took her hand. 'I'm so sorry,' I said.

She shook her head. 'Oh, it's all going to be all right. She's just in a state. Ten years from now, we'll remember this as a stage.'

'No, not about Polly,' I said. 'I meant I was sorry about what happened between us. In your basement. I'm afraid I was upset about Portia.'

'Oh, that,' she said. 'Forget about it. How is your hip now?'

'Fine. But –' I pinched my nose in an effort to stop the tears from coming ' – well, Portia died, you know. I had to have her put down just before Christmas.'

'Oh Barbara!' She took my hands as if to pull me into an embrace.

'Yes, it's very sad,' I said, holding her off. 'But there it is.'

'I'm so sorry, Barbara.'

'Come on.' I opened the car door. 'Let's be off.'

I had come with the intention of telling her about Bangs. I knew that it had to be done. But sitting in the car, I could feel my courage slipping away. The prospect of her anger made me weak. How to even start? *There is something I must tell you, Sheba . . .* I couldn't.

'What's up with your chin?' Sheba asked, as we drove through west London. She leaned across to examine my rash. 'Is it an allergic reaction to something?'

'No, no,' I murmured, batting her away. 'I'm just run-down, that's all.'

'God, I know how you feel. I'm *exhausted*.'

I nodded sympathetically. 'You must have been worried to death . . .'

'Well I was, yes,' Sheba said. She paused. 'Of course I was also up very late last night with Steven.' She grinned naughtily.

'Oh,' I said.

'I'm afraid I did a rather dangerous thing,' she went on. 'I sneaked him into the house after Richard and Ben had gone to bed. We were in the basement together for an hour.'

I glanced at her, less astonished at the risk she had taken than at the evident satisfaction with which she reported it. 'Steven was wearing a hideous sweater that his parents had given him for Christmas,' she went on blithely. 'Powder blue. V-neck. *Horrid* . . .'

'Please, Sheba,' I said. 'Can we not talk about Connolly now?'

She shrugged. 'Fine.'

'No, I don't mean to be . . .'

'No, no. I understand. I shan't mention him again.'

She gazed out of the side window.

'You know,' I said at length, 'I had lunch with Bangs the other day.'

'Oh?' Sheba looked at me. 'When?'

'On the Saturday before term ended. He –'

'On the *weekend*? Barbara!'

I blushed. 'No, well, he –'

'No, that's *great*, Barbara! Did you have fun?'

'It wasn't like that. It was just a casual thing.'

'You *are* a sly dog. No wonder I haven't heard from you lately!'

I hit the steering wheel in irritation. 'For goodness' sake, Sheba, don't patronize me! I'm not *quite* so desperate as to regard Bangs as a potential boyfriend.'

'Oh.'

'No, the only reason I bring it up at all, is that . . .' I paused. She was half turned in her seat now, looking at me intently. 'The thing is, I got the sense that Bangs knows about you and Connolly.' I hadn't planned this last-moment evasion. I surprised myself with it. But even as I was urging myself to stop, go back, correct the lie, Sheba's mouth and eyes were growing round.

'What? No! How could he?' she whispered.

Tell her the truth, I ordered myself. *Tell her what you did.*

But she was already speaking again, in an anguished, fearful rush. 'What do you mean "got the sense"? Did he *say* he knew?'

'I . . . I don't know how he knows or exactly what he knows,' I said, 'but he dropped some heavy hints that he knew something.' *Too late, now. Can't go back.*

'What hints? What did he say? Tell me.' Sheba clapped her hand to her forehead and kept it there. In spite of myself, I was mildly gratified by her horror.

'Well, he said something about "our mutual friend" having "an unusual relationship" with one of the pupils.'

'Fuck! Was it clear he meant me?'

'Who else would he have meant?'

'Why didn't you tell me before now? What did you say?'

'Oh, I played dumb, of course. I said I didn't know what he was talking about.'

'Tell me *exactly* what he said. How did he bring it up?'

'I can't give you line for line dialogue, Sheba. We were eating lunch and talking generally about school and then he said something like, "I notice that our mutual friend seems to be very close to one of the pupils."'

'He said "close to"? Or "unusual relationship"? Which one? I can't believe you didn't tell me this before, Barbara.'

'Er, both I think. He said, "close to" and then I said, "What are you talking about?" and then he said, "Well, our friend is conducting a rather unusual relationship with one of the Year Elevens." Something like that.'

'What sort of tone did he use? Did he seem disapproving?'

'Well, he didn't seem delighted about it.'

'Oh God. Oh *Christ*. Did you get the feeling he had proof? Or was it just a hunch of his?'

'I couldn't say, Sheba. He seemed pretty sure. Look, I didn't tell you until now, because I didn't want to worry you.'

'Worry me! What were you thinking?'

'I wanted you to have a nice Christmas . . .'

'Oh Barbara. Oh *fuck*. This is bad.'

'I know.'

'How *did* he find out? Do you think he's going to tell?'

'I don't know. He didn't say he was going to. But Sheba, I think you really do have to consider putting a stop to this thing, now.'

Sheba pressed the heels of her hands into her eyes. 'Bloody fucking Bangs,' she said.

The plane to Scotland was full of people returning home for New Year's and the mood on board was festive. We were made to wait half an hour on the runway, during which time several passengers broke out flasks of whiskey and began singing. Behind the galley curtains, even the flight attendants were taking sneaky sips from little paper cups. Sheba, visibly agitated by the news I had just imparted, found the general gaiety irritating. When the captain came on the tannoy to give a chatty explanation for the delay and to thank us for our patience, she turned to me and said with uncharacteristic vehemence, 'Why is he thanking me? I'm *not* being patient.'

Soon after the plane took off, a female flight attendant came tinkling down the aisle with a trolley, offering sandwiches and drinks. 'Meat or cheese?' she asked Sheba. Sheba queried the identity of the meat – 'Is it beef, or, or what?' she asked – but the flight attendant only sighed. 'That'll be cheese, then,' she said and dumped a triangular, plastic pack on Sheba's tray table. 'She's drunk,' Sheba hissed as the woman walked away.

We took a taxi from Edinburgh to Peebles. This was an extravagant thing to do, but Sheba said that the train would be too slow. She was in a hurry now to get back to London and talk to Connolly. In the cab, I tried to distract her by asking about her mother. She was not very forthcoming at first, but after some coaxing she became quite animated on the subject.

Her relationship with her mother had never been good, she said. Eddie had been the favourite child. She had always been made to feel that she was a failure. 'I didn't go to Oxford and then I completely messed up by *marrying* someone who didn't go to Oxford. Mummy has always spoken about Richard in this commiserating tone – as if it's generally understood that in the great egg-and-spoon race of spouse-getting, he's a third prize. She's an enormous intellectual snob, Mummy. A lot of wives of academics are but, in Mummy's case, it's particularly pathetic. She's got absolutely nothing to be snobby about. Her only adult accomplishment is having organized children's walking tours of "Historical North London" in the early seventies. And even then, her friend Yolande did most of the research.' We both laughed at this.

'The thing is,' Sheba went on, 'Mummy essentially pities anybody who wasn't married to Ronald Taylor. When Daddy was alive, she clung to this idea that Richard hero-worshipped him. She made a great thing of fending Richard off, as though, had she let down her guard for a second, he would immediately have started slobbering over Daddy and trying to get his autograph or something. It was mad. I mean, economics bores Richard and he couldn't have cared less about Daddy. But you couldn't tell Mummy that. Whenever Daddy told an anecdote, she would place a heavy palm on Richard's knee, as if to console him for the miserable misfortune of not being Saint Ronald.'

'Do you think,' I asked Sheba, 'that your mother will approve of me?'

'What?' Sheba looked startled. 'Oh, don't worry about it. She'll hardly notice you. She'll be much too busy getting at me.'

Mrs Taylor's 'little cottage' on the outskirts of Peebles was in fact a Georgian manor house with a couple of acres of land for its back yard. Sheba and I were standing in the driveway, getting our bags out of the car, when Mrs Taylor emerged on the front doorstep.

'Ah, I thought I heard you,' she said. 'Come in! I've just made tea.' She was dressed in a shapeless Aran sweater and stirruped ski-pants that had gone baggy at the knee. Her beaky face was framed by a Joan-of-Arc pudding bowl.

'This is Barbara, my friend from work,' Sheba said.

Mrs Taylor nodded at me coolly. Her eyes were vast and staring. 'Hello,' she murmured.

We carried our bags up the stairs and into the front hall.

'Was the journey absolutely bloody?' Mrs Taylor asked.

Sheba shrugged. 'No, no, not too bad.' She was looking at Polly's Doctor Marten boots which were lying underneath the coat rack.

'She's upstairs in her room,' Mrs Taylor said, following Sheba's gaze.

'Which one's that?' Sheba seemed vaguely taken aback to find that Polly had already been allocated her own room.

'The attic,' her mother said. 'I've had the walls repapered a marvellous tartan. Polly took one look at it and said that was where she wanted to stay.'

'What's she doing?' Sheba asked.

'Sleeping,' Mrs Taylor said. 'Golly, how she sleeps! I'd quite forgotten about the amazing phenomenon of adolescent torpor.'

Sheba grimaced. 'She never let *me* sleep at three in the afternoon,' she whispered as her mother turned and began walking away down the hall.

'Now, darling,' Mrs Taylor was saying, 'let me get you a cup of tea and we can have a nice chat before she wakes up.' She led us into her living room – a chilly, rather depressing place with grubby-looking kilims on the walls. There were one or two good pieces of antique furniture including a nice dresser, but everything else in the room seemed to have been purchased from office supply shops. Mrs Taylor advanced suddenly on her daughter and plucked, in a rather hostile fashion, at her waist. 'Is that a new belt?' she asked.

'Yes,' Sheba said. 'I got it at a shop round the corner from us. It's nice, isn't it?'

'Hmm,' Mrs Taylor said. 'You're not wearing a slip again. You'll have to borrow one of mine if we go out. I don't want you frightening Clem in the post office. Now sit down, dear, and let me get you some tea.'

'The belt got her in a temper,' Sheba whispered when her

mother had left the room. 'Mummy never buys new clothes. She thinks it's vulgar to take an interest in that sort of thing. When I was a teenager and I was first beginning to be interested in make-up and all that, she absolutely tortured me. If I even showered more than once a day, it was a major issue. Excessive hygiene is very lower-middle class in her book . . .'

'It was such a pity you couldn't come for Christmas this year,' Mrs Taylor called out from the kitchen. 'We had *such* a nice time.'

'Did you?' Sheba called back. She rolled her eyes at me.

Eddie and his family always go to Peebles for Christmas and Boxing Day but Sheba hasn't been up for the last five years. Her excuse is that Richard needs to spend Christmas with his daughters. (Marcia and the girls go to Richard and Sheba's for Christmas dinner.) But it is only an excuse. The truth, she says, is that Christmas is far too important a holiday to have it spoiled by her mother.

There was a long pause during which we sat listening to Mrs Taylor clank about with teacups. 'You don't want anything to eat, do you?' she shouted after a bit. Her tone was discouraging, faintly disgusted.

'No thanks, Mum,' Sheba called back. She turned to me. 'Would you like something, Barbara?'

'No, no. I'm fine . . .'

'I haven't got much in,' her mother went on. 'But if you need something, I've still got some cold turkey left.'

'No, no,' Sheba said, 'we're not hungry.'

There was another long pause. Then Sheba called out, 'Mum, I just want to say, I really appreciate your being so great about all this.'

'Don't be silly.' Mrs Taylor re-emerged now, bearing a tray. 'I love having Polly here. And God only knows, I understand how difficult it is when one's children decide they hate one.'

Sheba folded her arms. 'I wasn't aware that Polly hated me.'

Mrs Taylor set the tray on the table. 'Oh darling, don't be touchy,' she said. 'Have a biscuit. You're clearly not her *favourite* person at the moment. Polly's going through an absolutely typical teenage stage. You mustn't take it personally.' She smiled, revealing her rather daunting, tombstone teeth.

Sheba gobbled up a biscuit furiously.

'So, are you familiar with this part of the world at all?' Mrs Taylor asked, turning to me.

'Well,' I said, 'I've spent some time in Dumfries . . .'

'I see.'

'But no . . . I don't know Scotland very well.'

There was a dank pause. 'And do you have children?' she asked.

'No. No I don't.'

'Oh.'

'I have a niece and nephew.'

Mrs Taylor studied me for a moment in silence and then abruptly turned back to her daughter. 'I gather the weather in London has been beastly,' she said.

'Yes,' Sheba said. 'Hailstones, the lot. Actually, I quite like it.'

'Oh!' Mrs Taylor pressed her lips together as if to indicate that she thought Sheba was being perverse, but that she was not going to be provoked.

'I expect Richard finds it very oppressive, though,' she said, still hopeful of finding someone whom the weather was making miserable. '*Poor* Richard, cooped up in his study. How is the book coming?'

'Oh, Richard's all right,' Sheba said. 'He's taking a break from the book right now, to write a conference paper. He bought himself a little portable radiator for the study so he's happy as Larry.'

'My goodness. How grand.' (According to Sheba, one of Mrs Taylor's favourite themes has always been the inexplicable extravagance of her daughter and son-in-law's lifestyle.) 'And how's Ben?'

'Good,' Sheba said. I could see she was silently gnashing over the radiator comment. 'He's got a . . .' She evidently decided against telling her mother about Ben's girlfriend. '. . . a lot of things on at the moment. He's on very good form.' She sat up. 'Look, don't you think I should go and wake Polly? Let her know I'm here?'

'No, darling, don't do that,' Mrs Taylor said. 'She'll be horribly grumpy if you wake her up.'

Sheba slumped. 'She's going to be grumpy whatever I do,' she muttered.

Her mother cocked her head and tutted. 'Now, now.'

Sheba ate another biscuit. And then another.

Presently, her mother said, 'You know she thinks you're having an affair?'

Some people live in constant fear of having their secrets found out; others have a kind of arrogant certainty that anything they wish to keep private will remain so. Sheba belongs to the latter group. It amazed her – briefly enraged her, I think – that her daughter should have succeeded in knowing more about her than she had chosen to tell.

'Why on earth would she think that?' she asked, laughing.

Later, she told me that she had read an article in a magazine about how one could spot liars by watching for certain involuntary expressions and gestures associated with duplicity. In responding to her mother she had tried very hard to look her in the eye and keep her hands perfectly still.

'I don't know, darling,' her mother said, looking straight back at her. 'Female intuition?'

'Oh, for God's sake,' Sheba said, 'how preposterous. The

fact is, Polly comes from a very happy, stable home. She obviously feels she needs something to justify her teenaged horridness, so she is now resorting to invention –' She broke off suddenly. Somewhere during her last sentence she had turned her gaze to the floor, and begun massaging a biscuit into dust on the tablecloth.

Mrs Taylor studied the destroyed biscuit in silence. 'She seems to think that you tell Richard you've been working in your studio when you haven't,' she said. She glanced at me. 'Sorry about this, Barbara. Family business. Would you like another cup of tea?'

Sheba jerked forward into Mrs Taylor's startled face. She was wagging her index finger. 'No,' she shouted. '*No*. I won't tolerate this, Mother. It's very decent of you to have put Polly up and I'm glad you've developed this new interest in your granddaughter's welfare, but you haven't earned the right to start interrogating me. You're not going to start playing family bloody counsellor at this stage in the game.'

Mrs Taylor shut her eyes as if in pain and shook her head slowly. 'Darling,' she said, when Sheba had finished, 'what *is* the matter with you?' She looked at me. 'I'm *so* sorry about this.'

'Oh give it a rest, Mother,' Sheba said. '*I'm on to you*, all right? I know you think you've formed some special bond with Polly now. But I can guarantee you, the only reason Polly came here in the first place was because she knew it was the best way to irritate the shit out of me.'

Sheba stopped for a moment, as if registering amazement at her own courage. 'And I know you'd love to sit here all day,' she continued, 'finding out who I'm shagging and ferrying tactful little messages between me and Polly. But it's not going to happen.'

Mrs Taylor was looking away across the room now. Her

face was crumpled in dismay. Sheba misread this expression at first. For a moment, she told me later, she was persuaded that her rage had made an impact – that her mother had been listening for once and that some sort of breakthrough had occurred. In one of those mad, split-second vaults of the imagination, she pictured her mother and herself finally hashing out all their old resentments: finding, in the autumn of their relationship, a new, warm way to be with one another. Her mother would come to London on weekends. They would visit galleries together, have fun lunches at Italian restaurants, discuss men, swap recipes . . .

Then she caught sight of Polly standing in the doorway.

'"Shagging", Mum?' Polly said in her stagy, teenager's deadpan. '"Shagging"?' She turned on her heel and ran upstairs, slamming the door behind her.

'Polly, darling . . .' Mrs Taylor called out, getting up to follow her.

'No, Mum,' Sheba said grimly. 'I'll go.'

After she had left the room, Mrs Taylor and I sat at the table, exchanging embarrassed smiles for a minute or so. Then Mrs Taylor stood up. 'I think I had better go and check on them,' she said.

I got up to go with her, but she gestured me down again. 'No, no. You're not needed,' she said rudely. I waited for what seemed like a very long time after she had left the room, tapping my fingers on the table. I could not help but regard this latest development with some relief. If Sheba's own daughter suspected her of adultery, my telling Bangs was surely a less heinous betrayal than I had believed. Who knew how many other people suspected the affair?

After five minutes or so, I heard shouting coming from the top of the house. I sat for a bit longer, uncertain of what to do, and then I decided to countermand Mrs Taylor's orders and go up. As I climbed the stairs (carpeted with a shockingly filthy coir runner) Polly's screams began to resolve themselves into comprehensible sentences. 'You don't care about me or Ben or Dad,' I heard. And then, 'You try to make out that you're so nice and sweet.' And finally, 'You're a bitch!'

On the second floor of the house, I found Mrs Taylor standing at the foot of a ladder that led to the attic. She turned when she heard me, and fixed me with her formidable poached-egg stare. 'Really!' she said. 'You're not wanted . . .'

There was no point in debating with her; I simply began to climb the ladder. This was trickier than I had anticipated. The ladder was very steep and I was wearing a skirt. As I ascended in rather ungainly fashion, I was keenly aware of Mrs Taylor gazing angrily up at my knickers from below. When I reached the top, my head was poking into a tiny slant-ceilinged room. Sheba stood in one corner. Polly was lying on a bed in another. Mrs Taylor's new tartan wallpaper was a lurid shade of red and everything in the room – including Sheba and Polly – was bathed in its reflective glow. 'Sheba?' I said, peering over the top of the ladder. 'Is there anything I can do?'

'Oh, not fucking *her*,' Polly exclaimed. The crimson cast of her face gave her a dramatic presence. She looked like a little she-devil.

'Don't you dare speak like that to one of my friends!' Sheba shouted. I was flattered to hear her so angry on my account.

'Oh fuck you,' Polly said.

Sheba folded her arms. 'Please don't talk to me like that, Polly,' she said.

'Why not?' Polly demanded.

'Because it's not what I deserve.'

'And what do you deserve, then?'

'Well, a bit of respect for a start.'

'Yeah?'

Sheba went over and sat on the bed. Polly swerved away from her. 'Piss off!' she shouted.

Sheba looked over at me and smiled. 'You know, Barbara,' she said, 'I think this might be easier if we were left alone.'

'Of course,' I nodded. 'I'll be downstairs if you need me.'

When I reached the bottom of the ladder, Mrs Taylor looked at me triumphantly. 'I *did* tell you not to . . .' she said.

'Mum?' Sheba called from above.

'Yes, darling?' Mrs Taylor shouted.

'You too, please, Mum. If you don't mind.'

'Oh, but darling . . .' Mrs Taylor called back.

'Please, Mum. Just give us a minute.'

Reluctantly, Mrs Taylor followed me down the stairs. She had the tread of an ogress. The whole house vibrated as she descended.

At the first-floor landing, I stopped. 'Come along, Barbara,' Mrs Taylor said as she came up behind me. 'I'll show you where you're sleeping tonight. I've put a camp bed in Ronald's study for you.'

'I think I'd better wait here, for a bit,' I said.

'Don't be silly, dear, that won't be necessary.' She grasped at my elbow. 'Come on.'

I stayed where I was. 'No, I think I ought to stay. Just in case.'

Mrs Taylor studied me with an expression of irritated surprise. She was not accustomed to being disobeyed. 'Just in case *what*?' she asked coldly.

'In case I'm needed.'

'Oh!' She chuckled angrily. 'Well, Barbara, I hardly think –'

The end of her sentence was cut off by the commencement

of high-pitched screaming from above. It was Polly. The two of us immediately started up the stairs again – me first, Mrs Taylor in hot pursuit. When we got to the ladder, there was a brief, somewhat undignified struggle as to who would go first. I won.

At the top of the ladder, I found Sheba and Polly in roughly the positions that I had left them, except that Polly was now sitting up on her bed, holding her hand to her cheek. When she saw me, she broke off from shrieking for a moment. 'She hit me!' she gasped.

'For God's sake, shut up, Polly!' Sheba said.

Polly leaned forward now and made a clumsy effort to claw at her mother's face. But Sheba was quicker than she was. She grasped Polly by her thin little wrists and held her at arm's length. For a few moments, the two of them rocked back and forth on the bed, as in some children's game.

'Stop it at once. Both of you!' I shouted, but neither of them paid any notice.

Sheba, gaining a momentary advantage, pushed Polly back down into a recumbent position on the bed.

'You cow,' Polly panted. 'I hate –'

Before she could finish, Sheba swooped down and slapped her again. It looked to me as if she put some force into it. When her hand met Polly's cheek, there was a distinct and not unsatisfactory *thwack* and Polly's cries seemed to rise at least an octave higher.

Mrs Taylor was scrambling off the top of the ladder now. 'Sheba!' she shouted. 'Sheba! What have you done?'

Sheba looked at her mother quite blankly and then she burst into tears. 'Oh bugger you all!' she cried. She walked over to the ladder and began to climb down. I followed her of course, but when I reached the top-floor landing, she called up to me to leave her alone. Then she ran down the rest of the stairs and shortly after that I heard the front door slam.

I hovered on the stairs for a while, uncertain of what to do. I opted, finally, for going back down to the living room where, for the next hour or so, I sat on the sofa, flicking through back issues of the *New York Review Of Books*. (Mrs Taylor never reads them, according to Sheba; she's just too vain to cancel her late husband's subscription.) Polly and Mrs Taylor remained upstairs. Presently, rain began to speckle the living-room window. I was rather hungry by now and had started to think wistfully of Mrs Taylor's turkey left-overs. But I didn't want to risk being caught helping myself, so I stayed where I was and read a very long article about the Balkans.

By the time Sheba came back, I was ravenous. I hurried out to the hall as soon as I heard the front door click. 'Where are they?' she whispered when she saw me. Her face was ruddy and her hair was sticking to her scalp like a cloche. I pointed upwards. 'Oh God,' she said. 'I *am* sorry, Barbara. I didn't realize I was letting you in for this.'

I shook my head. 'No apology needed. Come on, let's get you out of those wet things.'

She sat down on the stairs and I began pulling off her shoes. 'Would you be a love, Barbara,' she said, 'and call the airline for me? Find out if we can get on an earlier flight tomorrow?'

I was just beginning to dial directory enquiries for the number when there was a loud cough from the first-floor landing. Looking up, we saw Polly, staring down at us. 'I'm not going back with you, you know,' she said.

'Oh yes you are,' Sheba replied.

Mrs Taylor appeared now, at her granddaughter's side. 'Perhaps,' she said, 'it would be for the best, Sheba, if she stayed here a bit longer.'

'*No*,' Sheba said.

The two of them retreated murmuringly. I went ahead and called the airline, made the arrangements for an earlier flight. When I'd finished, the two of us sat listening to the faint mewlings of Polly in her grandmother's bedroom and the thunderous rumblings of my stomach. After a while, Sheba said dully, 'I don't suppose I would ever have had children if I'd known it was going to be like this.'

Later, after everyone had gone to bed, I got up to use the toilet and found Sheba in the hall. She was sitting in the dark, dialling a number on the phone. She quickly replaced the receiver when she saw me.

'Is everything all right?' I asked.

'No,' Sheba said. 'Of course it isn't. You know it isn't.'

'No, I meant . . . you were on the phone. It's so late. I thought maybe something was wrong at home.'

Sheba shook her head. 'No.' She paused. Then she dropped her head into her hands. 'I was trying to ring Steven,' she said.

The taxi that took us to the airport arrived at six the next morning. Mrs Taylor was still in her dressing gown when she came out onto the doorstep to bid us goodbye. As the car moved off down the driveway, Polly, who was sporting a faint red weal on her left cheek, knelt on the back seat and waved plaintively through the rear window at Mrs Taylor's receding figure. Sheba, sitting up in front, stared stonily ahead.

When we got back to Highgate, I insisted on seeing the two of them into the house. As we entered the front hall, Richard was running downstairs from his study, three steps at a time. 'Polly!' he cried, hugging his daughter to him. 'Darling, please don't ever do that again. We were so scared . . .' He held her away from him to look at her. 'What happened to your face?'

'I hit her,' Sheba said quickly. 'We were having a row.'

Stirred by the recollection of her sufferings, Polly pressed her face against Richard's chest and began to sob. Richard stared at Sheba with a puzzled expression.

'What?' Sheba said to him, irritably. 'Oh, for God's sake!'

She turned to me. 'Barbara, thank you so much for everything. You must be getting home now.'

I offered to stay awhile and help prepare supper, but she was adamant. 'You've done more than enough,' she said, leading me to the front door.

We kissed goodbye and I left. Just as I got to the bottom of the front steps, she came back out again. 'Barbara!' she called. 'You will let me know if you hear anything more from Bangs, won't you?'

I nodded. 'Of course.'

After I went home, Sheba went straight up to her bedroom and rang Connolly's pager. She waited for five minutes, but he did not call, and when she came downstairs again Polly was huddled with Richard in the sitting room, recounting in a tremulous whisper Sheba's terrible behaviour the night before. Silently, Sheba picked up her handbag and coat and left the house.

For the next three hours, she rode aimlessly through London on her bicycle. At first she stopped every fifteen minutes or so to ring Connolly's pager, but she gave up after a while. He must have turned the pager off, she decided, or else have left it at home. It was two days before New Year's Eve and London was still in its post-Christmas lull. The streets were almost empty. There was a sharp, silvery quality to the air, and when Sheba breathed in deeply, she felt as if she were inhaling splinters. Slowly, as the afternoon wore on, a freezing fog descended. The light on Sheba's bicycle was not working and she began to keep, where possible, to the pavements. Occasionally she would encounter pedestrians – bundled-up figures looming suddenly out of the soupy grey. One woman called out 'Happy New Year' as she passed. A little while later, a man stopped and cursed at Sheba, with startling passion, for not having a light on her bicycle.

By five o'clock, she was frozen. She rode through the deserted City, looking for a café that was open. In Clerkenwell, she found one – a cramped, overheated place full of cooking fug and the tinny clatter of cutlery. She ordered eggs on toast and a cup of tea and then, as she peered through the café's misted-up windows at the dark street outside, she considered what to do next. She ought to go home, she told herself – placate her peevish daughter, explain herself to her reproachful husband. She knew they would be worried about her by now. But she couldn't. To go home without at least speaking to Connolly would be intolerable, she felt. Somewhere in the back of her head, there was a conviction that if she didn't manage to talk to Connolly that night, she never would again. Then an idea came to her. She would go to Connolly's house! She could not present herself at his front door, of course. But she could call up at his window; throw pebbles if necessary. As her plan took shape, the gloom that had been hanging over her throughout the afternoon fell away. She grew exhilarated at the prospect of seeing Connolly. She paid for her meal and left the café.

It was a long ride to Connolly's estate and when she got there, she spent a frustrating half-hour getting lost in the maze of buildings. By the time she found his square, she was quite worn out. She went up the back alley, as she had done the first time with Connolly, before remembering that his bedroom was on the other side of the house. She turned and wheeled her bicycle round to the front. When she saw a light on in his window, she let out a small yelp of happiness. At last, a lucky break.

She stood looking up for a few minutes, willing Connolly to sense her presence. After a while, she called his name quietly. She was uncertain how to pitch her voice and at first it came out as a broken squawk. She kept on. *Steeee-ven. Steee-ven.* There was no sign of Connolly, but in the window of the next-door house a curtain twitched and a woman's face briefly appeared. Sheba stopped when she saw this. It wouldn't do to have to explain herself to a neighbour. She looked about her on the street for appropriate missiles to throw at the window. But there was nothing. Not even a bottle top.

Then a second idea came to her. She would go to a phone box and ring Connolly's home phone. She didn't know what the number was – she and Connolly had always chosen to rely, for safety's sake, on his pager – but it was sure to be in the directory. If Mr or Mrs Connolly picked up, she would pretend to be one of his school friends. She couldn't imagine why she hadn't thought of this sooner.

The first phone box she tried was out of order. She was luckier with the next one, which she found outside an off licence on Albany Way. It smelled of wet cigarettes and old pee, but it was operative. Once she had located the Connollys' number in the book, she stood for a moment or two, practising her teenager's voice. Then she picked up the receiver and dialled.

The receiver was clammy against her ear. When Connolly's mother answered, she was so astounded by her own temerity that, for a moment, she was unable to speak.

'Hello?' Mrs Connolly repeated. Sheba could hear the noise of a television in the background.

'Yeah, hello,' Sheba said. 'Is Steve there?' (I once persuaded Sheba to do a bit of her London schoolgirl for me; it's astonishingly unconvincing.)

Mrs Connolly didn't reply. Sheba thought for a moment

that she had put the phone down. But then she heard her shouting, 'Steven! The phone!'

After a few moments, another phone was picked up and Connolly came on the line. 'Hello?'

'Steven? It's me, Sheba. I've been trying to get through to you all day but you've had your pager off or something.'

'Oh.' She could tell by the nylon crackle in the background that he was lying in his bedroom on his Grand Prix bedspread.

'Are you all right?'

'Yeah. Fine.' His voice was blank.

'Don't worry,' she said. 'I pretended to be one of your friends. Listen, I'm nearby. On Albany Way. Can you come out for a bit and meet me?'

There was a long silence. 'Steven?' she said.

'Nah, not really,' he replied. 'It's a bit difficult.'

'Please. I've been dying to see you. I need a hug.'

'Nah, I can't make it.'

'Polly ran away,' she said. 'I had to go and get her from Scotland.'

'Right.'

'Steven?'

'All righty then.'

'Steven.' Sheba was struggling now, she recalls, to keep the anger from her voice. 'I've got important things to talk to you about, Steven,' she said.

'Well ta for phoning,' Connolly said. 'See you around. Ta ra.'

He put down the phone.

Sheba stood staring at the phone-box wall for a full minute, she says. Then she replaced the receiver and stepped back out onto the pavement. She wheeled her bike across the street back into the estate.

She had almost crossed the square and was about to start

down one of the little alleys that led back to Hampstead Road when she heard voices across the way. She looked around to see two young people – a boy and a girl – leaving Connolly's house. Behind them, standing on the doorstep, was Connolly. 'Take care,' she heard him say. There was more conversation that she couldn't quite make out. And then Connolly came down the steps and kissed the girl. Sheba gripped her bicycle. She felt dizzy. She hadn't been able to see whether the kiss was on the girl's lips or her cheek. The other boy said something now that she could not make out and the three of them laughed. 'Fuck off, yer only jealous,' Connolly said in a jovial tone.

The boy and the girl turned and began to walk down the street towards where she was standing. Sheba scurried on. 'Oh Jesus, oh Jesus,' she remembers moaning to herself, as she broke into a trot. 'Please God, don't let him be in love with someone else.'

When Sheba got home that night, Richard was waiting for her. She found him in the living room, perched primly on the leather armchair.

'For God's sake, Sheba,' he said when she came in. 'This is the limit. It was bloody irresponsible of you not to phone. I already have one teenager to deal with. I don't need two.'

'Please . . .' Sheba said. She was still in her coat. Her hands were prickling in the sudden warmth.

'Please, what?' Richard demanded.

'Just . . . please.' She leaned wearily against the door.

'I'm *so* sorry to bother you,' Richard said. '*Of course* you're much too busy to be bothered with trifling family matters. Let's just cut the talk from now on and deal with our daughter by slapping her about . . .'

'Oh!' Sheba said. She walked across the room and sat down on the sofa. 'I knew you'd punish me for that.'

Richard folded his arms. 'Actually, I've been very careful to avoid expressing any opinion until I could hear your account.'

Sheba lay back on the sofa and looked at the ceiling. 'Wise judge!' she said.

∽

Richard and Sheba did not attend any parties on New Year's Eve. They had talked of having people round for a small supper. But they both agreed now that neither of them was feeling up to playing host. Polly went out to a concert in Brixton, and the remainder of the family had a quiet dinner at home.

I had no celebrations to go to myself, but that was as expected. Over the years, I have created my own traditions for the high days and holy days. This New Year's, as on every New Year's for the last decade, I bought in a bottle of sherry and spent the evening getting slightly sozzled while re-reading Jane Austen's *Persuasion*.

Sheba and I spoke a few times on the phone in the first week of the New Year. On each occasion, she seemed to me to be borderline hysterical. Connolly was still not returning her calls and she was finally confronting the possibility that she had been dumped. She speculated obsessively about the possible reasons for Connolly's loss of interest. Had she become repulsive to him? Or was there a new girlfriend? Did that little tart she had seen outside his house have anything to do with it? Since I had no useful contribution to make to these rambling enquiries, I mostly kept quiet.

The only other subject that Sheba showed interest in discussing during this period was Bangs – whether or not he had proof of her affair, whether or not he was going to report her. By this stage, I was feeling more sanguine about Bangs. With each day that passed, the threat he posed seemed to me to grow less credible. I began to suspect that I had exaggerated my indiscretion in his flat. I hadn't said *that* much, after all. And what I did say he may well not have believed. 'Bangs is not a boat-rocker,' I told Sheba over and over. 'Bangs wouldn't say boo to a goose.' To which Sheba would always reply with pathetic eagerness, 'Oh do you think so, Barbara? Do you really think so?'

Fifteen

On the Sunday evening before school term began, I came back from the launderette to find the light blinking on my answering machine. Most unusually, there had been three calls while I'd been out. On the first two, Sheba repeated my name a couple of times in a rather sepulchral whisper and hung up. On her third try, she left a longer message: 'Barbara? Where are you? Barbara? Pabblem called me this evening. *He knows.* I think he knows. He wants me in at eight o'clock tomorrow morning. He said a serious charge had been made against me regarding inappropriate conduct with a pupil. Please, *please*, Barbara, call me as soon as you get this.'

She picked up straightaway when I rang back. She had been keeping the portable phone by her side. 'I'm having a melt-down,' she said. She was in the middle of making the evening meal and the children were near, so she spoke quietly. 'Bangs must have said something, the bastard. What am I going to do? Tell me what to do.'

'You don't know it was Bangs,' I said. 'It could have been anyone. It could have been Polly . . .'

'Oh who bloody cares! The point is, what am I going to do?'

'Listen to me,' I said, trying not to sound too anxious. 'You have to get your story straight. Have you said anything to Richard?'

'No, he's not back yet. What on earth would I say in any case?'

'No, well don't. Don't say anything. This is all going to

blow over. When you see Pabblem tomorrow, you'll tell him that you are friendly with Connolly, that you've given the boy help with his artwork from time to time, that you have had *no physical contact with him whatsoever*. You must be adamant about that. Be outraged.'

'But what if Bangs has seen us together somewhere?' Sheba objected. 'What if he has proof ?'

'I don't think he has,' I said carefully. 'I think he would have told me that. And even if he *did* see you two somewhere, it's still his word against yours. Tell Pabblem that Bangs has a thing for you – that this is his revenge for being rejected by you.'

In spite of herself, Sheba laughed. 'I can't believe this is happening, Barbara,' she said when her laughter trailed off.

'Neither can I,' I said. 'But it's all right. It's going to be all right.'

I didn't really believe that. I knew well enough that trouble was on its way. But I could never have predicted quite how rapidly the trouble would arrive. A little less than an hour and a half after Sheba got off the phone with me, her doorbell rang. She was up on the top floor at the time, giving Ben his bath. Richard shouted out from his study for Polly to answer the door and then, when Polly did not reply, Sheba heard him swearing lightly as he stomped down the stairs himself. She didn't hear anything else for a while after that and she assumed that the caller had been a girl guide or a Jehovah's Witness. Then she became aware of raised voices downstairs. She left Ben in the bath and went out onto the landing. She could hear a woman's voice below and the bass rumble of Richard.

She walked down a flight of stairs to the next landing and leaned over the balustrade to see what was going on. The front door was still open and in the entrance hall a short blonde woman in a thick coat and woolly hat was standing, wagging her finger at Richard. 'Don't you talk to me like that,' Sheba heard her say. 'I've got proof. It's your wife that's the liar.'

Here it is, Sheba thought. *The calamity has come.* Her impulse was to flee – to dash across the landing into her bedroom and lock herself in the bathroom. She was actually turning to retreat when the woman looked up and saw her.

'You!' she shouted. 'Are you her? Come down here.'

Polly came out into the hall now, from the living room. 'What the hell is going on?' she asked her father indignantly.

'Get out!' Richard roared. 'Go back inside!' For once, Polly had no rejoinder. She glanced briefly up at her mother and then went back into the living room.

Sheba stood still, looking down at the woman's fierce, red face.

Later on, she would come to see how much of the mother there was in the son: the brown complexion, the bullish physique, the tragedy-mask eyes. At that moment, though, the woman's features seemed so alien and hostile that Sheba was momentarily persuaded she wasn't Connolly's mother after all.

'You're scared now, aren't you?' the woman jeered. 'Come on – get down here. I want to talk to you.'

It was electrifying, she says, to have a stranger shouting commands at her in her own house. Richard was peering up at her too, now, his face very pale next to the woman's. Sheba could tell from his bewildered expression that he had not yet understood. He still regarded himself as in league with his wife against this dumpy intruder in their hallway. *I have only a few minutes left of my old life*, she remembers thinking, as she began walking down the stairs.

'The headmaster rang us today,' Mrs Connolly said. 'He wants us to come in and see him tomorrow about Steven.

Won't say why on the phone. I say to Steven, "What can he want to see us about?" And he starts *crying*. Sobbing his heart out! I got it all out of him. He's told me everything. I've even seen those dirty letters you've been sending . . .'

'Now hang on a minute –' Richard said.

'No, Richard,' Sheba interrupted.

'That's right,' Mrs Connolly said. 'You can't deny it, can you? Why don't you tell him what you've been doing with my son?'

'You must control yourself,' Richard said. 'There's a child in the house.'

Sheba suddenly remembered Ben, still sitting in his cooling bath. 'Polly!' she shouted. 'Go upstairs and watch your brother.'

Mrs Connolly's mouth silently opened and closed like a fish's maw. 'Don't be telling *me* to control myself! I've got kids too, you know.'

Polly emerged from the living room again. 'Could someone please tell me what's going on?' she demanded.

'Shut up, Polly, and go upstairs,' Richard said.

Polly trudged sullenly past Sheba.

Sheba was standing on the last step of the staircase now. Tears were coursing down her face.

'That's right, cry,' Mrs Connolly said, 'you perverted bitch –'

'I'm sorry,' Richard broke in. 'I'm going to have to . . .' He put his hand on Mrs Connolly's arm, and tried to turn her towards the front door. But she writhed away from him.

'Evil cow!' she screamed at Sheba.

There was a brief struggle in the course of which Richard's spectacles fell to the floor and Mrs Connolly's hat came askew. 'Don't . . . you . . . touch . . . me!' she screeched at Richard. For a moment, the three of them – Sheba, Richard and Mrs Connolly in her tipsy hat – stood still.

Then, Richard bent down to retrieve his spectacles. He was putting them back on and had just begun to say something to Mrs Connolly in the fruitily appeasing tone that Sheba calls his 'Come now' voice, when Mrs Connolly made a running lunge at Sheba.

The contact lasted only a few seconds, but when Richard pulled Mrs Connolly off, she was holding a surprisingly large amount of Sheba's hair in her hand.

'No more!' Richard roared. He took hold of Mrs Connolly's shoulders. There was scuffling and shouting. Sheba stood clutching the hall table, sobbing. She recalls, with some amazement, seeing Richard clasp Mrs Connolly from behind and attempt to carry her, in an awkward bear-hug, to the door. Mrs Connolly's crêpe-soled winter boots dragged on the hall carpet like a corpse's.

After the door slammed, there was a tiny window of silence and then the doorbell began to ring. Richard stood with his back to the door, breathing heavily. Sheba sat on the floor. They stared at one another across the hallway, listening to the long urgent alarms of the bell and, just audible beneath them, the muffled opera of Mrs Connolly screaming on the front step.

∞

Sheba did not ring me that night after Mrs Connolly left. Her hands were full with Richard, I suppose. The next day she chose – wisely enough – to stay at home and skip her scheduled interview with Pabblem. I tried ringing her from school several times that morning, but she did not answer. As a result, I was in the dark for much of the day, forced to piece together what had happened from the scraps of frantic gossip being exchanged by my colleagues. Sheba had been found out having an affair with Steven Connolly, people were saying. There had been a fist-fight between her and the boy's mother. It was possible – even probable – that she had seduced other boys. The police had been called in.

At first break I found Elaine Clifford in the staffroom, surrounded by a crowd of glinty-eyed teachers, as she relayed the latest dispatches from Deirdre Rickman in the head-master's office. At that very moment, she reported, Pabblem was 'in conference' with the police and the Connolly family. Sheba had been called in to face the music, but she had refused to come and the police were now on their way to her house to arrest her. Pabblem was in a terrible state by all accounts. Just an hour ago, he had shrieked at a work experience student for making his coffee too milky. Deirdre Rickman attributed this behaviour to feelings of guilt and anger. Pabblem could not forgive himself, she said, for the fact that Sheba's lurid misdeeds had occurred on his watch.

Personally, I doubted this theory. If Pabblem was in a nasty mood, it seemed much more likely that he was racked with regret at having lost the opportunity to bully and humiliate Sheba. Had it not been for Mrs Connolly's precipitate action – her insistence on barging into Sheba's home the night before – Sheba would have come to school that morning and Pabblem would have had her in his clutches for at least a couple of hours of thundering interrogation. Now, she had escaped him, and there was nothing for him to do but surrender control of the investigation to the police. Poor old Pabblem had been robbed of his sadistic moment.

Somewhere in the middle of Elaine's performance, Mawson came in to hand out copies of Pabblem's much-delayed 'Where We Go Wrong' report. Pabblem had been scheduled to give an introductory talk at lunchtime about the challenging new ideas contained in its pages, but now, owing to what Mawson called, with redundant discretion, 'an unforeseen matter', he was obliged to cancel. A small cheer went up from the staff when they heard this – succeeded by a loud groan when Mawson announced that a new meeting had been set for the following week. Pabblem, he assured us, was still very much looking forward to hearing staff 'feedback' on his proposed initiatives.

On the way back to my classroom, I spotted Bangs scuttling along the ground floor of Old Hall. His name had not come up yet in any of the staff discussions I had overheard. Everyone seemed to be under the impression that Mrs Connolly was responsible for uncovering Sheba's affair. I knew better. His eyes met mine just as he was about to enter the staff toilet. He froze, like a surprised cockroach. His mouth opened to say something and then he seemed to decide against it. 'Little shit!' I spat as he closed the toilet door behind him.

At around four o'clock, I finally managed to get Sheba on the phone.

'Sheba!' I said when she picked up. 'Thank God. I've been trying to get you all day. Are you all right?'

'No . . . well, it's a pretty awful mess here. As you can imagine.'

'Have you seen the police?'

'Yup. Yup. They came this morning. Richard went with me to the station. There was a lot of stuff they had to do. Fingerprinting and so on. We only got back an hour ago.' I had expected tears and screams, but she was weirdly matter-of-fact. It was the shock, I suppose.

'How is he taking it?' I asked.

'I don't know. I'm terribly worried. He's still not answering . . .'

'What?'

'Oh, sorry, Richard you mean? He's . . . I don't know.'

'Shall I come over?'

'No, better not. I don't think Richard wants visitors. And we haven't spoken to the children yet.'

The next day, there was a small item about Sheba in the *Evening Standard*. It wasn't much – just a paragraph at the bottom of page four about a north London teacher being charged with indecent assault on a pupil. But I knew then that the floodgates were about to open. I spoke to Sheba briefly at lunchtime. She was even quieter now – almost catatonic. She still didn't want me to come to the house, so there was nothing for me to do after school but go home and fret.

On Wednesday morning I was called in to see Pabblem. It did not occur to me that he was going to talk to me about Sheba. I assumed that he wanted to discuss Year Nine's special history project on Ireland. According to a rumour floating about at the time, he was hoping to honour the sufferings of Irish peasants during the potato famine by having the children observe a day-long fast.

There was no preamble to our business on this occasion. Pabblem merely nodded when I entered his office and started talking before I sat down. 'As you know, Barbara, Sheba Hart is in quite a bit of trouble.'

I nodded. 'Yes, I'm aware of that.'

'Quite a bit.'

'Yes.'

'I gather you're close to her.'

'She is my friend, yes.'

He looked at me meaningfully.

'Is there something you . . . ?' I began.

'No, I won't beat about the bush, Barbara,' he said. 'It's been brought to my attention that you may have known about Sheba's relationship with Steven Connolly for some time.'

'What?'

'You heard me.'

There was a heavy silence.

'Brian Bangs tells me that you spoke of the relationship to him before Christmas. Is that or is that not the case?'

'I advised Brian of my suspicions, that is true.'

'Oh? Brian seemed to think you were more than suspicious. He seems to think you were pretty certain.'

'Well, he's wrong.'

'Very well. But did it not occur to you to share your suspicions with one of your senior colleagues? With me?'

'No. As I say, they were only suspicions. I am not a gossip.'

'You are aware, of course, that Sheba's conduct with this boy is a criminal offence? A very serious one?'

'I am aware of that.'

'Are you also aware that failure to pass on information about a criminal offence may be construed as criminal in itself?'

'I see what you are insinuating, but I'm afraid you're mistaken. I had no information to pass on. As I have explained, I am not in the habit of trading in unsubstantiated rumour.'

'And yet you were happy to pass on an "unsubstantiated rumour" to Brian?'

'Look –' I began.

Pabblem stood up now. 'You and I don't get along, do we, Barbara?' he said. 'It's not for want of trying on my part, I think. I've certainly tried. I know you've been unhappy with my leadership of St George's. I know you find my way of doing things a little' – he made a quotation gesture with his fingers – '"newfangled". But I think you'll admit that I've made a real effort to see your point of view. Haven't I? Wouldn't you admit that?'

I looked out of the window at the headmaster's garden. A

lone sparrow was pecking hopefully at the sheet of ice covering the bird bath.

'I think we've both tried to be civil with one another,' I said.

'Yes, and it's still not working between us, is it?'

'We're not obliged to be friends.'

Pabblem walked around his desk and crouched down next to my chair. 'I'll tell you the truth, Barbara. I find myself in a bit of a bind, here. I am extremely reluctant to believe that you acted as Sheba's accomplice . . .'

'Excuse me –'

'And yet,' he said, raising his voice, 'and yet I am under a very clear obligation to pass on any relevant information regarding my staff to the police. It's a tricky situation, you can see.'

'I wasn't an accomplice. I have done nothing wrong,' I said.

He laughed and stood up. 'Come on, Barbara! If you tell me you didn't know about Sheba, then I believe you. But you must understand that if you stay with us, I shall have to put the police in touch with you. As long as you're a member of my staff, I need to be sure there's not even a *semblance* of wrong doing.'

'This is nonsense –'

'It shouldn't be a big problem, talking to the police about this. Not if you really didn't know. I just thought it might be something you'd want to avoid. So I've been wondering . . .'

'But look –'

'Please!' Pabblem held up a hand. 'Let me finish, Barbara!' He paused for a moment, before continuing. 'As I say, I've been wondering how I might help you out. It occurs to me that this might be a good opportunity for us to take stock . . . to, you know, *reconsider* your role here at St George's. Since you are of an age – forgive me – at which retirement is a plausible option, I'm thinking, well . . . perhaps that might be the best course of action for you now.'

I stared at him. 'What are you saying?'

'I'm saying that you have two choices –'

'One choice, two alternatives, I think you mean.'

'Whatever.' Pabblem shrugged. 'I'm offering you a dignified exit.'

Not trusting my own composure, I did not reply.

'Look,' he continued, 'you needn't decide now. It's a big decision. Why don't you go away and have a think about it?'

He planted himself against the door as I got up to leave. 'I'm glad we had this talk, Barbara. You'll let me know what you decide, won't you? ASAP?'

I did not reply and he remained standing in front of the door.

'Can we agree on, say . . . tomorrow afternoon as a deadline?'

Finally I nodded and he moved to one side. 'Atta girl,' he said.

I was halfway down the corridor when he called out to me again. 'By the way, Barbara, have you had a chance to look at this?' I turned to see that he was holding up a copy of 'Where We Go Wrong'. I shook my head. 'Oh Barbara!' he said, cheerfully. 'Tut tut! Do try and give it a read. There are some very exciting things in it, if I say so myself.'

Sixteen

Eddie rang yesterday to let Sheba know that he and the family will be returning from India in a week. Sheba relayed the news with such glazed-eyed indifference that I was sure I had misheard her. 'A week?' I repeated. We have always known that Eddie would be back in June, but I suppose I had been counting on some last-minute reprieve.

'Yes,' Sheba said idly. 'He wanted to know how the garden was doing. Have you been watering it at all, Barbara?'

'Don't worry about the bloody garden,' I said. 'What about us?' Sheba looked at me, startled. Then she shrugged.

'Do you think there's any chance he'd let us stay on for a bit?' I asked.

'Oh no,' Sheba said. 'I don't think so. He told me to leave the keys on the kitchen table when I go.'

'And where, pray tell, does he think you'll be going? What are we going to do?'

Sheba said nothing.

'Are you listening to me, Sheba?' I said. 'We can't camp on the streets . . .'

'Oh God, oh God,' she cried suddenly. 'Don't shout at me. I can't bear it.'

There was silence in the room.

'*Ohh*, you mustn't mind me,' I said after a moment. 'I'm just a worry-wart, you know that. We'll work something out.'

'No, no,' she said, suddenly remorseful. 'I oughtn't to have snapped at you.'

'Not to worry,' I said.

She shook her head. 'Poor Barbara. I must be a nightmare to live with these days.'

'Nooo,' I said, getting up to put on the kettle. 'Not at all.'

After we had had some tea and I judged her to have recovered from her little outburst, I went to the shops to get something for our dinner. I left her lolling in an armchair in the living room, watching television. But when I returned an hour or so later, she was lying on the living-room floor and her eyes were red from crying. I thought at first that she had been mulling over our impending homelessness. But then I saw that she had been reading something. Spread out before her, on the carpet, was my manuscript.

I am usually scrupulous about putting my writing away. But Sheba has been so self-absorbed, so incurious about her surroundings of late that I guess I had allowed my precautions to become a little lax. The previous night, instead of taking the manuscript up to bed with me and putting it under my mattress as usual, I had placed it on the bookshelf, inside one of Eddie's large photographic volumes.

'You told Bangs,' Sheba said when I walked in. Her voice was trembling slightly.

I put down my shopping bags. 'What?'

'You told Bangs about me and Connolly.'

'What on earth are you talking about?'

'Stop it!' Sheba screamed. 'Don't lie to me. I've read it all in . . . in . . . your little *diary*.' She scrambled up from her prone position and brandished the manuscript at me. 'What is this? What are you doing with this?'

'Sheba . . . don't get het up. It's something I've been writing –' I began.

'I see that. How dare you? *How dare you?* What are you planning to do with it? Sell it and make a million?'

'I . . . I thought it would be useful to put everything down.

I thought it might help with the court case.' I stepped forward to try to wrest the manuscript from her, but she darted away.

'Help?' she said. 'To hear about me buying thongs and . . . and . . . hitting my daughter? What a wicked, wicked person you are! You betrayed me! You told Bangs.'

'For goodness' sake, Sheba,' I said. 'You would have been found out anyway. Your own daughter knew you were up to something. And the letters! How could you have expected not to be caught?'

Sheba stared at me. 'What an idiot I've been to trust you. All that filth and lies you've been writing . . .'

'There are no lies in there, Sheba. There's nothing in there that you didn't tell me yourself.'

She made a strange, guttural noise of exasperation. 'You're mad! How did I never see it before? You're mad! You really believe this stuff is the truth. You write about things you never saw, people you don't know.'

'Well, that's what a writer does, Sheba.'

'*Ohhh*, you're a writer now?' She began to laugh. I lunged forward, to get at the manuscript, but she danced away again, holding it high above her head.

'Look, Sheba,' I said, 'you haven't read it properly. You can't get the idea of it from just flicking through it. I'm writing in your defence.'

'What absolute shit!' she exploded. 'You're not defending me. You're exploiting me, that's what's going on here. All this time, you've been pretending to be my friend and what you've really wanted is, is *material* . . .'

'And how do you think it's been for *me*?' I said, suddenly angry myself. 'Acting as your bloody lady-in-waiting . . .'

She wasn't listening, though. 'Those awful things you write about my family,' she went on. 'About Richard. How much you must hate us! I suppose that's the spinster's consolation, isn't it? Examining the machineries of other people's marriages and pointing up the flaws.'

'Sheba, how can you say that? I have only ever –'

'Don't tell me what I can say!' she shrieked. 'I'm the Most Hated Woman in Britain! There's every chance I'm going to end up in prison! I can say whatever I want!' She was staggering about the room now like a crazy person.

'Sheba!' I shouted. 'I lost my job because of you! Think about that! I have suffered too, you know. We're in this together, you and I. If we're going to get through this, we have to find a way . . .'

'*What?*' she snarled. 'What *is* all this "you and I", "in this together"? You're insane! Richard was right. He always said you were an incubus.'

'I'm sure he did. Richard was always jealous of me –' I broke off, seeing Sheba's eyes widen with outrage.

When she spoke again, her voice was low and menacing. 'You have such delusions of grandeur, don't you? It's fascinating. You actually think you're somebody. Listen. Let me tell you something. You're *nothing*. A bitter old virgin from Eastbourne. *You aren't fit to shine Richard's shoes.*'

Seventeen

~~Damn her. Damn her. Lady Muck. Skinny bloody cow. She always made the big point of downplaying her advantages, behaving as if we were just two middle aged ladies confronting life from equal positions. Oh Barbara don't put yourself down like that! And the moment I take her at her word, presume on our equality, rather than waiting for her to magnanimously assure me of it, she is beside herself. Outraged. Ha! Her, who can't boil a bloody egg without me. Ungrateful bitch.~~

∞

Forty-eight hours have passed since Sheba uttered her last hateful words to me. I left the house soon afterwards and when I returned a few hours later, she had gone upstairs, taking the manuscript with her. She has been holed up in her bedroom ever since, refusing to come out, refusing to talk to me or to eat the food that I prepare for her. She emerges only to go to the loo and to make snacks for herself when she knows I've gone to bed. I find her little messes in the kitchen in the morning. Late last night, I was awakened by the sound of her crying – howling, in fact. It went on for hours. I grew so alarmed at one point that I nearly called Richard. She stopped eventually, some time around dawn, but my nerves this morning are absolutely shattered.

Luckily I have housework to keep me occupied. Eddie will be here in a few days and I've been Hoovering and dusting and washing like a dervish to get the house ship-shape in time. I've grown to rather love this house, I realize. The time we have spent here has been terribly sad, of course. But terribly intense too and even wonderful in its way. I keep staring at things, willing myself to remember them: the faded blue dressing gown that Sheba is always leaving draped across the sofa or lying in a heap in the hall; the antique Moroccan tiles in the kitchen; the velvet-clad hangers in the closets. Of course, memory is not really as obedient a faculty as that. You can't consciously decide what is going to adhere. Certain things may strike you at the time as memorable, but memory only laughs at your presumption. *Oh, I'm never going to forget this*, you say to yourself when you visit the Sacre Coeur at sunset. And years later, when you try to summon up an image of the Sacre Coeur, it's as cold and abstract as if you'd only ever seen it on a postcard. If anything unlocks the memory of this house for me, years from now, it will be something – some tiny, atmospheric fragment – of which I'm not even aware at the moment. I know this and yet still I persist in making my little inventory, trying to nail down my recollections: the queer taste of the herbal toothpaste that Eddie's wife uses; the long-finger shadows that the trees in the street cast on the living-room floor in the afternoons; the steamy sweetness of the bathroom after Sheba has been in there.

Mrs Taylor rang at 10.30, to announce that she is off in a fortnight, to stay with friends in France. She'll be gone for six weeks, perhaps more. Sheba's infamy is taking a terrible toll on her, she said. She 'can't bear being in Britain another moment'. Seeing my opportunity, I leaped in. Would it be possible, I asked, for Sheba and me to stay at her place while she was gone? She *hated* that idea, you could tell. But she'd already admitted that the house was going to be empty, so it was hard for her to say no. She raised all sorts of objections, naturally. Surely there were other, more convenient places for us to stay? Surely Sheba wanted to be near Ben? Surely we wouldn't be able to handle her temperamental boiler? But, in the end, she had to bite the bullet. As long as we have *absolutely no other alternative*, she is prepared to let us stay in her house for no longer than a month. I got off the phone awfully pleased with myself.

Since then, various hitches in my brilliant plan have occurred to me. For one thing, I'm not sure if the terms of Sheba's bail will allow her to travel so far. And even if they do, Sheba may refuse to let me go with her. I have been trying to prepare myself for this possibility, but the thought is intolerable. How will Sheba ever manage on her own? Who will do the shopping and cook her meals? Who will make sure she showers every day? I'm not sure I can bear it if I have to go back to being on my own again.

Eighteen

The crisis is over. Sheba and I have reconciled. What an exhausting day it has been! This morning at about nine, Sheba came out from her room and went to the attic. I took the opportunity, while she was tramping around up there, to slip into her room and retrieve my manuscript.

Much as I had feared, her room was in a dreadful condition. Every available surface was littered with crumpled pieces of paper, bits of clay and dirty clothes. A half-eaten tin of baked beans was sitting in the middle of the floor. Sheba had left the window open throughout last night's rain and the carpet near the window was sopping. I found the manuscript soon enough. She'd left it lying on her desk. I was just beginning to gather it up when I caught sight of a clay model parked on the floor at the end of the bed. This was the secret sculpture that Sheba has been working on: the mother and child. It was much larger than I had anticipated – almost three foot in height. It looked impressive. Then I walked around to inspect it from the front and my stomach seemed to tip up on its side.

The cross-legged 'mother' figure had been fashioned in Sheba's image. She had long, skinny limbs, heavy, romantic eyelashes, a slightly crooked nose. Even her hair replicated Sheba's messy bun. As for the hideous, pink boy-man spilling fatly across her lap – he was a crude, but unmistakable likeness of Connolly. I dare say that even a person unfamiliar with the circumstances to which it alluded would have sensed something unwholesome emanating from the sculpture. For me it was an utterly obscene object.

I did not hear Sheba returning from the attic until she was directly behind me.

'What are you doing in here?' a voice exclaimed and I swung around to find Sheba in her nightdress. Her hair was hanging loose. There was an unpleasant musty odour about her.

'I . . . I was looking at your sculpture,' I protested stupidly. I was afraid.

'Get out! Get out!' she screamed. We stared at each other and, for a moment, I thought that she was going to attack me. Then, quite suddenly, she sat down – or rather collapsed – on the floor. 'What is going to become of me, Barbara?' she sobbed. 'What is going to become of me?'

'Oh poor Sheba,' I said. I knelt down and put my arms around her. Her hair was sticking in clumps to her wet face.

'Get out,' she muttered half-heartedly.

'Sheba, please,' I said, 'come on. Stand up.' She kept sitting for a few minutes and then she allowed me to help her up.

We stood holding each other. When I judged that she was capable of standing without my support, I let her go. We gazed at the sculpture together.

'You know it can't stay,' I said.

'Oh?' she said. Her tone was dreamily neutral.

I picked up the manuscript from the desk. Then I bent down and heaved the sculpture into my arms. 'I'll take care of this,' I said as I carried it from the room.

Downstairs in the kitchen I sat the sculpture down on the table and hid the manuscript in one of the cupboards. Next, I got out the tool box from under the sink. Eddie's tools are terribly expensive and grand. I was nearly seduced by a hand-carved mallet with an ivory handle. But I settled in the end for a small, steel axe. (Less beauty, more power.) I opened the French doors and carried the sculpture out into the garden. It was one of those overcast mornings with a grumbling, mauve-coloured sky. The garden was looking wonderfully jungly and lush. I went back inside to fetch the axe and some old newspaper.

The sculpture wasn't nearly as tough or as dense as I had expected. I missed it with my first swing but as soon as I actually made my target, I crushed the boy's torso straight off. Tiny splinters of clay flew through the air. One large shard landed in Eddie's compost heap. I glanced up at one point, and saw Sheba, watching me from her window, a solemn Victorian wraith. I waved cheerfully and then I went on. With my second blow I took the top of the boy's head off cleanly, like an egg. Within five minutes, there was nothing left but Sheba's crossed legs and a small jagged remnant of her abdomen.

Somewhere, far across London, thunder began to growl. I gathered up as many of the smashed pieces as I could, wrapped them in the newspaper and took them inside just as it began to rain. Sheba had come downstairs now. She was standing in the kitchen.

'Is there anything else I should know about?' I asked her.

She shook her head.

'Are you sure?'

She was silent.

I stuffed the newspaper in the bin and then I ran back upstairs to her room. She must have had an idea of what was going on because she gave no sign of surprise when I returned with her handbag. She watched me intently as I fished the photographs out from the bottom. When I fetched the kitchen scissors she did begin to cry a little, but even then it was more in resignation than in protest.

After the photographs were cut up, I went to her and took her very gently in my arms. Sheba's body is so slender these days, one feels one could almost crush it. 'Come on,' I said. 'It's all right.'

She began to cry more energetically. Great, shuddering sobs. But I kept holding her and speaking softly, and presently she quietened down.

'What's going to become of me?' she asked again. 'What's going to become of me?'

'You're going to be all right, darling,' I said, stroking her hair. 'Barbara's here.'

I felt her droop, as if in surrender.

We stood in the kitchen, rocking very slightly back and forth for a long while. Then I sat her down and I made us some lunch. Fried eggs and bacon. Mugs of strong tea. Cosy food for a grey day. She must have been starving, because she gobbled it all up like a navvy and then demanded seconds. Darling girl. Darling, darling Sheba. I made her take a nap after lunch and when she got up, half an hour ago, she was in much better shape. The rain had stopped by then and she wanted to go for a walk. I let her go alone. I dare say she'll be all right by herself. She seems quite steady and calm after her rest. And she knows, by now, not to go too far without me.

Acknowledgements

Thank you to Juliet Annan, Jennifer Barth, Jonathan Burnham, Gill Coleridge, Lucy Heller, Clare Parkinson, Mary Parvin, Margaret Ratner, Colin Robinson, Mark Rosenthal, Claudia Shear, Roger Thornham and Amanda Urban. Thank you also to Larry Konner, without whose advice, morale boostings and all-round *menschlichkeit* this book would never have got written.

If you enjoyed

Notes on a Scandal

then you will love Zoë Heller's brilliant new novel,

THE BELIEVERS